Taken to Heimo

Xiveri Mates Book 4

Elizabeth Stephens

Contents

Bo'Raku *(boh - rah - kooh)*
Ruler of the Drakesh planet, Cxrian; once an independent planet, but following a failed invasion of Nobu, the planet was absorbed into the Voraxian Federation

Centare *(cent-are-ay)*
No in Meero, the most common trading language; primary language of the Niahhorru

Cxrian *(ss - ree - ahn)*
The red planet, coined for its color as seen from outer space, as well as the red skin tone of its primary species, the Drakesh; the human colony is one of Cxrian's moons

Eshmiri *(esh-meer-ee)*
Second largest group of space pirates; known for their short, stocky builds, laugher-like language, and fighting pits on the asteroid Evernor

Hexa *(hex - ah)*
Yes in Voraxian

Kor *(kohr)*
Trading city located on in the grey zone between Quadrants 4 and 5; ruled by the Niahhorru species commonly referred to as space pirates; their leader is Rhorkanterannu

Krisxox *(chris - zawcks)*
Voraxia's chief battle strategist

Nobu *(noh - boo)*
Voraxia's largest planet; ruled by Va'Raku; characterized by icy climates and long, brutal winters

Nox *(noh - cks)*
No in Voraxian

Ontte *(aunt-tay)*
Yes in Meero, the most common trading language; primary language of the Niahhorru

Oosa *(ooh-sah)*
Species of Quadrant Eight; ruled by Reoran; characterized by large blob-like figures that illuminate from within whenever speaking or expression emotion; extremely difficult to kill

Qath *(kahth)*
An oasis city located within Voraxia; surrounded by harsh deserts, it is known for its extremely hostile plant and animal life as well as for being the training ground of Voraxia's elite warriors, trained and led by Krisxox

Ra *(rah)*
Male son of the Raku and Rakukanna; equivalent of a prince

Raka *(rah - kaah)*
Male equivalent of a Rakukanna (i.e. if the Raku or xub'Raku is female, then the Raka or xub'Raka is the title of her mate)

Rakuka *(rah - kooh-kaah)*
Female daughter of the Raku and Rakukanna; equivalent of a princess

Raku *(rah - kooh)*
Overarching ruler of the Voraxian federation and its seven planets; based on, and ruler of, its principle planet, Voraxia

Rakukanna *(rah - kooh - kah - nah)*
Mate of the Raku

Shrov *(shrohv)*
Common Meero curse

Va'Raku *(va - rah - kooh)*
Ruler of the Voraxian planet, Nobu; referred to as Okkari on Nobu

Va'Rakukanna *(va - rah - kooh - kah - nah)*
Mate of Va'Raku; referred to as Xhea on Nobu

Verax *(vair - axe)*
Explain

Voraxia *(voh - racks - ee - uh)*
Chief planet of the Voraxian Federation; base of the Raku; characterized by expansive werro woodlands and a sandy forest floor

Xhivey *('iv - ay) or (xhziv - ay)*
Good

Xok *('ok) or (tzok)*
Curse word used universally and liberally

Xora *('oh-ruh) or (tzoh - ruh)*
Cock, dick, your word of choice for it

To the believers, whether your faith lie in
A God or many,
The Universe
Ancestors,
Science,
Spirits
or
Magic.

1

Krisxox

"Svera!" I shout.

Her body is trembling, covered in slick, glistening red — *it's blood, human blood,* her *human blood* — but at the sound of my voice, she looks at me and comes to life. *Good girl.* She makes it to her knees. The walls of this ancient C-class transporter shimmer. They shake. Svera falls.

"You're xoking slow! Get *up*, human!"

She hates when I order her. Hates when I curse. Hates when I call her *human.*

A frown disrupts the irritating kindness that is her stupid, human face and that's fine, because it distracts her from her fear.

"That's it. Don't be afraid. I'm not going to let him hurt you."

But I'm lying.

I can't move. I can't feel my own body. I can't feel anything except for the heat of the C-class engines releasing energy in great clouds of steam. This ancient beast comes from another time. So old, I'd never seen one with my own eyes until I climbed aboard with every intention of saving the female that I hate most in this universe.

"I need you to come towards me," I say, trying to be gentle even though I'm never gentle. I don't know how to be. And I'm not going to change for *her*. *Then what is this, if not trying?*

"Svera, *please*."

The crinkles in her forehead smooth when I beg her. I never beg *except* to her and increasingly more often. Right now I'd give her both my legs if it meant she'd walk any xoking faster!

"Move!"

She takes one wobbly step, and then another. I tense and growl and grunt and wince with each move she makes. These human females are so disgustingly fragile. The tiniest little movement and they fall the xok apart.

"Come on…" She moves so xoking slow… "*Come on!*"

Svera's too wet gaze meets mine. I see pain shining in their green depths. As green as the leaves of the baby werro trees, those bright, brave little saplings.

Meanwhile, the blood on her face shines in the most alarming, visceral shade of red, a color not often seen in nature. But worse than that color is the sound the engines make. Somewhere in the recesses of this transporter, they're screaming the same word over and over.

Failure.

"Krisxox," she whispers.

Everything is a blur. The black and grey against the aquamarine of the floor-length covering she wears...the pale brown of her skin with its haunting, yellow undertones...the small wisps of her hair that have escaped the covering she fixes to them...and then the silver shadow that falls over her body.

The Niahhorru attacks.

"Svera!" I roar as the pirate falls on top of her, taking her to the slated, metal ground.

Bloodthirsty beasts, the Niahhorru pirates ascribe to no quadrant, have no honor, no laws, no treaties with anyone and are led by a king obsessed with finding the location to the human colony so he can steal and breed the human females to repopulate his species' dying numbers.

I'm going to tear him apart for taking her from me, starting with all four of his arms...

These beasts are born fighters, killers and thieves and Svera is a weak, pathetic human *with skin as soft as Qath's sands, unblemished by the suns or their winds, untouched by time.*

She doesn't stand a chance.

Xok me! Xok her. *Don't. Please, don't.*

I struggle. I don't know what has me, but its hold is stronger than iron ion and heavier than stalyx. I've never been caged. Never been rendered weak. I am Voraxia's Krisxox — its strongest fighter and battle strategist. I wage war and I have never known defeat. *Until now…*

Now, I'm left to watch the Niahhorru bring one clawed hand down and rip away Svera's head scarf, revealing her hair to the light. With his next swipe, he tears through the front of her shift, baring her body.

"Get the xok off of her!" I shout, but even my voice is weak and ineffective, growing fainter and fainter.

He holds her down easily and positions himself between her legs. His bare backside gleams up at me. He's going to violate her. Can she even take him? Will he kill her?

"Svera. Nox…please…" I say, and this is the first time I've despaired. This is the first time I've felt a fear heavy enough to bring me to my knees.

The full power of the Xanaxana that binds me to Svera explodes through my bones. I roast alive, heating, sweating, burning, shaking, *dying…*

And then I wake and the dream fades just as it did last lunar and the lunar before and the lunar before…

2

Svera

I'm lying in the dark, wide awake even though my eyes are closed. My whole body is tightly coiled against the sheets. Or well, not sheets. The Voraxians use furs and animal skins to line their curved nests.

The edges are so high I can't see over them and I fall into the center. Just a little ball, trying to hide from my nightmares. But there's nowhere to hide. They sweep in like the wind through the trees outside of my window — with blistering force.

"Kiy gadol yawveh mikol ha'elohim," I remind myself. "Allah alakbar." I pray to the Tri-God to chase away the visions.

Visions of being chased, of being caught, of being hurt. I picture the horrible four-armed, spiked male that tried to…do more. *Nondah. The pirate's name was Nondah.* I remember holding a little dagger and trying to cut at him in order to protect myself. I'm not a fighter. Hurting him had hurt me. I don't want to have to do it again. I don't get any pleasure out of it. I'm not a warrior. I'm not like...

The door to my room opens with a nearly silent *whoosh*. I freeze. My heart is in my mouth. *Allah al akbar. Sh'ma Yisrael Adonai Eloheinu Adonai Eḥad. Tri-God help me.* It's him. Nondah. The name of the pirate who tried to...

And then I hear a familiar grunt and the same angry stomping that I heard last lunar and the lunar before and every lunar since the two of us have returned to Qath. Since I was taken onto that pirate ship, knocked out when it exploded, and woke up to the sight of Krisxox's angry red face. He'd been holding me.

And here he is rescuing me again even if it's only from my bleak and brutal thoughts. *Thank the Lord and thank the stars.*

I exhale my first easy breath of the lunar as he stomps to the plush seat in the corner and takes it. He unfurls the blanket I left out for him and, for a while, I listen to his agitated breathing until it eventually deepens and I know he's asleep.

I know because I'm familiar with this sound by now — the sound of him stomping in angrily every lunar, and stomping out at solarbreak just as angrily. Then he'll go down the hall and start to prepare first meal *loudly*. And eventually, I'll get up and fold the blanket he'd been using and wonder the same thing I do each solar — if he knows that I know that he comes to my room, or if he even cares. At the very least, he must have realized that the blanket he uses doesn't fold itself.

But he never says anything and I never say anything and like this, we both keep pretending.

I sigh contentedly and my muscles loosen and the darkness ceases to feel quite so cold. I close my eyes, still wondering about Krisxox and his brutish silliness and his pretending to be clandestine and my pretending to be asleep until, with alarming quickness, I'm not pretending anymore.

I sleep dreamlessly.

3

Krisxox

She could sleep through a Muxung Boar attack.

No matter how the summer winds wail, every solar I wake up, she's out cold. Her little body sprawled wildly over her nest, the delicately woven vervu-fiber blanket tangled around her legs, the heavy fur splashed haphazardly over her body.

She keeps her hair covered even when she sleeps. A light-colored silk encases it, but there are still small strands of gold and ashy brown that escape near her face and curl near her cheeks.

I follow the long line of her neck with my gaze. It's so thin and delicate. She shouldn't even be alive. None of them should be. And this one *definitely* shouldn't be here sleeping the solar away in my city in my home in my nest.

But she is.

And I don't wake her. I can't. I need to be careful. I don't need her knowing that I spend each lunar in her room. I don't need her knowing that I dream of her. That failing her gives me nightmares. *I don't need her knowing about the pressure in my chest. The fire that spreads across it. The heat that's so vociferous it makes me stark-raving mad. The colors that sometimes...flare...oh xok...xok!* I can feel those colors now rising within me like a sickness, a disease that festers and corrupts.

I'm staring down at her ankles, exposed up to the shin. Her skin is a flawless light brown. The bottom of her feet, very pale and strange by contrast. It's disgusting. *It's beautiful.* I remember what it had looked like to see her full body bared. To hold it in my arms. To hold her. Her. *My Xiv* — nox. Never.

I swallow hard and turn from her, but the weight in my chest is enough to slow me down. I stagger once, but make it to the door. I wave it open and move down the hall. The farther from her I move, the more the pressure releases. The weight is almost totally lifted by the time I reach the cooking pit.

Only a few steps down and I'm in my lair. Everything is right here. My head clears. After the training flats, it's the place I feel most stable. I pull out a host of ingredients from baskets below the red werro-wood cooking surfaces. I light the fusion fire cooking trays and I forget that I have an *alien* living in my house. It's sickening and so is she. Not she. *It.* The alien. *What would my sires say if they saw me living with it?*

I wince as the fusion knife cuts into the edge of my longest finger. The blade is sharper than any I've used before. It's one of the new Rakukanna's designs. *What would my sires say if they saw me using it now?*

"Hefenena, Krisxox," Svera — *it* — greets me in the Drakesh language. Though distinct from Voraxian, she's somehow managed to master both languages in the short time she's been among my kind and speaks them fluently now with only the slightest *most charming* hint of an accent. Nox. Not charming. Despicable. That's right. *Despicable.*

I do nothing to acknowledge her. Setting the blade aside, I pull out a flat, stalyx knife and continue cutting into the tough roots spread across the wooden surface in front of me. *It feels so dull by contrast.* I shake away the thought and dump the roots into the fusion tray. Steam rises from them and with a quick flick at the controls, they brown beautifully. I spice them and then I pull out a second tray and toss in a few strips of meat. Svera, she...doesn't eat this meat. So if I want to feed her, then I have to cook the meat separately.

And I do.

Every solar.

Her heat reaches me before her scent as she steps up beside me. She smells like darkness, a danger not yet known. My hand flinches like it's going to reach out and touch her without my consent...pull her against my chest, brush my mouth over those soft, pink things she calls lips...Nox!

"Mmmm," she says. She says the same thing every solar. That small sound of satisfaction. My xora stirs and my hearts beat harder knowing that she is pleased with what I cook for her.

I tilt my head from side-to-side and it cracks loudly. "It smells delicious in here. What do you call that root? The purple one?"

She points to a block of gum root as big as her head, and that's only half. I hand it to her and grumble, "Viron."

"Ouch, prickly, aren't we?" I can't decide if she means me or the xoking root. I grunt again, scoop roots out of the tray with a spoon and dump them on a plate that I shove her way.

"Thank you, Krisxox," she tells me in her human tongue, for this gratitude is something they express more easily than we do.

She takes her plate to the low island behind me and pulls out a string of herbs I know she likes. She chops them using the smallest stalyx knife I have. It's still way too big for her, and I glance at her periodically, hating that I'm impressed by the way she wields it. There's a disturbing fluidity in her movements. I train warriors to have such grace. *Most don't come close to Svera.* I growl aloud. *To it.* To it.

I eat at the island standing across from her and I accept the herbs she's chopped for me. Does she know I don't care for the taste? How could she? I eat them every time she offers them. I like the idea that she wishes to feed me.

"You're welcome," she says, when I don't say anything at all.

It's tradition for us, at this point.

She has a small cushion she sits on every morning to eat, pressed right up against one of the walls. The one with the largest window. She didn't like all the windows at first, until she realized that the sleeping quarters are insulated and that even if they weren't, there's no one up here with us.

All of the homes sit elevated among the trees and among the clouds when they drop low. The village where I train the xcleranx is a short journey away, but the next village is a half span from that. Qath's many markets are chaotic, but here in my home, Qath almost seems like a quiet place. It's why I like it. Even if it's no longer quite so quiet.

She starts to hum. A melody so delicate and beautiful it hurts. Like sunshine through Qath's dense canopy of leaves, it touches me gently, in a way that makes me want to tilt my face up to the light.

My stomach twists. The flavors that were bursting in my mouth a moment ago turn to ash all at once. *Nox. Nox nox nox.* The *pressure.* It rushes up from my stomach and presses down from my throat. *Nox.* I scrape my wooden spoon across my plate loudly and choke down whatever's left. *Who gives a xok?* Just so long as the pressure...just...just *dies!* I've had enough.

I return to my room, pull on my training armor and attach a fusion ion gun and stalyx sword to my belt. I ordinarily would never walk through Qath armed, but these solars, things are different. I don't know why. *I do know why. Now, I have more to protect.* But only because I agreed to keep the filthy human alive. If it were not that vow I made to the Raku, I wouldn't care at all.

Right. I would have just let Nondah…

I stagger into the living area. *It* has moved into the cooking pit and is washing up both her own dishes and the ones I used. I've told her she doesn't need to do this many times, but the fool doesn't listen.

I open my mouth to tell her as much, but that's when it occurs to me. Where is her incessant chatter? Her relentless questions about all things Voraxian and Drakesh? Her pointing at things and asking me how to say them in Voraxian? Constantly asking for my help to improve her accent?

I step up to the edge of the pit, but don't take the few stairs to descend into it. I just watch her with my arms crossed, my jaw ticking, wanting desperately to know what in the xok is wrong with her, but wanting equally to just keep going and accept her silence as a win. I hate when she talks to me. I hate it when she doesn't.

"What's wrong with you?" I blurt out. *Xok me.*

Svera turns. In her long, graceful fingers, she dries a plate. Setting it down in a stack with the others, she smiles. "Don't you know?"

Xok. If I'd known I wouldn't have started this xoking conversation. I shake my head.

"We leave today."

We do? I don't acknowledge her, but my hand twitches towards my life drive. Perhaps there was some important directive I'd missed.

Svera rolls her eyes just a little and I panic when they twinkle. *It's pretty.* "She's giving birth in two solars. We leave this lunar to Voraxia. I'm going to the market one last time before we board our transporter. I'd like to get Miari..." Her eyes widen and she shakes her head quickly.

No matter how much time she, or any of the humans, spend with us, they all falter over our use of titles. They find it strange when one title is transferred to another, when titles change depending on the planet, when titles stack, when xub titles are taken... They always slip into the habit of calling one another by their slave names — the ones we each receive from our sires. These names matter so little, I sometimes forget I ever had one, but other times...other times, I wonder what it would sound like for her to call me by mine...

"I mean I'd like to get the *Rakukanna* a few gifts from the market and some other things I promised her. I've asked Tur'Roth to take me. He'll be here any moment. He'll bring me to the training grounds afterwards and you and I can go home together to pack our things. Does that sound acceptable?"

Nox. Nox, nox, nox. None of it does.

She is going to the market. She is coming to the training grounds. She is going with *him*. She calls this place home. She says us. And yet, I can't. say. anything.

I told her that she could have a protector in my absence even though *protector* is a generous term. Tur'Roth is barely a xoking warrior. So weak.

He's a Voraxian and though he's not Drakesh he's still pureblood. The way *he pursues her*. A pureblood Voraxian pursues one of these…alien things. He disgusts me. And since she disgusts me equally, it should be fine that he follows her around like a pup to a teat. But that she *likes* that he follows her… I don't like them together.

I don't nod. I don't even move. I just watch her smile and put away the dishes she and I both used. I hate that she cleans up after me like a servant while wearing a petulant little smile.

"I'm going to get ready now. I need to gather some supplies. I have things I specifically want included in my gift to the Rakukanna. Are there any things you'd like for the Raku?"

"What for?" I snap.

She gives me that look again — the one that says that everything is obvious and that I'm a xoking fool

— then says slowly, "They are having a baby. And they are having the first hybrid human-Voraxian baby born in this new era. Post-Hunt. It's an exciting thing. A beautiful one. Mashallah."

She makes a four-pointed figure across her chest, one gesture at either shoulder, one to her forehead, then one to her belly button. I don't understand it, but I've learned that it's a symbol of her Tri-God. *So many strange things she gives to him...and I'm jealous of them all.*

I grunt and watch her finish cleaning up, tracking her wherever she moves. I wish I didn't, but even when my life drive beeps with messages, all I want to do is watch her.

"Perfect timing," she says abruptly. "He's here. I'll see you at the setting of the first sun?"

I look away from her and nod.

"See you later, Krisxox. Have a beautiful solar."

She waves at me. I don't give in to the urge to respond and too soon, the door to my home slides open and shut and she leaves and the pressure in my chest swells like a wave, urging me to rush after her and drown her in my monsoon *and perhaps slay Tur'Roth in the process.*

I nearly rip the door off of the frame as I watch her go. Watch her cross the rope bridge. Watch the disgusting xcleranx Tur'Roth cross to meet her on an adjacent one. He bows and extends his hand. Svera grins. I can see it from here. She bows and offers him her delicate fingers. They touch.

I hallucinate a thousand ways to butcher him.

He has no right to touch her. She's *mine. Nox. She's too disgusting to be mine. I'm pure Drakesh and from an ancient line. What would my sires think seeing me with an animal like her?*

So, I don't stop her. And I don't slaughter him. I stand there and flay myself alive as I watch them exchange words. He says something to make her laugh and that sound xoking *wrecks* me. And when they finally take the rope bridge leading to the market square suspended among the xribar treetops and disappear among the foliage I feel…nothing.

The swirling, churning rage and fury and disgust and revulsion and bitter, tormented happiness I feel whenever she's near me is gone. Hollowness numbs out into an even greater hollowness.

My ridges betray a multitude of colors I can see reflected against the walls of my home. They're darker than they should be, filled with an urgency to follow her that I can will away in my body and mind, but not in the dark, lost chasm of my soul.

4

Svera

My bags are full and weighted with the gifts I've prepared for Miari. I can't believe the day has finally come! I can't remember *ever* being so excited. No Christmas celebration with my family and the other worshippers of the Tri-God on the human moon colony, no Yom Kippur, no Eid or Iftar has ever left me with such anticipation.

I find myself bouncing on the balls of my feet with every step, the rope bridges swaying a little more precariously than usual as I do. I just want to board *now*, get on that transporter and return to the human colony on Cxrian's moon.

I'm a little nervous to return, too, after so much time has passed. Now that I've taken on so much more responsibility as not just Miari's advisor, but Voraxia's advisor on *all* things human, it's left me feeling a little strange about my relationship with the humans and especially, the Antikythera Council that leads them.

it ll be good to communicate with Mathilda and the other Council members face-to-face to hopefully alleviate some of the tension.

To prepare, but also to help distract me, Tur'Roth joins me as we weave through the labyrinthine markets of Qath.

Stalls bearing beautiful, colorful blocks of fabric followed by vibrant spices in a dozen different shades unfurl before me. We eventually pass the foods and deserts — all of which I've tried, for better and certainly for the worse — and then end in clothing and technology. Each of these stalls is suspended among the trees. Rope bridges connect all of them.

I look over the wooden railings as often as I can. The world here is beautiful. The sturdy trunks and branches of the green-leafed xribar trees allow for the world of Qath to thrive despite the dangers lurking on the planet's surface.

Rope bridges connect tree-based structures that house all manner of trading stall, restaurants, manufacturing units, and homes. Occasionally, the bridges do break and those that fall to the ground are rescued as quickly as possible... Other times, beings fall from the rope bridges and go unnoticed... Then, they have to fight.

The creatures of Qath are large, scary, and remind me of the stories Miari and Kiki told of the eight-armed beasts who live on our moon colony. I'm grateful for the attention of Tur'Roth. As one of voraxia's principal warriors — a xcleranx — following me around should be beneath his rank, but he seems happy to do it. And I'm happy to have him.

"Do you need help carrying anything?" He asks.

He blinks his large, black eyes and I smile, again having to guess at his emotions by the muted colors of his ridges. They are a pale blue at the moment. Blue is typical of contentment.

"Nox. Thank you though, Tur'Roth."

He nods again and looks forward, helping me navigate a path among the many rope bridges and landings until we eventually arrive at Qath's training grounds. One of the few places that touches Qath's soil, the training grounds span a considerable portion of land. Here, the earth is dense and packed and the trees form a protective perimeter around the vast space, at least a thousand paces long.

I climb down the ladder, lower my packages with the surprisingly simple pulley system, and turn to face the open square with Tur'Roth by my side. My breath shortens, as it does every time.

The warriors of Qath are an impressive thing to behold. Spread out in a grid formation, each warrior is exactly the same distance from the warriors surrounding him — or her, though there are quite a few more males here than females. This lack is another thing I mean to speak with Krisxox about, though I'm certain he won't change his admittance policy on my account. Or even consider it. In fact, I think with a frown, my intervention could make the situation *worse* for the female warriors looking to be trained by him. I will just need to find more inventive means of tricking him into doing it. Maybe, I could suggest that there are *too many* females training under him. *Surely, he'd admit a dozen more immediately if I did that*, I think and laugh under my breath.

More than sixty warriors train under Krisxox's tutelage at a time. Each of them currently holds a large, bow-shaped weapon with outward-facing spikes. *Like Niahhorru spines...* I shudder at the memories, and subtly make the sign of the Tri-God across my chest before forcing all thoughts of the Niahhorru back to the depths where they have no life.

"What is this weapon called?" I ask Tur'Roth in Voraxian as we approach the arena-style bench seats that span the full length of the training ground. They are often full and this solar is no exception.

From where we sit, Krisxox's back is to us while his trainees face us. They mimic his motions as he makes them, though none come close to his brutal elegance.

I've seen Krisxox fight many times now and it's a mesmerizing thing, belying an endurance, a calm, and a stoicism that his attitude towards me does not.

"That is an erdpremor."

"Erdpremor," I repeat, tilting my head. "A star sling?"

Tur'Roth laughs lightly and leans in towards me conspiratorially. His scent is like fresh straw and a deeper, heartier musk. It's attractive and so is he, with his jet black hair in tribute to his proud, Voraxian heritage, and his pure purple eyes, which are without pupil or iris.

"A star *saw*," he corrects and I warm.

"Ah. That does make more sense," I say quickly. I wrinkle my nose.

"You don't need to be embarrassed."

His dark grey-blue lips quirk. He has undoubtedly spent enough time around me to recognize my blush and its meaning, which naturally only makes me blush harder.

"Your Voraxian is very good."

"Thank you. And thank you for helping me learn."

I grip the glossy, dark wooden bench beneath me to keep myself from leaning back when Tur'Roth leans in even closer. *I hate it when he does this…*

"I'm happy to help you with anything you need."

He strokes the backs of his fingers down my cheek and, so subtly as to almost seem unintentional, over my bottom lip.

With a forced smile, I take his wrist and place his hand back in his lap where I give it a gentle squeeze.

"Tur'Roth, we've talked about this. Whatever feud exists between the two of you, you don't constantly need to exacerbate it."

He at least has the decency to look contrite. "Apologies. I just don't think it's fair that I should be denied the right to touch you simply because it pisses him off. Though you have to admit, it is fun pissing him off a little bit, isn't it?" He winks at me and I can't help but choke back a grin of my own.

"While that may be true..." And it is, though I'd never openly admit to it... "It is highly disruptive and with the Rakukanna and Raku so preoccupied, I don't need this devolving into an excuse for Krisxox to strike you." Which he has already, more than once.

"I don't mind being struck if it's for such a worthwhile cause," he says and my belly tightens or flutters or churns. I'm never really sure which, when he says these things to me. Part of me adores the attention. The other part of me worries that his attentions are bestowed for all the wrong reasons.

"I'd rather not see it."

He takes my hand in a gentle, platonic grip. "I'm sorry. I forget you are a sensitive female."

My lips quirk at that. Sensitive, or weak? I don't like that in the Voraxian culture, there doesn't seem to be much of a difference. I know how Krisxox sees me.

I nod and force a smile, returning my gaze to the training ground as Krisxox's tone picks up along with the pace of the warriors' next movements.

He stands elevated from the others, positioned in a spotlight. At least, that's how it looks with the way the sunlight filters down, illuminating the dark orange-red of his skin. It contrasts violently against the bright white of his hair. He has it tied up in a bun on the top of his head, but strands still break free of the knot and stick to his skin in sweat.

I swallow as I watch him move. If Tur'Roth is an attractive male, then Krisxox is a *very* attractive male. He is almost all muscle, yet he moves with the sinewy silence of a snake. Elegance. Grace. Words I would never have though to describe him, once. Now, I can't think of anything else.

He lowers into a crouch and his hide pants stretch taut around his rear. I quickly divert my gaze, only for it to land on the muscles swimming across his back. I admire the way they catch the light when they shift and swell. A single droplet of sweat claims my attention next, winding slowly down his spine, catching the sunlight. *So impossibly slow...*until he moves.

He's here and there and then he's not. He's remarkably fast. The other warriors attempt to match his speed, but it almost seems as if time has two different tempos — one where the rest of the warriors and I live, and a second where Krisxox moves alone.

A moment of stillness and then he thrusts his weapon forward like he might a spear before ripping it down. The motion draws my attention to the scars winding across his body. He's covered in light, silvery ribbons, like xamxin rivers winding their way across a crowded map, but no scar stands out so prominently as the one Tur'Roth gave him.

My breath formed steaming clouds as I struggled to control my anger. I felt filled with fire, like a dragon of ancient Earth's lore. Then came the charged whip. The way it sang when it met Krisxox's bare flesh. I was angry with him yes, but I didn't think he deserved that.

Tur'Roth raised his weapon to deliver Krisxox another blow — this one unsanctioned — and I will never forget it. Frozen in my thoughts, as the world was frozen around me on Nobu's icy fields, it was the first moment I saw Tur'Roth as...someone else. And the way Krisxox bore the first stroke of the flail and then, despite having heard it, patiently waited for the next... I was angry, yes, but I found that there was also something noble in that.

I suck in a breath as I watch Krisxox repeat the same motion, drilling it into his recruits over and over. And I can't help the warmth that spreads through my belly as I do. Okay, *lower* than my belly. I press my knees together and squirm as I try and relax the tensing muscles high in my thighs, because squeezing them only makes the pressure *there* worse.

While I have no experience with males short of a few chaste kisses with human boys, I have always been...easy to excite. For many rotations, I was ashamed of my thoughts — far too ashamed to touch myself in the darkness of the lunar — but after openly confiding in my mother about my body and its treacherous ways, she convinced me otherwise.

Your body is a pure, natural vessel of the Tri-God. He would not have created you this way, if it was not his intent.

After that, I stopped feeling so self-conscious and I learned how to alleviate the pressure myself, but... among the Voraxians and Drakesh, some of that old shame has resurfaced because the aliens...they can smell it.

"Svera," Tur'Roth grunts. His teeth are clenched and the ridges along his brow are a fluttering jumble of blues and purples. *Lust. Purple is lust. The darker, the more demanding.*

"I'm so-sorry," I stutter, smoothing down my skirts and breaking his gaze.

His hand reaches out and touches my thigh, just above the knee. I jerk up to stand. "I will just go down to speak with..." I glance around frantically. "...the Evras below."

"Do you want me to come..."

"Nox." I laugh nervously. "Nox, it's alright. I'll just be a moment."

Tur'Roth gives me a conciliatory bow before pulling back and allowing me to slip past him. I don't look back at him as I descend the arena-style seats. I don't look up at Krisxox either.

My name is said by many of the Voraxians gathered. I greet them in return and doing so helps my head clear and the heat knotted in my belly. I know these beings all by name — or occupation, rather —

and I know their families, their hobbies, what they like and even their hopes for Voraxia.

Taking a seat nestled among the Evras — those responsible for managing the food stores, including everything from harvest to import — I listen to them talk, enrapt, as I continue to keep my gaze focused and away from Krisxox as he lowers his star sling — star *saw* — and repeats new motions without a weapon.

Tel'Evra is in the middle of describing a new type of bean the Evras are trying to source from Quadrant Three when my life drive buzzes.

I glance down at the holographic image floating across my skin, like a constantly changing tattoo scribbled in letters that are as blocky as they are green. The message is from Lemoria. My heart stills. I flick open the holoscreen and view the full contents of her communication.

I leap out of my seat and have to catch myself on Tel'Evra's outstretched hand to stop myself from tumbling down onto the next bench as I shout, "The Rakukanna has gone into early labor!"

Natural labor. Her labor was meant to be induced on the coming solar from the safety of the moon colony's new medical facility, but something must have happened. *I hope it is a blessing. Not a miserable repeat of what happened to so many females who came before who lost their young ones, or even their lives.*

"Verax," Tel'Evra says, his lashless eyelids fluttering rapidly.

The younger male continues to grip my hand firmly as I stand up on the wooden bench beneath me and look up at the faces of so many Voraxians and Drakesh.

I find that most are already looking at me — the novelty of having a human among them has yet to fade for most, even after the half-rotation we have already shared together — and it does not take long to catch the attention of the rest.

With all eyes on me in swirling shades of purple and blue and black and orange and grey, I shout as loud as I can, "The Rakukanna has gone into labor! Voraxia will have it's Ra or Rakuka soon!"

A chorus of shocked murmurs gives way to cheers. Tur'Roth is clapping encouragingly and when I meet his gaze, he winks. My heart sings. I quickly hop down, stumbling a little in my long shift, but a heavy hand slides under my elbow and keeps me from falling onto my rear.

"Thank you," I say reflexively. Instinct leads me to believe it's Krisxox, but the scent is all wrong. Drakesh coloring and a warrior's uniform are all these two males have in common.

I start to retract my arm, but the male tightens his hold. He's smiling, but a flicker of black crosses his ridges that makes me tense.

"You must be thrilled that another bastard *oud* is going to be born into the world, just like your *Miari*," he sneers her name, meaning it as an insult. Though I don't share in this tradition of guarding names, I still hate that he knows it. "I hope she and the baby both drown in blood."

The chatter and chaos rise around us, but I still pitch my voice low and even and say, "You would do well to release my arm, warrior. Both the xcleranx Tur'Roth and Krisxox himself are tasked with my care…"

But he only grips me tighter and pulls me further under the umbrella of his heat. I grunt and my heart throws out bolts of lightning as I remember being handled much more roughly than this on board that ancient Niahhorru ship. My lashes flutter. I see the dark carcass of a Niahhorru pirate with each blink.

"Krisxox is the best of us. If he doesn't kill you outright it's only because he's doing his duty, but he won't stand in our way. And that spineless Voraxian, Tur'Roth?" The horrible male balks, "He's hardly going to be enough."

I rip my arm down, but he's already let me go. The momentum sends me stumbling backwards, straight into Tel'Evra.

"Are you alright?" He says, then immediately, "That is such wonderful news! I cannot wait to meet the little one when our Raku and Rakukanna are able to tour. You will have to send us images before then. Will you promise?"

It takes me a moment to remember where I am and what words I need to say and in which tongue. In the time it takes for my mind to catch up to me, I glance back to where the male had been, but he's gone, replaced by congregating bodies that are laughing and smiling.

"Advisor Svera?" Tel'Evra says.

I start. "Oh um…"

"Do you promise?"

"Images. Images of the baby. Of course. I'll send through as many as I am able. Under the directives of the Raku and Rakukanna, of course."

"Oh! Of course. Of course," he repeats, bowing to me again and again. "Did you hear that, Er'Evra? Advisor Svera will send us the first holo images of the new kit…"

He's already turning away from me when I'm pulled around by more voices. The next, Tur'Roth's.

"I saw Vendra speaking to you. Are you alright?"

He caresses my cheek intimately as he scans my face and body. It's touching, his care…*but it doesn't make my pulse quicken or the breath in my lungs catch. It doesn't make me heat between the thighs. It doesn't make me wet.*

"Thank you," I say, feeling stupid as that's not an answer to the question I was asked. "I mean, I'm alright." Physically, anyway. But that threat. There was something wholly sinister about it and, while I've gotten my fair share of glares and grimaces, none have been so bold as to threaten me like that. Not with such *hatred*.

Good, I... Tuf Roth's gaze pans past me and his expression falls. His shoulders square and his hands drop to form six-fingered fists. The surrounding talk quiets and the fuzzies on the back of my neck stand on end. And even if the cumulation of these things was not enough for me to know that we've been interrupted, it would be given away by his scent.

He smells like citrus fruit. Tangy and acidic with just enough sweetness to make it bearable. It's a smell I find myself thinking of late in the lunar and even a scent that I sometimes, daringly, touch myself to...

It affects me more than it should. More than I appreciate in this moment. The clenching of my stomach has become a sharp pang, the ringing of a gong whose ripples feel almost as powerful as the first touch.

"Krisxox," I say, voice too high to be mine.

I clear my throat and look away from his face, which is wreathed in an anger that most Voraxians are well-schooled not to show. Unfortunately, that leaves me eye-level with his ribs, or rather, the plates that are layered like rough cuts of wood on top of them and protect his vital organs.

He's still dripping sweat. Well, glistening really. And the smell of it...citrus and burnt sugar...I inhale a little deeper. I never thought that male sweat could smell so clean or so oddly sweet.

A small thimble of sharp, hot pressure spears my clitoris, like it's been flicked roughly with a callused thumb.

I straighten and meet his gaze and try not to breathe as I blurt, "Did you hear the news?"

"Everyone in xoking Qath heard the news. What were you thinking, announcing it like that?"

Tender wisps of white hair cling to his cheeks. They're hollow, framed by a stern jawline and high cheek bones. His dark vermillion lips are full. He's staring down at me with his enormous screa eyes. His nostrils are flaring. He looks ready to devour and in that moment, I feel ready to be devoured...

And then I register his words.

I spit, "I was thinking that it would be an excellent occasion for the people of Qath to celebrate their federation's newest member. What is happening now is the most significant event in the history of Voraxia since the dissolution of Cxrian's empire and the Drakesh absorption into the Voraxian federation. If you cannot see that, then you're blind."

"I can see it, human." He growls and ducks his head, patronizing me in that way he knows I hate. He crosses his arms and licks his dark red lips. "But it's not a moment worth celebrating."

I tense. I wish I didn't let him rile me like this, but he is either intentionally trying to hurt my feelings or he genuinely believes what he just said. The latter is a worse scenario than the former, but both hurt.

I decide then that Krisxox must have been placed in my path by the Tri-God's own hand in order to test my faith. Not in the Tri-God, of course, but in myself. In me. Can I endure him?

I close my eyes and exhale through my mouth. I count to three. *One. The weight of the sun pressing down on me from through the canopy. Two. The sound of the faraway rope bridges swinging as vendors and shoppers swarm the rowdy market. Three. Cold citrus drink on a hot sunny solar. The smell of Krisxox's skin.* I open my eyes. *Release.*

"I am very disappointed that you feel this way."

A muscle in his neck spasms and his whole head twitches. I'm under his skin, just as he's under mine. This is a battle between us, our every interaction. I lose often, but not as often as he does.

The Tri-God does not place rivers before us too wide to cross.

"You're disrupting my xoking training. Look at this. It's chaos." He isn't wrong.

Only about half of his warriors are in their original grid formation. Perhaps less. I don't care though. This isn't a day for training. This is a day for celebration, inshallah, and I refuse to let him ruin that.

"It's perfect timing to leave, then. Wouldn't you agree? Training looks like it's over."

"Why the xok would I leave now?"

I thought you said you heard me, Krisxox. The Rakukanna has gone into labor. We need to travel *now*, not this lunar as originally planned."

"We leave when I say we leave and I'm not letting some filthy hybrid ruin this training session or any other. You need to sit back down and shut up and wait until I tell you otherwise."

The insults I could stomach — at least that's what I tell myself — but the callous, listless way he speaks about Miari and the Raku's baby?

I want to scratch and claw and bite. I want to enter his arena and wage a war I know I'm unlikely to win...but that I *might*.

Words rile within me and I spit out the first ones that come, without thinking. "You are a foul, ruined thing and I *hate* you," I snarl and in this moment I mean it even though I've never hated anything.

He freezes. Even the strands of his hair, once caught in a breeze, seem to still. He narrows his gaze and red rolls across his ridges.

"Krisxox, settle down," Tur'Roth grits out at my back.

Krisxox is breathing hard now, shoulders lifting and sagging with each breath. Ignoring Tur'Roth, he leans even closer to me and that scent...that cruel scent. It plays tricks with my body that my mind is too weak to fight. I break. Wetness surges past my underwear and drips down the seam of my clenched thighs.

Krisxox's mouth opens. His hands flinch for me and he seems to be fighting a losing battle, too, because he brings himself even closer. My chest is one deep inhalation away from brushing his. I stare straight up at him. Purple flashes in his brow and he chokes and the sound is not full of malice, as I'd hoped, but thick with male desperation.

I quickly turn away from it. Krisxox *cannot* think that the arousal pooling in my core is for him. He *cannot* be rewarded for his degrading and demeaning behavior. I have to get myself out of this because if he comes any closer, I might *give in*…so, I do the first and only thing I can think to do.

I turn around, reach for Tur'Roth, raise myself up on my tiptoes and brush a kiss across his cheek. At least, that was my intention. But Tur'Roth turns and captures my mouth with his.

He moans into my lips, curves his hand around my head and holds me in place. We kiss, while the male I'd been so close to killing or embracing stands a pace away. Close enough I can still smell his skin and the sugary sweat that it makes. Even though I don't like the sensation of Tur'Roth's kiss, I whimper anyway at the effect that scent has on me. My head spins and Tur'Roth catches me.

Kissing is not common in Voraxian culture and it's clear he has no experience with it. His lips are hard and stiff and his tongue invades my mouth, sliding much too deep. I almost choke and carefully separate us with my hands, pushing against his abdomen to put some space between us. I'm in shock.

I've kissed three boys before this. The first two were boys from my congregation. Feeling rebellious, we pressed our mouths together after our Seventh Solar Youth Group. The third…the third was an attempt…to do more.

I wanted to be prepared for my time in the Hunt and I asked a kind, gentle boy called Raffa to…help me. Or well, he offered, but all he succeeded in doing was terrify me when he mashed my breast through my dress and then attempted to take my head scarf off. I retreated and have not been near a boy since. Until now.

"I…" I don't know what to say.

Tur'Roth is holding onto my arms, keeping me close. He's breathing hard — practically panting — and his forehead ridges are blazing purple lust blotted with bits of brown satisfaction.

He grins down at me and the shame in my gut doesn't do what it's meant to because it just liquifies, becoming one with my arousal. I can still smell him behind me. I can still feel him, like he's touching me, even though he's not. And Tri-God forgive me, I want to be touched…

And only by Krisxox…

"Let's go back," I say, not daring to look over my shoulder at Krisxox. All I know is that I need to get Tur'Roth away from here.

And then Tur'Roth's ridges grow an even brighter violet and I register what I've just said. *Oh comets. He doesn't think that I mean to go back to my nest, does he?*

"I didn't...I meant..."

"Svera." The word is spoken in a pitch so dark and rough, it sounds like a new language. "Step away from Tur'Roth."

My thoughts are firing. My belly is somehow both steel and liquid. Perhaps molten metal. It drags me down, begging me for something — anything — to alleviate the ache.

I need to think. Quick!

"Tur'Roth needs to help me...carry my packages! Come, Tur'Roth." I start away from him, still unable to look back and meet Krisxox's gaze.

Tur'Roth doesn't immediately follow me but instead watches the male over my shoulder, the one emitting a tension so palpable, the arena that was jubilant moments before has gone utterly silent.

My face is burning hot embarrassment. "Tur'Roth," I whisper-shout. "Please!"

His feet come unstuck and after another black-ridged glare at the male whose gaze I refuse to meet, he comes after me.

We ascend the rope ladder and cross the bridge and I still can't bring myself to speak. It's only outside of the stalyx doors to my home — to Krisxox's home — that I turn to him.

"I cannot invite you in."

He nods, but is still staring back the way we came. I notice he has his hand on the holster of the blaster at his hip and I panic, worried he is thinking the same thing I am — that Krisxox is going to slit his throat.

"Tur'Roth?"

"Hexa, Svera?" He looks at me and tries a smile, but his soul isn't in it. "Here you are." He hands me the packages in the basket he carries on his free arm.

"I am sorry," I say, taking them.

Confusion colors his brow. "Verax."

"I just..." I didn't mean to do that. I didn't mean to kiss him. "If Krisxox doesn't mean to join us, will you take me to the human colony as soon as I'm packed?"

His grin becomes a broader, more generous thing, then. "Of course. It would be my honor."

Why couldn't Krisxox ever say that? Or anything kind, for that matter.

"Thank you." I smile shakily up at him and he takes a half-step towards me that I quickly evade. I place my palm to the reader and the stalyx doors whoosh open and I step inside without saying anything more and, in the darkness, I breathe.

My legs are shaking as I set down my basket by my place at the window. I'm genuinely scared for Tur'Roth. I'm a little scared for me. I know that Krisxox hates me and does not want me, but he doesn't want anyone else to have me either. He's made that abundantly clear anytime any male so much as winks in my direction.

I'm sweating. Am I sweating? I wonder if my sweat would smell so good to Krisxox and wrinkle my nose at the thought, then I remember the way he smelled when we stood so close. Looking down at me, ridges a beautiful indigo, the scent of his skin. What would have happened had we been alone? Would I have been able to remember the teachings of the Tri-God and resist him?

No.

I enter my room and have to brace both hands against the largest basket against the far wall. The baskets contain all of my neatly folded clothing and even though I should be packing, right now all I can think is to take my clothes *off* and relieve the ache between my legs. It nearly hurts. There's a pressure in my stomach as well, like a bubble. It wants something...

To burst.

I mewl and the sound of the door whooshing shut behind me makes me tense.

"Krisxox," I gasp, trying to brace myself for war, but when I turn, the male standing there has the same red skin Krisxox does, but an entirely different face.

My fever breaks over ice. My stomach lurches into my throat. I'm going to be sick. I fall back against the basket behind me, nearly tumbling *into* it. I glance around for a weapon, but there's nothing here I can use. It wouldn't matter, either. I only have one weapon in this dangerous, bloodthirsty universe and I think he wants to kill me right now, too.

"He won't save you now. No one will," the one who threatened me says, as if reading my mind. Vondah? Was that his title? I don't remember. It sounds too much like Nondah, a name I know well.

When the others start forward again, I struggle to stay on my feet, knees shaking for an entirely different reason. I refuse to take this lying down, literally, so I'll stand until I'm unseated and I'll fight the best that I can.

I curl my hands into fists like Krisxox once taught me. He disparaged me then, because I couldn't throw a punch. I still can't. But as my spine meets the dusty wooden wall to my right, I know that I'll have to try because I'm weaponless now that I've wounded him, and I've got nowhere left to go.

Krisxox, my mind treacherously thinks. Because I begin to pray to him when I should be praying to my god.

5

Krisxox

I. don't. have. words.

I. can't. xoking. think.

Fury has undone the male that I once was. In its place is nothing. It swishes through me like wine in a jug. This feeling of emptiness. Of sorrow.

And above all else, of *want*.

She gave him something that was meant for me. It was *mine* and he had it! How many times have I dreamed of pressing my mouth to hers? How many females have I practiced on?

And it was all for her.

She thinks me a wanton — no better than a whore — and that's fine. I am. But since she arrived in my care, I haven't bedded one single female. I bring them home, hexa, and I kiss them until my jaw xoking hurts.

It isn't a practice of Voraxians or Drakesh, but now it's becoming popular and sometimes, when I'm weak, I imagine kissing her for the first time. I imagine her liking it. I imagine her forgetting her own xoking name and everything she knows until I'm all that's left. In these treacherous imaginings, I want to be her whole entire xoking galaxy *because she's already mine. She's already ruined me.*

And when I was off dreaming, Tur'Roth comes... he comes and just...presses his mouth to hers and holds her against him and I...I'm going to skin him alive and then throw the pieces down for the cavra cats to eat. And then I'm going to...then I'm going to *do something* to her.

Rage crests and peaks when I realize that I can't even think of what I would do. What *could* I do? I could...I could grab her...hexa, I could grab her...then I could force her up against the wall of her bedroom *and then I could steal that kiss that she so willingly gave to Tur'Roth. A kiss that was* mine *by right.* And then what would my xoking sires think...If I willingly tasted her...pressed my *lips* against hers...

Desire slashes into my gut like a blade and halfway across the rope bridge, I buckle. Other Voraxians stop, refusing to move past me. I shout them all away and a youthful female carrying a basket of live endor snakes, likely ready for skinning, winds around me at a run.

The rest pause and wait and let me get a grip on the railings — and find my own bearings — and toss me strange looks as I struggle. They whisper, too. I know that they whisper about me. They think I'm falling to the insanity that claimed Bo Kaku. He might have been right in his views on Drakesh superiority, but the way he forcibly coupled with human females is disgusting. They're human *aliens*, after all, worthless...

And if he'd forced my Svera to couple with him, I swear to Xana herself I'd have yanked his eyeballs out of his skull just so he could watch me xok him with my sword. I stagger on the rope bridge again.

"Krisxox, you will let me know if you require assistance," the Lira asks me. Head of the weavers, he carries long dried grasses in a basked on his arm. I grab the basket and yank it from his grip, tossing it onto the wooden bridge behind me. Many of the grass pieces slip through the slated grates beneath our feet. He's a respected elder and the look of surprise and horror that fills his face at so much hard work lost nearly brings me to my knees all over again.

"Don't speak to me," I roar.

The marketplace comes to a standstill. I push forward. Towards her. Following the angry pressure of my xora in my training leathers. *Disgusting.* I should xoking cut the thing off. *Xok! Xok me.* I'm breathing hard with the control it takes to hold back the emotions eager to blaze like sirens in my ridges, announcing to all of Qath — to all of xoking Voraxia — that *I, Krisxox,* last of a line of pure, proud Drakesh have a disgusting, wretched, pathetic human for my Xi...

43

Krisxox.

I look up. A sudden cold wind brushes my cheek, carrying the sound of my name. I cock my ear to the breeze and wait until I hear it again.

Krisxox.

The cold comes again, more violently now and I know by looking around at the others crowded on the rope bridge that this isn't a natural sensation. No one else feels it. This cold is something *other* and right now, it touches the place directly between my two hearts — *the place where Svera lives.*

I move forward faster than I ever have, dragging myself along the railings. I jump and land hard in the center of the bridge that leads to my home. The door is closed and the platform surrounding my home is vacant except for *him.*

His hand reaches for the blaster on his belt. Pink fear sweeps his ridges but I can't seem to channel my energy towards him. There's something more compelling than my need to impale him pulling me directly to my door and then past it.

The darkness of my home closes in around me as the door slides shut at my back. "Krisxox..." I hear her voice out loud, coming from her bedroom down the hall, and it's the same tone I've heard before.

Once before.

On the C-class, I thought I heard her whisper it...and then when I surged towards the sound, I found her under Nondah.

There's a thump and a scream and, for a moment, time is a lost thing.

Svera screams a second time and this fresh sound is a fist that reaches down my throat, grabs my insides and rips them all out through my shattered teeth.

The time it takes for my feet to carry me to her door feels like a lifetime. The door sliding open takes another eternity. I lurch inside her room where her scent touches everything — a fragrant smoke, a deep wood, a crimson spice — only to find that violent perfection ruined by foreign scents.

Males. Three of them.

One of them has his hand around her outstretched wrist. Her fists are balled — was she attempting to fight? The thought makes me wild.

One stands back watching.

One holds a knife.

"Svera," I say and my voice is cool, calm. Even. Nothing that I feel.

The males in the room tense and turn and see me and spread out, like they aren't sure if I'm here to reprimand them or to join them. I'm not here for either, though.

I'm here to eviscerate them. To make it so that they never even were.

Svera wrenches out of the male's grip, momentum sending her tumbling back onto the nest. She quickly pushes the end of her shift down to cover her feet. Her gaze locks with mine and is glossy and wet. Her chin is trembling. Rage rises and crests.

I cock my chin at her, directing her towards the far wall and she understands my meaning easily.

She crawls to the far edge of the nest and rolls over it, ducking in the narrow space between it and the wall so that she's safe from the blood that's about to rain.

"Krisxox," a male whose name I do not know or care to, says to me.

I nod at him, giving him permission to speak. His ridges flare white and black and red and I sense that he does not fear me. He thinks me an ally. Horror strikes my stomach at that dangerous realization. If this is what he thinks, is this what *she* thinks of me?

In a moment of weakness, I recognize that if this is the case, I will need to change her mind. *Everyone's. Perhaps, even mine…*

"We wanted to do you a service by getting this disgusting female out of your home," one of them says.

The third male adds, "Her kind is an abomination and she is the one making the rules that dictate how we interact with them."

"She wants us to breed with them on equal terms. To try to make pairs and mates. It's disgusting. We were going to remind her that she is nothing more than an animal by feeding her to the cavras." This one who seems to be their leader, he will die the slowest. He laughs.

He laughs.

He laughs and I grin to show all of my teeth. At whatever expression this grinning translates to, the males share a glance. The one on the right edges back. He will die second then, the most cowardly.

"You mean to tell me that you three broke into the home of your Krisxox to butcher the female in my charge?" I sound like my sire, right before he whipped me. To make me stronger, he said. It worked. And now I will show these males what strength looks like.

They share another glance. The one on the right wears his cowardice in his ridges now. A taupe color. He is uncertain.

The leader speaks. "We wanted it to be a surprise for you. We know that the only reason you keep her is because Raku ordered you to, but he's *weak*. It's disgusting the way he's allowed himself to be manipulated by the hybrid *oud*."

Oud. It's a term so foul I cannot recall the last time that I heard it. It fills me with a sickening sense of anticipation. It's the scent that floods the plain of battle right before an assault, that metallic perfume.

I nod. "And you believe this is the only reason I keep watch over the female? Because the Raku ordered me to?"

They all nod, but they don't speak. Not when I take a step closer to them and all three of them seem to shrink. I release the hold on my ridges and let the Xanaxana's power fill them with a color I spend the better part of my solars trying to deny.

"Xok," the leader curses.

Pink ridges flare all around. Fear. Nox, not fear. *Terror*. I want them as terrified as they made Svera.

"Think again," I whisper, and then I lift my left hand and as colors braze bright through me, I end all three of them.

I am controlled and calm as I settle into the battle trance where there is no time, only the next thing and then the next thing and the thing that comes after that. Motions become actions as I grab the leader by the hair and by the plate on his back.

He revolves and takes on a fighting stance — one I xoking taught him — and when he kicks out at me, I have to release him in order to avoid the blade he produces from his training kilt.

He comes at me again, charging, but it's like he moves in slow motion. I easily step aside, grab his knife-wielding hand and, as he stumbles past, jerk his arm behind his back and break it.

He shrieks and I kick both of his knees in from the side, breaking his legs. I shove him forward, grab the knife and fling it at the coward attempting to run away. It hits him in the lower back, right where I meant it. It severs his spinal column cleanly between the second and third vertebrae, which paralyzes his legs.

He falls to the ground and I turn to the remaining male. He drops into a fighting stance, but the moment I feint towards him, he tries to run away.

I meet him on the threshold, grab him by the back of the head and crush his face against the wall, then again hard enough to shatter the bottom half of his face, ruining his nose, mouth and jaw, but not hard enough to blind him.

Nox, I want him to see *everything*.

I grab the males in Svera's room and drag them into the hall by the hair. I drag them past the cooking pits out of the house and onto the platform that surrounds it. I do not look at Tur'Roth.

I feel his presence but, if I look at him, I will kill him and I can't kill this moron for simply being neglectful and stupid. Because then where will I be? Exiled to Kor? Joining the Niahhorru pirates trying to steal females? Because I will have to. Xana leaves me no other choice.

I will always come for her.

As I toss the males into a jumbled pile, I'm aware of the looks I receive from the crowd that's gathered. *Let them watch. Let them spread word of what happens to those who look at Svera and try to wrong her.*

I begin removing their armor until they're each completely nude, then toss their bloodied kilts off of the platform and hear the screech of the animals below as they excite. I hear the sound of larger beasts chasing away the smaller ones, and then the cavra's unmistakable growl. *Xhtbey. They will be happy with my next offering.*

"Krisxox, our Krisxox, we are your honored fighters," the coward shrieks. He's panting, spittle flying from between his teeth as he grabs at the wound in his lower back.

The male with the shattered face tries to say something, but can't.

The leader screams, "Xok the female! She is worthless. She could not even fight us. All she did was call for you."

Failure.

The word rings and rings and rings. I reach for the leader, then remember — *slow* — and I take the male with the shattered face instead. I throw him over my shoulder, rise to stand, and see *his* face.

And then I see black. The color is so pure and lovely. Bloodlust. I feel it again. I try to cut it down, but it's a sturdy werro, able to endure.

"Krisxox," Tur'Roth says, advancing on me with a weapon drawn. "Easy. Put the…"

"Where were you!"

His jaw works. His gaze flashes to the door to my home. "I…"

"Would have stood outside and listened to her killed. *That is where you were.* Now if you do not wish to be a feast for the cavras, step the xok aside!"

Tur'Roth falls back like the coward he is. He stumbles away from me, hitting the far rail. He inches away from it like it'll grab him and drag him to the feast.

"Run!" I tell him. "And do not return. If I see you again, I will remove your plates and strip your title. You are inept. A xoking disgrace to xcleranx. That I let you leave here with your title at all is only Svera's grace."

"I..." He tries to be brave. "You only dare speak to me like this because you're jealous of the kiss Svera honored me with."

"*You're xoking right I'm jealous! She is my xoking Xiveri!*" The colors in my ridges scream, becoming so bright I'm momentarily blinded by them.

My chest is heaving. I pant, "If you ever come between me and my Xiveri Mate again, I will annihilate you." I struggle to breathe. I get lightheaded. "I will annihilate you, Tur'Roth. *Leave.*"

His ridges are plastered white. His mouth hangs open. White radiates from the rope bridge around me. So many faces watching me now, there will be no coming back from this. The whole of Voraxia will know. Svera will know. My sires will know.

Humiliation should be what I feel, but it's ruined a little bit by another emotion. *Pride.*

Tur'Roth nods and meets my gaze. "My regrets, Krisxox. I...did not know." He nods again and I stare ion rounds through him until he eventually turns and pushes his way through the crowd, disappearing for his own safety.

I hoist the male higher on my shoulder and turn to the railing at the edge of the platform. There are thick, retractable stalyx ropes mounted at even intervals that allow for quick escape. I grab one now, hit the release and it unfurls in my palm.

Jumping from the platform's edge, I let the rope propel me downward at its maximum speed. I kick aside branches threatening to incapacitate me and, twice, have to pull the mechanism to slow my descent so I don't kill us. Nox, I need the whimpering, crying coward in my arms alive for this.

We don't even reach Qath's mossy ground before the first cavra leaps for me. I swivel the coward's body around mine, using him as a shield as the cavra king sinks his claws into the coward's thick hide. He takes the coward from me and I listen to his shrieks as the cavra male feeds his pride.

I yank on the rope and shoot up, up, up.

I repeat the process with the other male and by the time I get to the leader, the cavras are sated, returned to their den. The leader's shrieking corpse is left to the gevrao, then — large rodents who follow the cats at the top of the food chain, but who eat slow.

I watch them feast on his legs and arms first, tunneling their way in. They get tired after they chew through his thighs and that's when the shock sets in. He passes out. I'm sure he'll wake again at least once more before they kill him and am satisfied.

I breathe.

I climb the rope, retract the cable and kneel on the platform outside of my open door. Like a valve releasing steam, I feel more capable of moving, but little else. I stand and hold onto the wall so fiercely my claws sink into it.

It isn't rage that's suddenly made my legs so wobbly, and it isn't fear. It's the Xanaxana. Now that I've released it, it doesn't want to go back into the place I've hidden it. It wants to be *known*.

The battle is fierce but eventually I win and stagger inside, colors gone. I stumble into the hall and reach the door and when I look inside, Svera is standing at the foot of her nest, looking shaken and fierce and vulnerable.

She's holding onto the edge of her nest with one hand. The other reaches up to touch her head scarf which has fallen to one side, revealing a batch of fuzzy curls combed back into a ball at the nape of her neck.

Her throat works. She touches the symbols hanging on worn beads in the center of her chest. "Thank you," she whimpers and her voice breaks.

I forgot that Xana and I haven't been locked in a battle, but a war. She surges again, this time with even greater force, and my colors glow, showering the room with light.

I roar away from the wall where I stand and advance on Svera. I capture her in my arms and I take her entire weight as she gives it up to me.

"Are you hurt?" I say, voice jerking as my palms skim her body, moving over her shoulders and back, her waist and hips.

She looks fine. She's got tears on her face, but she's alive and here and with me.

"Svera?"

She nods. "Hexa. Are...are you fine? You have blood...all over you." Her chest hitches in a way that makes my ridges glow pink.

"Can you breathe?" I place my hand on her chest where I can feel her lungs struggling.

"He...hexa." But she still hitches.

"Svera, breathe." I capture her against my chest and let her wet, watery eyes leak all over my neck, soaking into the strands of my hair that fall there, smelling like salt, like metal.

I brush my thumb over the cartilage in her ear. It's so soft, so strange how it moves for me like rubber. "I shouldn't have pushed you away," I growl against her skin. Soft as ash. Dreadful. Despicable. Human. *Mine.*

I taste her hairline, the sweat that's formed there. It's something that shouldn't fill me with want, but does. Just like everything else about her.

I start, "I shouldn't have..."

"I shouldn't have kissed Tur'Roth."

Surprise. I wasn't expecting this from her, and feel my xora do a little dance. I trace my claws down the curve of her face... slide my hand around the back of her neck, wrench her head back.

Nox, you shouldn't have," I growl.

Her fingernails scrape down the outsides of my arms. Her mouth and eyes are puffy and swollen and she's never been so beautiful. She licks her lips and my xora hardens. I snarl and quickly shift my hips away from her so she can't feel it, but she follows the line of my body with her own, plastering herself to my chest.

"Easy, Svera…"

She isn't listening to me. Instead, a shiver racks her body and she whispers, "It was for you."

She's a bloodthirsty thing. I know it now for certain. Because when she leans forward, I have no choice but to surrender.

My body stiffens and I move to meet her. My mouth hovers over hers. My calves are trembling and I try to stiffen them, but my impulse is to lie down and rut her senseless. I might have, if she'd let me. If she hadn't been nearly assaulted in the very nest I'm hallucinating taking her in.

"Take it," she says.

I've been with countless females, but right now, I make a sound I've never heard. Like I'm strangled. Maybe I am. She has a hold on me I can't escape.

"You were just assaulted. I shouldn't."

"Krisxox…"

I wrench her to meet me and my mouth comes down hard over hers. I kiss her and even though I've been practicing, I'm still struck.

They weren't…

They aren't...

She shouldn't...be so *soft*.

The heat is xoking inferno and I'm rendered stupid by it. I don't react at all after the initial contact. I just absorb the sensation of her hot, swollen mouth as her lips meet mine and she tastes me so eagerly.

It's that eagerness that undoes me. That throws me. That makes my left knee buckle. I have to lock it in order to stay standing at all.

"Krisxox," she mewls, *needy*.

I'm failing her for the third time, now. And I will not fail her a fourth.

My instinct is to devour, but I want to be different. I don't want her to think of me like Tur'Roth, who shoved his xoking tongue down her throat right in xoking front of me! I can't have her thinking of any male when she's in my arms. I want her to be lost just like I am lost.

I form my lips to her mouth's shape, inhaling her breath, carefully tracing her tongue with my own. I kiss her tenderly, careful with how battered these tears have made her mouth look.

She tastes like a battlefield. An asteroid belt full of mines. And I crash into every one of them.

Black and bloodthirsty.

I taste it on her breath, like smoke after the air clears. I let it fill my lungs. I wrap my arm around her ass and hoist her up against my body. I hold her high enough that she can't feel my erection against her hot core and so that she's looking down at me, gasping a little gasp every third time our lips meet.

And then something strange happens.

She blinks and holds the sides of my face, like she's trying to stabilize herself as she sways. The black in the center of her eyes is fully blown and I dive into it, a lone swimmer against a thousand waves.

Something *shifts*. The air gets heavier, thicker, harder to breathe through. I feel the weight on my own chest release ever so slightly and just as it does, Svera moans.

Moans.

"Svera." My grip hardens around her body and I start to lower her, but she writhes.

"Krisxox," she whimpers the moment her chest comes into contact with mine. Ruthlessly, she *rubs* herself against me.

"Xok…"

"Touch me," she yelps. "Please."

"Svera, you…were just…" *Reasons! Find them!* She's a human. I'm Drakesh. I'm Krisxox. She still carries her slave name. There's nothing to bind us.

Nothing but the universe.

"Take me to the nest and touch me," she moans again.

I stagger, having to catch myself on the nest to keep us both upright. "This is where they almost…"

"But they didn't because you were there. You saved my life." She releases her weight against my arm, leaving me no choice but to let her fall back into the center of the nest.

Well, I had other choices, but I ignored them.

"Svera." I take a step back, but it's the only one I can manage. I reach for my xora and, through my thick kilt, I try to tame it.

Svera's eyes flare and she spreads her legs and my mind turns over and my tail whips through the air frantically.

"Krisxox, *please.*" She begs me. My Xiveri Mate is xoking begging me to rut her.

And I'm standing here debating this?

Hexa, she's a human, I'm Drakesh, she's...*so xoking perfect.*

I lurch forward onto the nest, covering her body with mine, until I remember Nondah covering her in such a position and move to the side. I don't want to hold her down. I don't want to harm her.

She reaches for me, twisting onto her side to face me. She grabs my shoulder and I grab her neck and I tilt her head back and when she *whimpers,* all thoughts of restraint flit from my thoughts like fire from the end of a blow torch.

My tongue licks her mouth open and I spear the dark heat that I find. She grows more bold, biting my bottom lip between her teeth, before moving away from my mouth to my jaw to my neck.

Xok! The neck?

This...wasn't part of my training.

Nerves ignite throughout my body that I wasn't prepared for. Instantly, I want to see her reaction when I do the same thing to her.

I wrench her away from me, her hair cover slipping, and I devour her throat, biting hard on whatever skin that I find.

She moans my name and I can't xoking think. There is nothing but this. The weight in the air. The sensation of it binding us.

"All I could think about was being back on that ship with Nondah. I was so scared…" Her words contradict her actions when she grabs my hand and shapes it to her breast.

I squeeze all on my own and I'm shaken. Shaking with need. With despair. With relief. With a whole xoking host of emotions that she has drawn out of me.

"Me, too."

Her hands in my hair delve into the strands, even though she has no claws. She clutches me to her with all the strength she has.

"But you came for me."

Bang. Bang. Boom. *Krisxox.*

"You came for me again. Just like you did last time."

I meet her gaze and hold it and time hangs between us as I give voice to one fatal truth. "I will always come for you."

Her eyes water and her hand reaches between us to my kilt, but I shift away from her touch. I can't. Not like this.

Momentary hurt flashes across her expression and my gut twists. I want to explain to her what I'm feeling, but I don't know what that is. So, I go back for her throat, kissing my way up and down. Experimenting. What else will elicit these wonderful, beautiful moans from her?

I taste her ear, suckling the lobe and biting down on that soft, rubbery shell. "Ahh!" She shouts. Her back arches and she pushes my hand down from her breast, down, down, down until I can feel the thatch of her curls through her shift.

"It's hot here. So xoking hot," I moan, growing delirious as I rub her.

She's writhing uncontrollably now and I'm about to spill my seed all over her and I haven't even seen her yet. And I *need* to see her. I will not rut her, but I will not leave her like this.

I grab her shift in a fist and pull. I half expect her tell me to stop since her god requires her to remain covered, and I *don't* expect her to lift her hips and yank her shift up even more. I'm going too slowly for her.

I laugh and when I pull back and look at her face, I see it.

Lost.

Purely lost.

I pull her shirt up to her waist and reach down until my fingers finally touch fur. It's a denser curl than that of her hair, but the same color. And it's *soaked*.

"Are you wet for me, human?"

Her eyes narrow, black dots in them contracting... but only until I feel my way past the fur to the small, soft bit of skin just below it.

She gasps, her hand catches my shoulder and she digs her blunted claws into my skin. "Krisxox! Stars!" It's the closest to a curse I've ever heard from her and it makes me grin all over again.

"You aren't familiar with this, are you?" I ask and when she shakes her head, I feel awash with satisfaction.

I swirl my fingers around the skin that makes her writhe and twist, then slip them lower. She closes her eyes. I kiss the space between them.

"I haven't blunted my claws yet, so I cannot enter you."

She's panting, face twisting in what looks like pain but is its opposite. "Krisxox...I need..."

"Shh. I'll tell you what you need and you'll take it, won't you, human?"

Her eyes fly open and she looks frightened as I use my entire palm to massage her core. She tries to pull her legs together, but I wrap my tail around her knee and keep her open and exposed to me.

You have nothing to fear, Svera. Not with me. Not ever. Just trust me through this."

She nods even as tears well in her eyes, even as the pressure of my palm against her core becomes more intense, even as my fingers carefully flick the skin that is most sensitive.

Rivers of her magnificent aroma spill out across my hand as she shudders, struggling to take in air. Her mouth opens in a silent gasp and she grabs me so hard, I can see her arms, how they shake.

I rub my palm more gently against her tender skin and watch as the first orgasm rises up in her body. Every inch of it is twisted by the pleasure I give her and as it peaks, she shouts a curse I *never* thought I'd hear her say to the roof.

"Xok!" She's holding onto me for dear life and droplets of water are spilling from her eyes and her heels are digging into the fur beneath her and all it takes is my hips grinding into the nest beneath me for her orgasm to draw one out of me.

I try to suppress it so I can stay present for her, but it's too powerful. It hits me over the head, just like Xana hits me over the head. With one conk. I'm out.

I arch over her and press my lips to hers and even though this can hardly be called a kiss with how tight we both are, I want to taste her as she comes for me for the first time.

The first time of many.

What would my sires —

xok: This time, the curse is entirely mine.

The kiss breaks as I hurtle to cover her body, face-planting in the furs over her shoulder while my hand continues to pump unevenly against her wet, watering slit and my hips continue to piston onto the nest, rutting, rutting, rutting...*xok!*

Seed rips out of me and I feel it spurt on the inside of my kilt and I'm xoking furious that it isn't spilling all over her. I want to see her soaked with it. I want to see it on her breasts, in her pussy, on her tongue.

"Svera," I shout at the same time that she shouts, "Krisxox!"

She's screaming loudly now, holding onto me anywhere she can. Her hips lift from the nest and grind into my palm as she works her own orgasm out the way she wants. I match the pulses, match the turns, match the beat until my xora spills its last drop and her ragged gasps even.

Time passes. A lot of it. I blink my eyes open to the sensation of her fingers on the outside of my arm.

I'm lying beside her and she's looking at me. "Was that..."

"Just the beginning," I answer and I feel a fool right after. She's *still* a human. I'm *still* Krisxox.

"Oh stars. What have I done?" She says and she covers her eyes with her hand.

thing, panic grips me to hear her say it. I take her wrist with my sticky, wet palm and pull it aside.

"Verax, Svera. What is it? Did I hurt you?"

"Nox. Nox… Just." She shakes her head. "The Tri-God. This is wrong."

"This is Xana. You had no more choice in it than I did." And it isn't over. The rutting rage of the Xanaxana will take longer than this between us. This was just an isolated blip in time. An accident.

That will happen again and again…

Xok. What would my —

"It doesn't matter," I grunt. "It's over. It won't happen again."

She looks between my eyes, as if searching for truth. I don't know if she'll find it, but I'm happy to let her look. "You don't even like me."

"Nox. And you find me a terrifying monster, so we're even. It was just biological. It couldn't be avoided. Your god will forgive you for this. In fact, this didn't even happen. You're in shock."

"Shock?"

"Hexa. It's not even real. I'm not even here now. I'm outside shouting at warriors and you're in here, preparing for departure. None of this happened."

A corner of her mouth quirks. Her expression softens. "It does feel like a dream."

That's because it is a dream. Go back to sleep and when you wake up, everything will be right in the universe."

She touches the edge of my jaw, but I see how her eyelids get heavy. I glance down and my hips jerk forward, towards her. Her shift is still up around her hips and my hand is still tickling her fur. I bring it up to her stomach, then to her chest mound — her *breast* — and I squeeze it.

She inhales and blinks many times.

I'm ready for more. I *need* it. "This isn't happening either."

I pull back, aware that we're on dangerous ground, and kiss her quickly, just once more.

Alright, again. Just one more time.

And another.

When I pull back, I drag a blanket over her and make sure I'm still on the outside of it. The barrier is flimsy, but needed. She's sleepy, traumatized, in shock. She doesn't need me rutting her on accident. Already, this was too much.

She exhales, "Thank you, Krisxox. Even if this never happened, I'll always remember that you came when I called you…"

She closes her eyes and her breathing mellows out almost immediately. She melts against me, resting her head on my arm, but as she does, she melts me, too.

The boat I'd been shoveling water out of has fully capsized and I'm drowning happily now. The bond I'd been trying to break has won. It already won and now it sits there laughing at me. It rips, tears, pushes and pulls.

It winds into and out of me, like a thick needle through thin skin, stitching itself into the fabric of my existence. My colors bathe the entire room in light. I know that she's seen it and that I should care, but as she sleeps and I watch her sleep, I wonder…what's the point?

Her small, delicate fingers against my skin.

Her heat.

Her wet eyes and her red cheeks.

She still has scars. And I still have scars. If she disappeared from my arms this instant — if she'd been *taken* from me by those xoking fools — I'd still carry her like this with me forever. And she'd be just as heavy. She bought me at an auction I didn't know existed at a price I'd never have agreed to. And that price? Just my soul. Just every piece of my shriveled xoking hearts.

Silently — *painfully* — I slip out of her nest and gather her things. I pack clothes for her, what I think she'll need, anyway. I make sure to grab multiple scarves for her hair.

I grab everything out of her washroom. I even pack the gifts she bought for her kinswoman and the new kit and, when everything is ready, I pack Svera up, too.

I cradle her in my arms and let her sleep as I issue the order for the xub'Ixria to fetch us from my home in a glider and take us to the transporter so that Svera does not miss the birth of the hybrid. Not because I feel any differently towards the Rakukanna and her new kit, but because I know that my Xiveri Mate would not want to.

6

Svera

We're together in one of the domes. I know we shouldn't be, but I pretend that this is okay. I haven't been given leave to stay in other quarters on Qath, so I'm not sure I should even try here on Nobu for such a short stay, and I'm not willing to risk Krisxox's wrath. Not on this lunar. Not after so much war has been worn across the bright white cold that blankets Nobu. Not after so much bloodlust has been sated.

Inside the dome, it's cold despite the flames gathered in the stone pit in the center of the small, cozy space, casting heat. It's cold despite the layers and layers of furs bundled around me. It's cold and still Krisxox sits shirtless on a short stool in front of me. He wouldn't let Nobu's healers stitch him, but when I pressed, he said it would be alright if I did it. I told him I'd never stitched skin before and he told me he didn't care.

Ordinarily, Lemoria would have passed a healing torch over the wounds, sealing them quickly and painlessly, but because this was a trial and Krisxox interceded when I should have been allowed to choose my own champion freely, he is being punished. It feels as if I am, too.

I work silently, sticking the pointy end of the curved needle through his skin again and again, trying to blink past the pain I feel seeing another creature in pain. Even one as deplorable as Krisxox. We don't speak at all. I'm still furious with him and he doesn't care.

The longer he goes without speaking, the angrier I get. I want to yell at him. To scream. I want to pound on his back with my fists. My fingers start shaking with that desire and I finally drop the needle, let it dangle from a single black string sticking out of his back like the forgotten noose of a victim long dead.

And then he says evenly, glibly, like it doesn't matter at all, "If she were not Xhea, I'd be tempted to invite your human to train with the warriors on Qath."

The words I'd been prepared to launch like lances shove back into my mouth, down my throat and into my belly where they stand rooted. Tension deflates from my shoulders. They sink down my back. I didn't realize my face was all screwed up until it releases. A small smile flickers over my mouth and I look up into the long mirror leaning against the wall in front of Krisxox. His ridges are brightly colored again, but when he meets my gaze, the color cuts and a sensation bubbles in my chest that I haven't felt before.

He says stoically, "She has a warrior's heart."

The bubble gets bigger, swelling until I feel like it's about to take me off of my feet. I have to catch myself on something and the only thing near is Krisxox. I place a single hand on his shoulder and his ridges go wild with color, but only for less than a blink.

I swallow hard and my voice is teeny tiny when I say, "What are we doing, Krisxox?"

"Nothing," he grunts, avoiding my gaze.

"I mean, what are we?"

"Ruined," he grunts again, though this sound is tainted by humorless laughter.

I nod, understanding, and return my fingers to the slender needle. "There is a proverb that says, 'When I am with you in the ruins, I am in the garden, but when I am without you in the garden, I am in the ruins.'"

More humorless laughter. Krisxox shakes his head. "What is this? Some ode to your precious Tri-God?"

I smile, but it does not fill me with pleasure, but with sadness. Perhaps a touch of both. "Nox. My grandfather used to say this to my grandmother. It is a proverb about love."

I wake from the memory confused. Not just because it's the first dream I've had in rotations that hasn't featured Nondah, but because I'm lost and I'm not in the garden.

Where am I?

I tense against the sheets, my heart battering around in my chest. I try to inhale and exhale deep breaths, but they don't come to me easily. I'm scared. Terrified.

And worse than all those things…I'm *aroused*.

Flame. It rips through my sternum, like a struck match, and sets fire to the patch of hair between my thighs. I squeeze them together. *Where am I?* All I want is the answer to that question. All my body wants is *him*.

The sensation doesn't belong here and is so out of place, I feel a blooming headache in the front of my skull and no matter how I twist and turn in the pallet beneath me, it won't let me go.

"Krisxox," I whisper, needy in a way I don't recognize.

I reach up and thread my fingers through my hair. There's a head scarf lying next to me on the pillow, but it must have fallen off.

I pull the band out of my hair and shake my curls free, hoping that satisfies the headache. It doesn't. Instead, the bubble in my gut swells, threatening to tear through my skin. My cheeks fill with fire and likely color, too. I wonder, do the Voraxians think I'm angry all the time?

The thought makes me want to laugh. Instead, I release a painful sob, "Krisxox!"

My body curls up, like it's trying to protect me from some external foe when the enemy is here, inside…

The doors whoosh open and Krisxox sweeps his blaster around at the space. He carries two blasters, a sword, and too many daggers to count — and is that a grenade?

"Where," he snarls, "Svera, where is the enemy?"

"Nox," I beg. The sight of him makes the fire raging through me worse. "Please." I reach for him at the same time the doors slip shut at his back.

The calm battle god looks hollowed out. He drops his blaster. He drops his other blaster. He frees his weapons' belt and the rest of the weapons clatter at his feet.

"Xok," he curses. "The Xanaxana is strong in you, isn't it?"

I don't know. I don't anything except that I need him. I *need* him.

"I need you inside of me."

I've seen Krisxox struck many times and I've never seen him react like he does now. He falls back, crashing against the wall beside the door. One of his hands runs up through his hair. The other goes to the band securing his trousers. He pushes the release and they drop to the floor. It's all sleek grey and, judging by the pallet surrounding me covered in crisp, standard-issue werro-fiber sheets, I know we're on some kind of transporter.

Something about Miari. She's doing something important this solar, but I can't remember what it is.

Looking at his xora — the first one I've ever seen — I can't remember my own name.

"Svera," he barks. He shakes his head, but his hand is already on his xora, touching that long shaft. It's gorgeous. "Nox. You worship a god...you can't."

A small voice in the back of my mind tells me he's right, but I can't recall why that matters. "Why do you care?" I rasp. Is that me? Or is someone else working me like a puppet? This is not who I am. I am...

"Svera," he balks.

"Nox! Krisxox, please!" I reach for the collar of my shift. "Tear it. You have to tear it. And move your hand. Let me see..."

His fist drops from his xora and my mouth waters. The arousal heated in my core pours down the insides of my thighs. I should be squeezing them together to try to staunch the flow, but I don't do that either.

Instead, I roll onto my hands and knees, spread my thighs and stare a hole through Krisxox's crotch. His xora is so long and thick. Dark red and throbbing, it has ridges up the back of it. They fire with color the longer I look at them, radiating a whole host of indigo shades.

"Krisxox, *now!*"

"Augh!" He storms forward, reaching me in two short strides. He grabs the collar of my dress in his enormous hands and rips it straight down the middle. He curses as my body comes into view.

Krisxox… I reach for him and let my fingers trace the outline of his xora. I touch it, grab it, *fist* it.

"Nox. Nox…" He reels back. His chest is heaving and his colors are mutinous. I can't read any of them.

Anger riles me and I release his xora and pound my fist on the pallet. Pain. It needles the center of my sternum, like a tree taking root where it isn't supposed to. It grows and flowers and all of its branches are covered in thorns.

"You find me so disgusting?"

"Nox."

I clutch my chest, trying to staunch the growth of that pain. It doesn't work. "Then *why*? Why do you insist on torturing me like this?"

"Nox," he roars, meeting my gaze. "Nox. I'm not…I would…the things I would…I would lay *waste* to armies just to have you once. But I haven't *mah'ree* you."

"*Mar'ree?*" I say, repeating the Drakesh word for fruit. "What does fruit have to do with this?" My voice twists, panic warping it.

"Nox," he snarls, pulling at his hair now. Yanking at it. "The human word you use *mah'ree…may'ree.*"

Married. He hasn't married me.

"Married?" I repeat, aghast. "You want to *marry* me? You don't even know what that is. You don't even like me. You *hate* humans. You hate *me*."

"I never xoking said that," he shouts, grabbing his xora again. Blue beads on the tip. I want to taste it. I

74

want it *in* me. It has to be in me. That's the only thing that matters. "And I never said I wanted to xoking *may'ree* you. I just said you don't have to do this. Your god won't let you without *may'ree*."

I level him with a stare. One I've never used. I glance at the door to his left. "Then get out of here and send in Tur'Roth."

"You bloodthirsty xoking human..." He roars and suddenly he moves in that Krisxox way he does. He's by the wall, and then he isn't.

He's kneeling on the foot of my pallet and his hand is on my chest. He pushes me back very gently and then hooks his hands under my knees. He spreads my legs around his hips and snarls down at me.

"Don't you xoking say his name. There are *no other males for you.* There is only me."

I scoff, feeling wild, feeling crazy. "You have no claim over me. Not with the harem of females you keep."

"They're all practice." He drops onto his elbows over me, hips positioned between my thighs. My legs are trembling. My heart is racing. I can't catch my breath. I can't...do...anything...

"Practice for what?" I humor him, but only because he still hasn't touched me. His chest is so close, but he doesn't drop it close enough to scrape the peaks of my nipples. "Krisxox..."

Practice for you, idiot. I'd never kissed anyone before we discovered your species. I wanted to be sure I knew how to ruin you…"

Anger. I clasp my fingers behind his neck, then yank violently on his hair. He hisses, but resists when I try to pull down his mouth down to meet my own.

"You expect me to believe that? I've heard their moans through your door in the middle of the lunar."

"You can believe what you like and you…" He freezes, exhaling a breath a little deeper than the last. I can taste his sweet, citrus scent in the back of my throat a dagger of pleasure splits my clitoris in half. I'm going to burst. *I need to burst!*

"Krisxox!"

"Xok!" He reaches between us and covers my entire core with his palm.

I whimper wildly, thrashing now, but he refuses to move. He holds me down, fingers tangled in my hair, anchoring the back of my head to the mattress. With his palm on my crotch, he pins my hips.

"Krisxox!"

"Nox! Tell me. Were you listening at the door to my room in the lunar?"

"Hexa!"

"Why?"

I shout the truth. "I didn't like that you were with them."

He growls and the color in his ridges explodes. "You didn't like imagining me sinking my xora deep into the body of another female?"

He starts to move his palm, massaging me. Distantly, I remember him doing this to me before and it felt...simply...no, there is no simple. It felt treacherous and incredible. Full of both hate and love.

"Svera."

"Nox," I pant, "I didn't like that. The sounds. Hearing her moans."

"What else did you hear?"

"Grunts. The sound of your bodies..." He removes his hand and all at once, replaces it with his xora.

"Ooh!" I scream at its heat. I glance down between us, pushing on his shoulder until I can see the engorged head of his xora pressing against my clit. "Stars...Krisxox..."

His fist looks enormous around his xora as he begins to trace patterns across my clit, sweeping up and down through my sopping folds. They hurt. They hurt so badly...

I hook my arm around his neck and try to kiss him, but he won't let me. "Please..."

He meets my gaze, gently strokes his hand through my hair, gliding his claws across my scalp, forcing a shudder through my body. "I only kissed those females Svera, and only to practice for this. I dismissed them before the rutting and, after they left, I fisted my own xora just like this and always to thoughts of you."

"I touched myself to thoughts of you," I heave, hardly listening. I'm sure he's lying anyway. There'd be no reason for him to tell the truth. Not when he's about to get the only thing I'm sure he's ever wanted from me. The thing I've guarded and kept safe. And now I'm throwing it at him and he's reticent to take it.

The Tri-God has a wicked sense of humor.

Only, I'm fairly sure the Tri-God has nothing to do with this.

It's blasphemous.

It's exhilarating.

Whatever it is feels so unimaginably good. I suddenly understand the lives that sinners lead, drinking and scheming and lying and rutting. Rutting. I want to rut!

Krisxox sucks in a breath between his clenched teeth and the wind it creates shoots down the front of my body to caress my nipples, bringing their peaks to painful points.

"Krisxox…" I grab onto his shoulders, using him for strength.

"You…touched yourself thinking of me?"

"Hexa. Now *please.* Rut me. Breed me. Take me. I need your xora in me. It's so big, so hot. I imagined it often, what it would look like. Yours is the first xora I've ever seen."

"And it is the *last* xora you'll ever see."

His chest rumbles, vibrating in a way that makes me worry that the ship is shaking apart. I wouldn't care if it did. All I care about is the bubble in my abdomen and shredding it.

"Krisxox..."

"*Yess*. Look down at my xora now, Svera. Watch closely."

Surprise at hearing a human word in his throaty Drakesh accent stalls me. My lips flutter, like I'm searching for some question or acknowledgement that I can't find when Krisxox shifts — not a lot, just a little — but enough to bring the engorged head of his xora to the folds of my womanhood.

I look away even though he told me to watch, preferring to focus on his face in the hope that it will make the little voice in the back of my head go away. Because I don't want him to stop.

"Svera," he breathes. "You don't have to do this."

Can he read my thoughts?

"Mmmm," I bend and break. The bubble is stretching me past my limit. I shake my head. Tears wind out of the corners of my eyes, or maybe not. My eyes are burning. "I need you inside me."

"You can fight it, Svera. I've been fighting the Xanaxana for rotations."

"It hurts..." There they come. The tears leak.

Krisxox hisses at the sight of them. He starts to pull back, but I dig my nails into his shoulders and hold him still. "Nox. Please. I'm not..." I lick my lips.

I'm not a fighter. I'm not like you. I can't win against this."

"But your god…"

"Your god is stronger."

He nods and I know he understands. He kisses my chin, my nose, each of my cheeks. Then he licks the seam of my lips and, like magic, they part. He catches my mouth with his and kisses me so deeply, more tears well in my eyes. I'm lost in the universe.

"Exhale on the count of three," he tells me. I slip one hand around his neck, the other around his thick upper arm.

"One." I nod once and feel the huge rod of him begin to make a maddeningly slow march forward. Goosebumps cover my arms and when he reaches out and trails just the lightest pad of his fingers over them, I close my eyes.

"Svera," he growls.

I cut him off. "I want to do this. But I…need you to lead. I don't know how."

Krisxox's hair hangs towards me, the long tendrils creating two curtains on either side of my face. I blink my eyes up at him and stare at him between my lashes. He's holding his breath. Time slows and stills.

"Two," he says, sliding a little further forward, *inside me.*

I gasp as my body grips him like a glove around a hand. The pressure is already so intense and I feel so full and I…

"Is this it? Am I still…a virgin?"

He barks out a desperate laugh. "Hexa, Svera. You are still a virgin. I'm not all the way inside you yet." He laces his fingers with mine. He presses his lips to the center of my forehead.

"Are you…cold?"

He laughs again, more fully this time, and his whole body shakes with the sound. "Nox, Svera. I'm on *fire*."

"But you're trembling."

"You," he grumbles, voice so low I almost can't make it out.

"Verax."

And then a little louder. "You make me feel like I've never done this before."

"Are you…" I hesitate, and in the haze of my fever, the word tumbles out, "nervous?"

"Xoking terrified. The garden is a beautiful place and I'm scared to enter it with you because I may never leave it. I shouldn't want to stay there, but I…I think I do."

I shiver, and that small voice surges, demanding to be heard. *This is more than flesh. This is Xanaxana. What will joining now mean for us?* But it doesn't matter when I inhale his sweet citrus into me.

I writhe, trying to get some friction against my clit. "Take me to the garden, Krisxox," I mewl.

The indigo in his ridges blazes even brighter and he releases a brutish grunt. He meets my gaze and nods just once.

"Three."

He pushes forward with one hard jerk and every muscle in my body tightens in unison. I scream and it is a *pained* scream. I'm trying to get away, but Krisxox is holding me still, steady. He plants strangely sweet kisses all over my forehead and throat. *Strange for a male incapable of love that he should be so loving…*

My eyes squeeze shut tight, but Krisxox is murmuring in my ear. He bites the lobe, laves the inside and then kisses the tender skin behind it. I'm suddenly distracted by the rush of warmth that cascades down my left side. He tells me to breathe, so I breathe.

Whoosh. That's the sound of my soul leaving my body. Aaahhh. That's the sound of my soul resettling over my limp frame.

"That's it," he encourages. "There…" His voice sounds more pained than I feel and he barks into the curve of my neck when his hips retreat just a hair, then move forward.

He repeats the motion, hardly moving at all, and snarls again. Meanwhile, I'm going through my own spiral. Competing sensations are warring over my body. Desire versus fear. Warmth versus ice. Pleasure versus pain. With another soft roll of his body over mine, pleasure finally wins.

"Krisxox…"

His hips shift back even further until almost all of him is out of me. I push back on his shoulders and look down at the space between our bodies, the product of my virginity shimmering on his rock solid erection in shades of pink.

"Oh stars…"

"Xok!" He roars at the same time. "Svera, I…I just…" He doesn't finish that sentence. He doesn't finish any sentence, even though he starts a dozen. Or a hundred.

My legs are spread around him so wide they start to shake and burn. Which is good, because this way my outsides can match my insides.

"Fill me, Krisxox. I want your seed inside."

"Xok! Svera!"

The shadow of a smile falls across my lips when he pulls back just enough to look into my eyes. He is shining with a legion of colors, white and lavender screaming louder than the rest. Surprise. Somehow, that fuels me more than the sight of the purple. Krisxox, who has been with so many females he has likely sampled all Voraxia has to offer, is *surprised* by me.

"Verax," he manages to grunt, though it's hardly intelligible.

I'm still thinking about that surprise. It's brighter than the lavender. Does that mean it's a good surprise? Or not good? Gasping and panting, I manage to squeeze out the words I need to.

"Do…I…please you?"

He guffaws. *Guffaws.* The sound is the most unattractive he's ever made and his hips suddenly lose their rhythm. He stops fully sheathed inside of me and reaches between us to knead my right breast, finally giving me what I've wanted this whole time. I shout with need.

"Do you please me? You do not *just* please me. You make me forget who I am," he rumbles.

"You are Krisxox," I tell him, darkness closing in as the spiral tightens and the bubble lifts me up, up, up, through the ceiling, out into the cosmos.

"Nox. Not anymore. Krisxox would never have rutted a human."

I gasp when he starts to plunge his hips forward again, electrifying so many places inside of me that I squeeze convulsively around him.

"Don't worry…this…isn't…happening!" I gasp on each thrust.

He picks up his pace and smooths his hand over my hair, cradling the back of my head. He kisses me slowly, lips raw heat and desire.

Against them, he says, "And it won't happen again and again and again."

I close my eyes in an effort to block him out and the sensations that his words stir within me. I fight to remember that he isn't a good male, that he has said and believed terrible things against the Tri-God's teachings, that even if he may worship me now, it's possible he doesn't even like me and he certainly does not respect me yet, but...Krisxox is a ruthless battle strategist, and he may win this war yet.

His other hand switches under my hips and while he holds himself up on one elbow, he manages to wrench my entire lower half up off of the pallet. The angle changes and his xora charges deeper inside of me, activating a hidden control panel and only he knows the codes. My whole body reacts. He *owns* me.

I curl my nails into his skin so hard I think I might draw blood, but I can't relax my hold. "You?" He says to me as I gasp and grunt and moan. "Do I please you?"

I'm strangely touched. Even though I worry about his pleasure, I did not expect him to care about mine. My head falls back and I heave, "Hexa, Krisxox...I am in the garden now. Are you...here... with me?"

"I'm here," he growls, shouting, moving faster, more frantically. "Xok, Svera! I'm here..."

He growls against my mouth before invading it with his tongue. He tastes like me. Like salt and like some sort of poisonous flower. I feel drugged as he breaks free and swallows in air, while below, his hips continue to pound into me with the same stultifying pressure. How does he not falter? Where does he get his strength from when I can barely lift my head?

He releases my hair, then snakes his hand between us to touch the sensitive bundle of nerves just below my curls. He brushes it with all six of his fingers, just feathery touches, and I erupt.

"Oh!" My shoulders jump up beneath my ears and I panic. He holds me steady and does not release his pace or the hold he has on me.

"Hexa," he whispers and then when I start to shake with violence now, "*Yess...*"

"Arck!" I yelp, torso jolting off of the pallet like I've been touched by the cold hand of electricity. My soul leaves my bones. I float up into the universe surrounding us on all sides. I see the cosmos in Krisxox's eyes, unsure where the edges of the room that's swallowed us end and where he begins or where I fit into the mixture.

He is suddenly *everything*.

I'm bruised and wounded, cut open and sewn shut and as I blink away the water that fills my eyes in a sudden rush, Krisxox touches his forehead to mine and a warm breath jerks out of his throat and he says my name and his back muscles tense beneath my hand and his hips rock and rock and rock...

Warmth. It explodes inside of me and I feel suddenly dizzy and disoriented. There's a pain in my gut and a fuel in my core where I feel his hot desire pushing through me.

I didn't think this through.

I didn't think *any* of this through. How could I have? I wouldn't have expected that I could get addicted to sin. I thought that the Tri-God would spare me from this punishment. I didn't expect that I would ever feel the Xanaxana in me like this.

I am not a Voraxian and their beliefs are not my own. I am not in love with Krisxox. I thought Xanaxana was stronger than lust, but it isn't. Because as I spiral out of control and squeeze my eyes shut tight and Krisxox barks my name, demanding my attention and our eyes lock and the light of his ridges drowns out the sight of the room around us, I know that I'm lost to pleasure. Lost to the small flecks of good that tether me to him. Perhaps I always was.

Perhaps this is sin.

Perhaps this is heaven.

I don't know anything anymore except that the bubble has burst. Shattered. The voice is gone, too. The act is finished. There's no taking it back.

He's breathing hard, but no less hard than I am and no more.

And then the second wave of the orgasm shatters me, splitting my skull like an overripe fruit. I fall apart in Krisxox's arms while my hips buck and writhe and I rub my clit ruthlessly up and down his body. He matches my uneven thrusts like he knows where I'm going, even though I don't know where I am.

He makes gurgled sounds that should be embarrassing, but they only pull more of my soul through that tether, binding me to him. Xanaxana. This is it. *Tri-God help me. Tri-God save me from this.*

Only, I don't want to be saved. Lost in the garden now, I have no desire to be found.

"Svera," he chokes. "Svera, are you alright?"

I blink my eyes open, but the colors all shift and blur together. My fingers are tangled in his hair, my arms slack around his neck.

I shake my head and he hisses, "Xok. I'm sorry. I didn't...I..."

But there's nothing to be said.

"I'm your Xiveri Mate." I sniff. The wildfire in my chest has dimmed to a small bonfire. I still hurt. Still ache. Still want. But I can think. I know my name.

I know my shame.

"Where are...where are my beads?" I say.

Krisxox is still inside of me and I'm talking about my beads. "Verax." He looks confused. He should be.

"Can you please..." I push on his shoulders tentatively, scared to touch him. Scared to look at him. If I do, I'll start this all over again. Even now, I can feel his xora like a hot ember inside of me. I want more. More. I never want to stop!

Oh stars. What is happening to me?

I try to wriggle out from under him, but he holds my shoulder gently. "Wait. I don't want to hurt you," he mumbles under his breath.

"Oh…that is…kind."

Krisxox grunts out what sounds like my name, but I don't react to it. I just keep my gaze trained on the space where our bodies meet and watch Krisxox sit up and reach between us.

Slowly…*so, so slowly*…he works his length out of me. We both hiss as his engorged head finally slips free of my core. He's still erect and my throat bobs at the sight of it. "Did you…"

"Hexa," he growls, smearing blue across the inside of my left thigh. It trembles under his touch, all the way up to my lips, which gasp. "Harder than I ever have before."

"You're still…*stiff.*"

"Hexa. Because I am ready for you again. A thousand times more." Even as he says what he does, he still reaches for my knees and slowly…so, so slowly…pushes them back together. I expect pain, but he moves so gently that all I feel is a dull ache through the outsides of my legs and rear, up my back, in my arms, my hands…everything aches.

I start to roll out from beneath him and reach for my shift, but when I pull it over my lap, I remember that it's torn. I palm the empty space around my neck as my panic rises.

"What's wrong? Talk to me. What hurts?"

Krisxox shifts towards me and covers the hand on my chest with his own. Right between my breasts. Right over my heart. I meet his gaze and say nothing. There is nothing to say.

"My nagoom-cross?"

He hesitates, trying to read my expression.

I can't stand it. His gaze fills me with fire. I can feel nothing but liquid between my legs. His blue seed, mixed with my own syrupy orgasm, plus a little bit of pink. *I'm not a virgin anymore.*

And I'm not married.

"Krisxox." My voice is three notches higher. I start to sweat.

"It's here." He reaches to the edge of the pallet. There is a small pull-out table there with my nagoom-cross next to a small packet of water. I reach for both simultaneously, rip open and drain the packet, loop the cross over my neck and try to get out of bed. It's… difficult.

Not only because my legs aren't cooperating with me, but because I want to stay. I want the bubble to come and erase the little voice again. Only there is no little voice and maybe there never was a bubble.

Maybe there is only me.

"You can go now," I say as I waddle awkwardly to the wet room attached to this one, trying not to let any of the seed still lodged deep in my body spill out on the floor.

But I thank you," I add over my shoulder. My voice catches. It's shaky. Everything's shaky.

I expect the door to the wet room to close behind me, but it beeps in alarm. I turn and see Krisxox naked in the doorway, blocking it with his body.

My breathing starts to accelerate. I want to go to him, *run* to him, taste the way I taste by licking his xora clean.

Oh stars. Tri-God…no! *No, I can't turn to him now unless it's to beg forgiveness.*

"Krisxox, I…"

"You begged for me and now you're dismissing me." His voice is cold, his ridges, for the first time, expressionless.

"Hexa."

He snorts, his hair ruffling in the wind his breath creates. *Oh stars, he's an attractive male…* Why does he have to be so attractive?

"Why?"

I shudder. "It shouldn't have happened."

"You said that you wanted it to happen."

"I did."

"You said that you knew the consequences."

"Well, I'm a sinner now. I lied."

He's silent and I don't look at him as I step into the water tube in the center of the room. I want to beg him to leave, but I don't want to talk to him. I want to get clean and pretend…

I don't know what I want.

we both did," he growls and he slams his fist on the wall hard enough to make me jump.

Water rushes over me as I grip the beads around my neck in a vice. "Please leave, Krisxox."

"Nox."

Anger. I rub my face roughly and turn away from him, so he can't see my front. Water washes over me, sending blue lines streaking down my legs. "Krisxox…" My voice is shaking.

"Nox."

"I don't understand why leaving me alone now is so difficult for you." I try to sound strong, but my voice is shaking. "You hate humans."

"I don't hate you."

"I am human. You can't have it both ways. I…I heard what you said about Miari's baby…"

"And I heard what you said when I saved your life from my own kind. I killed them for you."

"You…verax."

Krisxox shifts, but he doesn't break my gaze. "I killed them. It was within my authorization from the Raku. I didn't do anything illegal."

"But you…they're dead because of me?"

"They're dead because of *them*. Because they came into my house and threatened my Xiveri Mate."

Irritation flares as hot as the water pouring from the overhead grate. "So, you killed them because they dishonored you."

"Hexa." He stiffens. "Nox. That isn't…"

it is. And I'm sorry. I didn't think you would care this much." I didn't think *I* would care this much. I'm not sure I was thinking at all.

My heart...gapes. It feels like...like my heart's been torn out of my chest and shoved into his. He stole it and I'm not strong enough to recover it. Not against the Krisxox of Voraxia.

"Svera, you can't deny this! You showed me the garden. I belong there now. We both do."

"Nox, Krisxox." Hot water rushes over me, erasing what has been. "Now, we are just ruined."

He roars and punches the wall again. "This is not over between us, Svera."

"You're right. Because this never happened. There is no us."

7

Svera

The moment he leaves, I drop to my knees and lower my forehead to the floor. I pray. I stand and kneel and stand again. I hold my nagoom-cross so tight in my fist I plan to leave bruises on my fingertips.

Maybe they'll match the marks he left on my throat.

I tried rubbing at them and blotting them with a cool cloth, but there are visible marks on my neck I can't ignore. They stand out in dark plum against my light brown skin.

What did I think, that I'd be able to hide from it? Maybe I did.

I stare down at the head scarf on my pallet, wondering what to do. I'm not allowed to wear it anymore. I'm a ruined woman. Only virgins wear the scarves. Everyone will know I'm not married. Everyone will know that the Xanaxana came for me and I failed the test of the Tri-God.

Krisxox...he's felt *this* for me for so long, but he's managed to fight it. I felt *this* long enough to open my eyes. To consummate it from that point took me less than the next moment.

Maybe he's more deserving of the Tri-God's love than I am. The Tri-God, like Krisxox, values strength and he is nothing if not strong.

The way he carried me, taking my body's full weight. The way he moved me around where he needed me. Where I didn't know I needed to be. The way he took control and held me through the initial pain.

Tears prick my eyes as I start to heat all over again. "No, no. Please. Tri-God." I drop to my knees and pray for forgiveness. *What will my father say?*

He and my brother will try to kill him, of that I'm sure, and Krisxox won't waste a second in slaughtering them for the insult. He *hates* humans. Nothing I can do or say can change that if he's unwilling to change it in himself.

"He hates humans," I whisper out loud. "And he's my Xiveri mate."

Just hearing it guts me at the same time that it sets my thighs alight. I *can't* get wet again. I've already washed twice.

I swallow hard and press my kerchief to my forehead. For as clean as I am, I can't seem to get cool. Everything is hot and strained. The garden is still full of flowers and all of them are calling my name.

I need to distract myself. I need…to work. Yes, working will help me.

It's an unreasonable hour to attempt to make contact with the Voraxians, but as I won't be able to reach them on the coming solar since I'll be with Miari, I figure that recordings will be better than nothing.

I pull out the retractable desk against the wall and power on the holo screen behind it. The moment my bio-signature is recognized, I pull up the most recent report from the Evras. They have been working closely with Voraxia's biologists to determine which foods we might have any luck harvesting. Turns out, our options are limited.

But limited is still a place to start.

I am familiar with our agricultural practices on the colony since I often helped Kiki and her father harvest cane. We have plenty of it, too, so I bypass all suggestions for sugary crops, as well as the more um…adventurous Voraxian spices, and search the Evras' log for something heartier. Something that can sate the true hunger so many on the colony know.

There.

I make a note at the large purple root. Viron is what Krisxox had called it before he handed me my tray. *Hate? Then why does he still feed me each and every solarbreak?*

I shake off the thought and draw up the recording device, signaling it to make a note at the viron so that when I return this report with my recommendations to

Miaii, the Evias and the biologists, they'll know what I'm talking about.

I clear my throat. "Viron would be well suited for the human palate. It's a purple, hearty root, rich in vitamins *and* protein. It can be prepared in a variety of ways and would make an excellent complement to…"

Whoosh. The door opens. My muscles fire with tension. My core melts. My shame starts to flap its wings and fly away.

I blink many times and pause the recording. Without looking over my shoulder at him, I say, "You can stay like you do every lunar, but I don't want to talk about it."

Silence. It's eerie. But after a bated breath, I hear the door glide closed and his heavy feet pad over the floor to the seat I prepared for him.

I hear him ruffle the blanket I placed there — another crisp werro-fiber sheet — and itch with the urge to look back at him. I want to see his face, his expression, what he's wearing. Mostly, I want to shout at him for taking my virginity even though it was my idea and he tried to stop me more than once.

Maybe, it didn't work. Maybe my virginity's still intact and he needs to try again just like he promised.

I press play. "Complement to the wild rice as a staple diet. Like the rice, the viron grows underground and can survive with very little water. Perfect for colony soil. My recommendation is that we begin with viron and see how it takes before moving on to other tubers. This way, we can ensure that the colony has the ability to produce a well-balanced meal for every inhabitant, even if something were ever to block or delay the next import from Illyria."

I hit send and move on to the next task quickly. I have dozens of them that I need to get to with relative urgency. I'm acting as the Rakukanna, of sorts, while she's absent, and despite the fact that the universe is changing with the kit she's about to bring into it, the universe is also not standing still. Things are still happening and so much is going on in the colony, it's hard to keep up with everything.

I send three more crop recommendations through to the Evras, as well as a list of food supplies we'd like to see imported. I also update the list with items we no longer need — the acidic krell shrub that was *supposed* to resemble a leafy green ended up hospitalizing three humans.

I'm about to move onto my next task when behind me, Krisxox's low voice says, "You liked the viron?"

I tense. His voice is almost as seductive as his scent. "Hexa. I enjoyed it."

"Xhivey," he grumbles. "Then you should suggest the Ickeron. We have trouble growing it on all planets except Cxrian. Grows on a vine above ground and needs direct sunlight. It's three times the size of a viron and has more flavor."

I consider, too distracted by the fact that he gave me a good suggestion to even realize that he gave me a suggestion at all. "Water intake?" I say, scanning the list as I search for the item.

"Little."

"Oh hexa," I say, arriving at it. "I had considered this before, but it's covered in these thorns. They're poisonous."

"Hexa, but your humans don't skin these. You get Echalhas to do it. You ordered a herd for breeding and milking, correct?"

I nod, turn and look at him. "Hexa."

He shrugs one shoulder and quickly looks away. "Then you grow your Ickeron in their pen. They eat the skins and leave the gourds behind. Your humans can collect them."

My lips part. I search for something to say. Something to make the brutal pounding of my hearts slow. Because right now it feels like even though my heart is gone, I've been given a replacement. Two of them.

And they hate humans.

Or at least, they're supposed to.

I swivel back around and make a quick recording with Krisxox's suggestion. As I move on, I quietly say over my shoulder, "Thank you for your help."

He just grunts and offers neither answer nor explanation.

Next, is the arduous business of explaining to Voraxia's city engineer, Rehurion, why the Tri-God congregation is unhappy with the proposal to rebuild the Tri-God center for worship. The center is built directly on top of fragments of the shattered Antikythera satellite and my congregation reveres them.

Again, as soon as I've finished speaking, Krisxox buts in. "How many are you?"

"Verax." The word jerks out of me. I...shouldn't have answered at all. I shouldn't have placed the blanket for him on the stool in the corner. I...shouldn't be breathing in his sweet citrus, the one scent in the universe that acts as an immediate balm to my soul and chases all doubt away.

"In your Tri-God? How many of you are there who worship it?"

"Hm. Well, there are one thousand seven hundred and four humans in the colony — soon to be one thousand seven hundred and five — and of those, I'd say about two-thirds are worshippers of the Tri-God, but only about half of those are devout like my family is."

I go back to my holo screen and draw up the file I was last working on deciphering. Found in one of Mathilda's many boxes as a scrap of folded parchment, I scanned it and have been devoting a considerable amount of time and energy to it. The script is one that puzzled me. It's *Meero*, the language of the Niahhorru pirates.

"And the rest?" Krisxox mumbles, distracting me.

"Verax."

"The others who aren't believers in this god of yours, what do they believe in?"

I sigh, "Well, some have faith in some version of a higher power, whether it's the Tri-God or not is not clear. Some believe in spirits and ancestors and pray to them just as I pray to my Tri-God. Some believe in karma — a notion that means that your good and bad deeds are repaid onto you in this life or the next — some believe in some cosmic force in the universe — "

"Xana and Xaneru?"

I shrug. "It might very well be, but by another name."

"And the others?"

"Some believe in nothing at all. That we are all just here living together in this universe as a happy accident. That we are all just products of the machinations of the elements that created us."

He is quiet long enough for me to refocus on the screen, and then he interrupts me again. "Your Rakukanna and Va'Rakukanna don't believe in your god."

"Nox," I huff, annoyed and not just because I've been interrupted, but because this is the longest conversation we've ever had and it's when I'm angriest and most vulnerable. *He is a clever strategist.*

"The Rakukanna is a devout believer in science, but after she found her Xiveri mate, I've heard her say things that dare me to believe she's questioning that. I believe she's found a little faith in something else."

"In what?"

"Magic." I grin against my better judgement and look at him over my shoulder.

Color blasts through his ridges that makes my whole abdomen clench. My legs tighten even though they're terribly sore and I wince.

Krisxox clears his throat loudly. "And your... Va'Rakukanna? What does she believe?"

I'm breathing harder as I say, "Up until very recently, she believed in the same thing you do."

"What is that?"

"Hate."

I go back to my screen, but Krisxox, the brute, is insistent! "And now?"

"Now? Oh, I don't know. Perhaps the Xana. Perhaps nothing. Perhaps only the Va'Raku, her Okkari. She worships him just as he worships her."

"Is that why she is not the advisor? Because she does not worship the right god?"

"Nox! Of course not!" I whirl around to face him, fingers forming fists. "She is not the advisor because she is Xhea to her people. She wouldn't have the time."

"And you do?"

I do. And I care. In a universe where we are wanted only for our ability to bring pleasure, someone has to care about us."

His jaw clenches and his teeth press against his tense upper lip. He opens his mouth to speak, but I...I am not myself. I don't let him.

"Don't! Don't Krisxox. Don't say something you don't mean."

"I..."

"Shut up!" The words whip out of me and he flinches back from them harder than when he was whipped in front of me.

Shame. It hurts me down to my toes.

I feel it grip the backs of my eyes. I swallow it down.

Reaching for my nagoom-cross, I turn back to the screen before me and quickly return to the translations I've pulled up next to the original text.

Decades of history transcribed in all manner of methods leaves a lot of work for me and my team. Some of it we were able to decode from ancient hard drives, some of it still sits within ancient electronic storage boxes that we have no way of opening, some of it is even handwritten on paper, parchment and papyrus, and all of it spans dozens — if not hundreds — of different languages no longer known.

I am fortunate to have the assistance of three talented young Voraxian scribes helping me with this specific undertaking, but I felt *odd* asking them to help me with this particular file. I had a strange feeling about it. I still do.

Not strange, *bad*. A bad feeling. Downright dreadful.

I might have mistaken the half-torn page as a piece of scrap paper miscellaneously filed in this storage unit marked *Grain: Rotation Eleven to Thirteen* had it not been for the distinct repetition of some marks. Like ink blots all dropped to be exactly identical. Impossibly perfect, I recognized it for what it was after closer inspection.

A script. *Meero.*

I've been studying Meero for some time now, determined to have something to arm myself with the next time I cross the Niahhorru.

I'm not like Kiki — I can't wield a spear.

And I'm not Miari — I can't build one.

But I can learn and my father always said that knowledge is power. And when my mother went through the Hunt, she proved it. She wasn't injured by the male who claimed her. She was able to speak with him and though she won't ever tell us what happened to her during the Hunt, she says it wasn't bad.

I pull out a stick of charcoal and the actual piece of paper I'd been working my translation out on since I uncovered this strange file.

To you — Fifty mornar treyxna. Three fereranin. Twelve geeran.

To his highest — One oud.
The Hunt. First light.

My amended translation reads right next to it:

To you — Fifty sacks of Ebo nut (nuts that can be ground to flour, pressed for milk, creamed and made into paste — rich in nutrients and the primary staple of the common populace of quadrant six). Three tuns of fereranin (hooved creature that is easily bred and farmed and whose meat is a common staple of the people in quadrant one). Nine tuns of geeran (hooved creature that is revered by worshippers of the Tri-God, like me).
To his highest — One oud (??).
The Hunt. First light.

I circle the word *oud*. Somehow, it sounds familiar. But where have I heard it before? And, more importantly, what is this paper for? What is Mathilda doing with it?

Mathilda has not been forthcoming with information since I was named human advisor to the Rakukanna. I've uncovered a lot that she never shared — information Kiki would say that she kept hidden — though I don't like to believe her capable of such deception.

I learned that there were two additional satellites launched from the home world: One called *Isfahan* that took humans to the planet called Sasor. Located outside of the eight known quadrants, it is too far to reach. The second satellite, Balesilha, carried humans to Quadrant Five. They *are* within reach and, since discovery of the coordinates to Balesilha, I've begun plotting with Ixria and the xub'Ixira to voyage to the satellite, recover the humans and fold them into the Voraxian Federation.

Strange that Mathilda would have kept these coordinates a secret. Strange that she and the Council never told us that there were other living humans left in the cosmos.

She maintains that it would have been bad for morale, knowing that there were other humans out there that we couldn't reach, but I still don't know that I agree with her. It would have given us power to know we weren't the only ones. Something to hope for when the suns were at their brightest and the soil was too dry to yield crops. At the very least, I believe in truth.

I do not like to think it, but I believe that Mathilda, more than truth, believes in power.

This is clearly a trade. A treaty. A bargain. A pact. But as I stare at the words and run my fingers over my nagoom-cross over and over again, I cannot figure out who signed either end of the transaction. It cannot be Mathilda, because the colony neither saw the product of any part of this trade and certainly could not have been expected to give the items listed in the first section.

What is an oud?

What does this have to do with The Hunt?

And if this is written in Meero, what did the Niahhorru know of the Hunt and what goes on in the colony? What *do* they know?

"What do you have a Meero document for?"

I scream. Krisxox is standing right over my shoulder staring at the holoscreen with a look of pure menace. It radiates off of him like stellar coronas from the sun, exploding and lashing everything in their path.

I quickly shift to put space between us. I try to hold my breath so I don't smell him when I answer, "I found it among the Antikythera Council documents."

"Verax."

"It's clearly a trade of some kind, but what I can't figure out is why the human Council would have this. It's written in Meero."

"You speak Meero?"

"A little." Actually, quite well.

"Then you'll know that it's not all Meero. This word here," he says, reaching over my shoulder to tap the paper spread out on the desk. His claw taps the word *oud*. He hisses under his breath, "This is Drakesh."

I gasp and look up at him and suddenly the unanswered questions that linger between us are relegated to this urgency. I remember. Oud.

"That's what the male who attacked me called Miari and Raku's baby. It is a *derogatory* term then?"

"So foul not even I would say it. I have only heard it said three times in my life used to describe beings that are not Drakesh, or are an impure mix of species. Once by my female sire, once by Vendra," I wince. *Vendra, that was his name. Not his title, his name.* "And once by Bo'Raku."

"Oh God," I belt out, taking the lord's name in vain. "Oh." I lift my hand to my forehead and with my free hand, fan my face. "Mm-mm. This can't be. This can't..."

"Verax," he barks. He looks down at me and his fingers curl around the back of my seat. He looks like he wants to grab me, but shows restraint. "What is this? What do you see?"

"I..." I have a suspicion. A terrible one.

I lick my lips and quickly reach for the drawer where more water packets can be found. I fumble with the latch and Krisxox molds his hand over mine, positioning himself directly behind me to do so. My fingers tremble and I heat as he presses my hand in the right pattern and the drawer slides open. He plucks a packet from the silver interior, rips it open with his teeth and hands it to me.

"Thank you, Krisxox," I whisper.

He is so close, bowed over me like he is. The long strands of his tangled white hair tickle my shoulder when he moves. He looks like...he's going to...No!

I quickly drain the water, set the packet down and heave, "Mathilda must have been engaged in a trade with Bo'Raku and the Niahhorru."

Krisxox stares up at the screen, gaze reading over the Meero again and again.

"But the trade couldn't have gone through."

"Verax," he says.

"The kits, they didn't survive. If that is what is meant by *oud* here, then it would have been a trade for a hybrid baby."

"He could have gotten a lot for one, if he was intending to trade with the Niahhorru. I don't think they were a part of this bargain. He is writing in Meero only to cover his tracks. But this." His claw taps on my parchment again. *Oud.* "This is a mistake. He couldn't think of one other word to describe the babies."

Babies. It's the first time he's ever acknowledged that that's what they are, regardless of whether they're human, Voraxian or both.

"You think this was a failed trade between Mathilda and Bo'Raku then."

Krisxox nods. "You?"

"Hexa, I do."

"She will need to be punished."

Ice spears me in the gut and it's strange, because as the sickening feeling arrives, I get the sense that he feels it. He crumples slightly, wincing as if in pain.

"That is all you ever think about, isn't it? Ways to punish humans?"

The unmistakable shudder of the engines interrupt whatever he might have said next. As soon as we steady our descent, I fold up my parchment, tuck it into the pocket of my abaya, then quickly check my hair.

It will be the first time any on the colony have seen it.

Braided back into two long braids, each one hangs over my shoulder to reach my breast. Fixed with small rubbery bands that match the color of my hair, I take another breath.

This is it. I can do this.

Shame hits me.

I don't know. Maybe not…

I smooth down the soft hairs at my hairline and take another fortifying breath. In. Out. Ahh. Be strong.

"What are you doing?" Krisxox barks as soon as I gather the basket with my things — *things Krisxox gathered for me* — and the second basket with gifts for Miari and head towards the door.

I stop and look at him, confused. My face scrunches. *Don't breathe. Stay strong.* "I'm home. I'm preparing to disembark."

Snarling, he snatches up one of the head scarves I unpacked and left on my pallet. "Your *hair*. Won't your Tri-God punish you for this? Or did you forget him already?"

Tears. They come with the shame that chokes my throat. I blink many times and shake my head, trying to feel anything but rage. But I don't.

"I don't need it anymore." I start towards the door.

Krisxox charges across the room, blocking my way. He shakes the veil in my face like a physical manifestation of the Tri-God laughing at my shame.

"Verax."

"I owe you no explanation." I try to side-step him, but he's too broad, filling up the doorway with his beautiful red skin. His chest is bare. It always is. I want to sink my nails into it, climb up onto him and rut him all over again.

The insides of my thighs shake, struggling to even keep my own weight. I'm so tired. Mentally and physically, I'm drained. And this was supposed to be a happy day. What sort of state will I be in for Miari? I'm supposed to be strong for her.

Shame.

"Svera, tell me. What is it?" His voice breaks and when I look up into his stark, angry face, he swallows several times and I feel...too tired to fight.

"Only virgins wear the veil. Women who are married or ruined no longer wear it."

He stiffens. "Ruined?"

"Hexa. Ruined. I am not married and I broke a tenet of the Tri-God. I will have to denounce myself before the congregation and the priestesses and priests will have to decide whether or not I'm removed from the congregation, or forced to repent in order to remain."

Krisxox is shaking his head. I've never seen his eyes so large and for a moment, I'm absolutely terrified of him.

"Krisxox, *please* move out of my way. These baskets are heavy." *And I'm still weak from rutting you so thoroughly.*

He takes the baskets from me so rapidly, my whole body pitches. He catches me against his chest, sets the baskets down and quickly, madly, begins wrapping the scarf he's holding around my head.

He covers my eyes and nose and my whole head. Is he trying to suffocate me?

"Krisxox!"

"You are *not* ruined."

"Krisxox, stop!" I flail out and manage to dislodge his hold. I back into the room and my calves hit the edge of the pallet. I plop down onto it, landing directly in my pile of scarves.

"I did not ruin you. I did not do this thing to you…"

His ridges are flashing now and the colors surprise me. They're grey. Grey is for grief.

Something twists in the place where my two hearts now sit. I reach up and catch my chest. I feel like falling apart. *Inhale. Exhale… Ahh… Breathe. Release.*

"Krisxox, you had no choice. I...provoked you. But it's done now. I am a ruined woman in the eyes of my congregation. It's fine. It isn't like I was going to have any luck finding a male from my congregation anyway. I'm too pale and even if I *were* desired, you're here. You wouldn't let me find another mate. You couldn't. You're my Xiveri. Even if you hate me, you have no choice but to defend me. So just...please get out of my way."

But he doesn't. My words seem to break something in him. He drops to one knee at my feet and grabs the pallet on either side of my knees. He bows his forehead to touch them, nuzzles his face between them, forces them to spread. He bites the inside of my knee and I gasp and when he jerks back upright, he is another male.

"Please, Svera," he says in Drakesh.

Please.

I...I'm not sure what to do in the face of that single word, and then when he repeats it in badly broken Human, I'm completely lost. "*Pulayeez.*"

I jump where I sit, and it has nothing to do with the fact that the transporter rumbles as it docks. "I...it would be wrong. A lie..."

"Lie for me. *Pulayeez.* Just for now. I will fix it. I will fix it, I vow to you, I will fix it."

"How?"

"I read your human manual." Shock.

"You...you did?"

He nods. "I read about *may'ree*. It's no different than the Xanaxana except for that Xanaxana is more powerful. We are already *may'ree* in Voraxia. I will explain that to your Tri-God people and then they will understand."

I notice that, at no point, does he offer to marry me in my own custom. Not that I would want him to offer. He is no husband. He is only Voraxia's battle strategist.

"Until then, wear your head cover."

My shoulders sag. I look down at the hijab in my lap and slowly, begrudgingly, put it on.

"Married people don't hate each other," I whisper as I tuck my braids beneath it and fasten it securely.

"Hate or not, it makes no difference," he says, grabbing my baskets from the floor.

"Nox," I whisper sadly. "I guess it doesn't."

8

Krisxox

I am panicked. I am also drunk.

The room around me is crowded on this side of the viewing pane. I should be more interested in what the Islu'Raku is saying to me as we wait for the kit to emerge, but I grunt and wave him off, too interested in the sight of my Svera's beautiful face on the other side of the glass.

Focus.

Xoking focus!

But my Xanaxana will not.

There. I xoking said it. My Xanaxana has gone xoking berserk for the female with the slit that smells like a burning banban tree, the type of smoke used to make ceremonial fires in the ancient Drakesh villages where they still practice the dark arts. *Magic. She teems with it and when it overflows, it falls onto me in layers of irrevocable curses.*

She thinks she is ruined? Ha.

The xoking human has ruined me completely. I was a proud male before but, as I stand on the other side of a plate of glass looking in at the Rakukanna's birthing chamber, all I can see is her. I do not see the Raku standing proudly beside his human, bringing water to her lips when she asks for it — like a slave.

I do not see the human Va'Rakukanna of Nobu standing at the Rakukanna's side, whispering in her ear. I do not feel the brush of the Va'Raku's arm against mine as he moves beside me, watching the birth about to take place.

I do not see Lemoria and her host of xub'Lemoria rushing back and forth across the woodsy womb of a room, complete with a plush birthing nest, checking holo screen after holo screen to ensure that the Rakukanna's vitals are within normal range as she finally begins to push.

All I see is Svera. The look on her face as, after a quarter solar, the hybrid emerges from the Rakukanna's body, all red and wet and glistening. Its little squeals can be heard even through the mirror, even louder than the agonized, grateful breath taken by the Va'Raku beside me and the cheers of the other xub'Raku gathered in front of the viewing pane.

And then I feel my body clench. Nox. The Xanaxana is gobbling me up. *Her dark magic is at work.* My xora is stiffening at the sight of the wetness on Svera's face. She is *crying* again, a practice only performed by kits and humans. So despicable and yet... I have not forgotten what it felt like to see the wetness on her cheeks when she shook apart in my arms. She was in pain, but she braved it, letting my xora bask in her warmth all the way down to the base. I was inside of her. I was xoking *inside of* her and the look on her face after? Pure grief.

I have bedded hundreds of females and not one of them ever looked at me like that. So torn. Shattered.

Ruined.

My heart — my sole heart, because I only carry hers now — slows and skips. I could *die* from the wound she ripped open inside of me.

I spent inside her, staring down into her eyes and she was so full of emotion. So full of flame. And then moments later, she pulled away.

Never again. She's mine forever.

What would my sires say?

Oud.

And if I ever heard them call her that, I'd bury them in the same place I buried Vendra.

My foot shoots towards the entrance Lemoria pronounced that we spectators would not breach, but Va'Raku catches my arm. Without looking away from the viewing pane, he says softly, "Your ridges betray you, Krisxox."

I tense and move my feet back into position and try to get ahold of myself. My ridges are bubbling with emotion, totally unlike the stuff Svera wears on her cheeks. This is dark emotion. Hateful towards her for making me feel like this, and even more hateful towards her congregation for making her feel like she does now. The most hate is reserved for me.

I should hate me for rutting her at all, but all I hate is the fact that I've failed her again, perhaps even more miserably.

"It is a beautiful thing, is it not?" Va'Raku says, pulling his own hands behind his back as he stares straight forward, ridges betraying not one hint of the satisfaction I can hear in his tone.

He inhales, "It is enough to make one wistful. And eager."

I just grunt. If I say something to disrespect his Xiveri mate now, I have no doubt that he will gut me and I don't have any desire to kill him. For one with mixed heritage, evidenced by his purple skin — a combination of the Voraxian blue and the Drakesh red — he is a decent ruler. He should likely have been made Raku — would have been had he been willing to relinquish his role as Okkari on Nobu. But he was not. It is his home.

Home.

I shuffle uneasily on my feet, unsure why the word bothers me so much and quickly reach for another hard ale from the nearby table.

Svera emerges from the birthing chamber some time later with the Va'Rakukanna and several of the xub'Lemoria. Ki'Lemoria pronounces the birth as a complete success — lauding it as a miracle that the

Rakukanna did not even have the assistance of our modern technology to pass the child, but was able to do it on her own, naturally. *As if that's some great victory. Females have been birthing kits for millennia before the advent of our health technology.* I ignore the fact that with his pronouncement, I exhale then a little deeper.

"And it's a girl!" The Va'Rakukanna shouts and she leaps at her mate and he spins her around, taking her off her feet. My lonely heart catches as I glance at Svera. I wish I didn't, but I do. She's looking at me with pink in her cheeks and as she looks away from me quickly and engages with another xub'Lemoria, I wonder if she's thinking the same thing I am.

I want her to greet me like this.

I'm agitated as the festivities carry on with xub'Raku of our great xoking quadrant making bold pronouncements like, "The humans have saved us!"

And other even more bold statements like, "We owe a great debt to the Rakukanna."

And, "May this be the first of many hybrid kits that are to come."

And finally, "The little Rakuka marks the beginning of a new solar in the history of Voraxia."

A solar in which *ouds* no longer exist. A solar in which Svera...carries...my...

Xok. What would my sires —

Uff. Thinking like this is exhausting. I haven't slept in a solar and I'm starting to feel it. I'm falling apart.

Lemoria, at long last, emerges into the waiting chamber and the xub'Raku gathered herald her like she's a xoking queen. She at least has the decency to hold up her hands and wave off the adulation, though she has to go and ruin her own reserved humility by touting the Rakukanna as the true hero. Something about her birthing canal being no wider than the other humans who were unable to produce living kits, yet managing to persevere with little guidance and produce a healthy baby.

Svera, meanwhile, partakes in all of it. She toasts with her pink beverage that contains no spirits while the rest of us toast in blue. I don't toast, but drink in the corner of the lavish room. And I keep drinking as the other xub'Raku settle onto the low divans and poufs in this waiting chamber, drawing up their holo screens to communicate the news to the farthest reaches of all quadrants.

Va'Rakukanna returns to the nesting chamber with her mate in tow. She holds the kit while the Raku helps to clean and dress his Rakukanna. Va'Raku's ridges beam with deep blue satisfaction and pleasure when he looks at the kit. As if it were his own. He even goes so far as to hold the sleeping bundle of rags when it's offered to him and he takes it without complaint.

I look away, back to my drink, which doesn't taste nearly as harsh as it should. So, I have another. Meanwhile, Svera and Lemoria leave the chamber and only Svera returns a few moments later. She doesn't go back into the birthing chamber, but starts towards me.

For a moment, I panic, thinking she's going to come speak to me and ask me questions that I won't be able to answer, but she steps right past me. She doesn't even look at me. It's almost like she didn't even notice me here even though she's xoking branded into my forehead. A beacon for me to carry for all time.

I charge out after her into the spacious hallway filled with doors to other birthing chambers, each just as opulent as this. There are hundreds of these on the new birthing center built on the human colony meant to serve human, hybrid *and* Voraxian females. It is meant to be the pinnacle birthing center across all Voraxia, as if they wanted to create a specific planet where children of all kinds were worshipped.

What will Svera's kit look like?

The thought makes me stagger and liquid rushes up my throat along with a heaping of bile. But I am not sick at the thought of Svera's potential kit.

I am sick at the thought that if I don't *fix this*, it won't also be mine.

I can scent the baby on her arms, its wet matter clinging to her clothing still. It's confusing me. Making my brain hurt. My Xanaxana is thrilled.

The memory of her naked flesh writhing beneath mine haunts me in the solar's light. It was, in a word, spectacular. It was xoking *everything*. Looking down at her on that low pallet, hearing her shred me apart when she asked me to get Tur'Roth. *That male shouldn't even be alive.*

Bloodthirsty thing.

I have known Niahhorru pirates without such savagery. She had been using me for her pleasure, the filthy little thing, making my xora hers. It won't ever be anyone else's. It isn't even mine. It is bent, broken to her will, already. She doesn't know it yet, but all she has to do is ask me for what she needs. All she has to do is ask me to ruin my pride and marry her.

But she won't.

Because I'm not even sure she wants me.

The thought suddenly hits me like a lightning strike. Pure and wrong. She doesn't want me.

She is my Xiveri mate and she. doesn't. want me.

And I don't want her, but she's mine.

Silence. It whistles through my ears, passing through empty space. What happened to my brain? Like a holoscreen shutting down because of a malfunction, I suddenly can't compute.

What am I supposed to do?

I...if we don't want each other, but are bound, are we meant to live like this forever? In pain?

Not xoking happening.

I don't like seeing her in pain.

She needs *me* to make that step. She needs *me* to ask. She needs *me* to fix it. To protect her. Even if is from myself.

"Svera! Stop!"

She's nearly at the door to the lift that will take her down to the planet's surface. We are on the highest of five floors of this new monstrous center for younglings and while the lift has railings, like a glider, it has no walls. She could fall. *I want to catch her.*

Her cheeks are round and smooth and her eyes are bright, but glossy. Something's wrong. "Are you going to confront Mathilda?"

"That's all you think about, isn't it? Punishment?" Xok me. What did I say?

I've never heard her like this. She sounds like she's in pain. "Are you hurt? What did that xoking little…"

"Oud? Is that what you were going to call it?"

The sound of hearing that word in her voice stands out as something wholly wrong and I suddenly hate that I ever revealed to her its meaning.

"Svera…"

But she just makes an aggrieved sound and turns away from me.

She waves her palm in front of the vein reader and a low, dark green light illuminates the threshold and lintel, letting her know that her request has been registered.

The carpet on the floor beneath my feet is made of a synthetic plastic. It is enough to mute my steps without carrying the dust mites that can affect the sick. "You can't leave without telling me. Especially after what happened. You might hate me right now, but I'm still your guardian…"

She cuts me off, as clean as a well-slit throat. "I have already put in my request to have you removed as my guardian."

"Verax!" Nox. I stagger as she rams that dagger into my heart all over again. Bloodthirsty creature, she twists.

"The Rakukanna will be remaining here on the human colony for the foreseeable future and I would like to stay with her until she returns to Voraxia. I will travel back with her when she leaves and then I will organize a werro for myself in Illyria or on Nobu. I've already been offered a dome in the Va'Rakukanna's village."

"*No.*" I know this word in her Human language. I've heard it from her often enough.

"Yes."

Rage. It pummels me like raining fists. I shake my head, feeling the effects of the spirits wash over me hard, making my emotions explode while the skin numbs on my fingertips. I can suddenly feel life firing through each and every one of my scars. I look up at her face, at the soft scar below her left eye. It's almost imperceptible now, but I can still see it glowering at me like a neon sign, ceaselessly blinking *failure.*

I choke, "Is this because of what happened on the transporter?" I told myself I wouldn't speak of it until

I found the right time, yet here I am xoking blabbering about it. Making it real.

"Of course it is."

"I told you, I would fix it."

"You can't."

"I can…"

"Nox, Krisxox. Unless you're planning to marry me, then you can't. And even if you were, I wouldn't want you to. I don't want you for my mate!"

Irony. It's a xoking bitch, isn't it?

I shake my head and watch the doors to the platform slide open behind her. I'm trying to catch up, trying to figure out what's changed.

The ripping in my chest is worse now and so is the nausea. I can feel Xaneru trying to anchor me while Xana tears at me from above. She's going to take back the Xanaxana and even though it's what I wanted and I refuse to give into it, I'm not strong enough to give it up.

Ruined. Hexa, I am. But in this moment, I wouldn't want to exist any other way. This is it. She is the garden. Her hot nectar only proves it. *Don't take me from the garden, Svera,* I want to tell her. I want to scream it until my lungs burn.

What would my sires think? *Xok my xoking sires!*

"Svera…" I choke, chest heaving as I catch myself on the wall. "Don't do this. I can fix…fix…it."

She takes a step back onto the landing and her arm is still blocking the door, but that's *all* that's keeping her here with me.

Without prelude, she rips her headscarf off and tosses it towards me. It flutters to the ground, closer to her feet than to mine, and just before the doors shut, she says three final words that tear me apart.

"You've done enough."

And then it comes. The wave. The horror. Every torture in history is inflicted upon me all at once as Xana, in her infinite wisdom, gives me what I've always wanted.

Freedom from the Xiveri that binds us.

The pain is too much to take.

I pass out.

9

Svera

My fists are clenched, my shoulders tight by my ears, as I finally extricate myself from the mob of people surrounding me, rejoicing at Miari's successful childbirth, just like I should be rejoicing. Many of them comment on my hair and who I've been married to and why they weren't invited, but I offer no answers or explanation.

But my shame can no longer compete with the suspicion — *accusation* — growing like an infection in the pit of my stomach, turning all that is good to rot.

I race as quickly as my flat sandals will carry me down the main street of the old town up to the hill where the new houses are being constructed. The Antikythera Council members are first to receive the Voraxian-built homes, complete with all the amenities of Voraxia's technology, coupled with some colony innovations of our own.

But I'm not headed to the Antikythera houses, seated high up on the knoll in a red dust-colored material that is impenetrable to the sand and sun and never stains. They're beautiful. *Like tomb stones are beautiful.*

My feet come up short as I glare up at the largest of the homes — well, the second largest after the house used by Miari, Raku and other xub'Raku when they're visiting, as they are now. Just as large as theirs, this is only Mathilda's and her granddaughter, Deena's. I use my hand to shade my eyes from the suns' rays as I stare. *Mathilda, what have you done?*

No. I'm not sure yet, so I can't rush to any rash conclusions. That's what I tell myself as I veer off of the main road and head to the squat, adobe house that my parents and brother share — *my* house, since it's the only one that belongs to me. The place I stayed in on Qath? Well, that's just a distant memory.

It should be.

It *will* be.

My house was one of the largest homes in the colony until the Voraxians began construction — and it still is. With large windows made out of *real* glass dotting both the first *and* second floors, it always seemed palatial compared to the ramshackle wooden home that Kiki lived in growing up, or the even more derelict tin shack Miari constructed for herself when she was old enough to move out of the orphanage.

Dust clings to the door when I knock and comes off on my sweaty hand. I had so looked forward to seeing my parents again, but as the door flies open and I take in the sight of my mother's glowing, golden face, all I can feel is the pain of a betrayal that I wish I could dismiss...

But there are lives at stake.

"Svera!" She coos and how I've missed the sound of her voice. Her eyebrows crinkle together over her gently sloping nose. "What is it, sheifala? Your veil! Did it fall off? Do you need another? Habibi," she calls over her shoulder, "Quickly fetch Svera a veil. Hers was..."

"Nox." I shake my head. *Be strong.* I meet her gaze. *Be brave.* "Nox."

Her eyes widen and her lips part, but before she can speak, I say, "I need to speak with you and dad. Right now."

"Of...of course." She opens the door and I step inside. When she closes it behind me and closes out the sunlight, I take a look around. My heart clenches. So much has happened and, here, nothing has changed.

The same leather futons are clustered around a shared eating table. It sits low to the ground and is made of a worn black wood that my grandfather stole from trees outside of the dome when he was young.

He was one of the hunters, then, but eventually was attacked by a small creature with sharp tusks.

When he was brought back to the village, there was only one medic — my mother's mother. After she healed him, she gave him a medical book her father had smuggled from the Antikythera satellite. He became her apprentice and they became great friends and their children, medics, who loved one another.

On the other side of the room a prayer mat is laid out, as if recently used. It is well worn, green, with beautiful calligraphy in the middle. Brought from the ancient world, it is my family's most prized possession.

"Sheifala," my father says, coming around the corner at the end of the hall. He starts at the sight of my hair and his gaze wanders down to my throat. The marks there are obvious. His hand comes to cover his heart and mine nearly breaks in the same moment. Both of them.

"Svera has something to speak with us about, habibi," my mom says. "But first, you must tell us. Did everything go well with the birth? We heard sounds of celebration in the streets and assumed that it was a success."

She clutches her nagoom cross, rubbing the beads worn, as mine are. She'll pass those beads down to my future child, should I be so blessed, just as I'll pass my own beads down to their child and so the cycle will continue and through the nagoom crosses, no life will ever be forgotten.

"Hexa," I answer reflexively before switching to human. "I mean, yes. Miari and her mate have successfully brought new life into this universe."

"Alhamdullah." Chimes my father's voice in time with my mother's.

"Where is Ibra?"

"He went to lead prayer with Corane." Good. He shouldn't be here for this. "They pray for Miari's safety. The entire colony has been in quite a state since she went into the medical center, hoping for her and the child. But you say the child was delivered safely? The...Rakuka?"

I nod, feeling a lump form in my throat that I can't swallow past. I touch my hair again. The way my dad is staring at it makes me feel self-conscious. *I better get used to it.*

"Yes, mom. And in private, you can call the baby Dora."

"The perfect name, mashallah," my dad says, making the sign of the Tri-God over his chest and then kissing his fingertips.

I nod. My mom sniffles and I fight the urge to hug her...then I give into it. "For Miari's mom."

"Yes," my own mom says, sounding weepy, "I know, sheifala, I know."

She squeezes me back tight and I forget that I'm advisor to the Rakukanna and partially responsible for all of the lives of all of the humans and hybrids still left on this rock, rotating in orbit around Cxrian, which orbits itself around one of Voraxia's suns. Instead, I remember that I am a human and that I, too, was a child once.

"Oh sheifala, you're shaking. Come here." And then more softly, my father whispers, "Whatever has happened, we will get through it together." He means my hair and I wince. Tears grip the back of my eyes. He does not even know the depth of my depravity, but he's already forgiven me for it.

Can I do the same for him?

My dad's arms fold around me and I breathe in the scent of the nightshade on his shirt and the slightly burned scent wafting from my mom's clothing — likely from her making a mess in the kitchen again — and I exhale deeply and we just stand like this in the entryway of our little adobe home while words rise up in my throat, choking me because I need to say them but I don't want to say them. I really don't.

"How about some chay?" My dad says.

My mom nods and I slowly extract myself from her grip. My nose is a little runny and my eyes are all foggy when I make my way into the sitting area. I take one of the low seats and fold my knees carefully beneath me.

"I…" *I don't want to ask them what I'm here to ask. Perhaps, it's better not to know.* "I'm sorry that you weren't part of the birthing procedure. Lemoria was overly concerned for this first birth and wanted to have her own staff. For the subsequent births that take place here, including Jaxal and Lisbel's, she'd like for you to be included. She asked me to apologize to you profusely. She knows you're skilled medics."

"It is no concern of ours, so long as the child was born and both child and mother are now healthy and safe," my father says, taking a sip of his tea and munching on a corner of cane-and-root bread. He glances at my hair again, then looks away while his pale cheeks turn ruddy. I got it from him, and am sure mine appear exactly as his do.

"We do not take any offense to being asked to step aside. The Tri-God does not tolerate such pride."

I nod and take a steeling sip of my nightshade tea, but right now I can't taste its floral spice. My tongue is swollen in my mouth, unwilling to get the words out.

And then I say, "After the birth, Lemoria expressed surprise that Miari was able to pass the child so easily through her birthing channel."

The change is almost imperceptible. My dad tenses. My mom's gaze flits down. But I still see it and I *know* and I'm horrified.

"Here I was, terrified to confess my own sins to you when yours outweigh mine a thousand times. Lemoria said that it was not possible for so many females to have died if they were passing hybrids just like Miari did. And *you* were the only medics there. You *both*."

I look between them, watch them watch me with terror in their faces and a shame even greater than mine.

"Svera," my mother says, then nothing.

No one speaks. No one dares. The world is so silent, I can sense a storm coming, but it's only inside of my chest and when I speak again, it makes itself known. "I need to know that they weren't *sold* to a Voraxian traitor. *Tell me.*"

"Svera," my father starts, but he chokes on his tea and a wracking cough makes it impossible for him to speak.

My mom gives him a gentle pat. She gives his shoulder a gentle squeeze. "She is the advisor now. The truth cannot hurt her."

"I need to know," I say and I'm shaking. "I'm responsible now for what happens to the hybrids. I'm the link between the two worlds. I can't be left in the dark. Not anymore. I know that Mathilda has been hiding so much from us — knowledge of the other humans, her treaty with Bo'Raku. I know that she was engaged in illegal trades with him. Did she make one? Did she sell a hybrid? And what happened to the mothers?"

"How...how do you know all this?" My father's lips quiver.

Hesitating, but only for a breath, I reach into my pocket and pull out the piece of scrap paper with my scribbled translation. As their gazes read down the list of demands I wrote in Human — *the exchange* — my father's already pale face grows dangerously ashen, and my mother's grip tightens around her cross.

My parents are quiet for a long, long time. They both stare at the note, reading it over and over. Finally, my father breaks. "We were told by Mathilda that we were needed to deliver the hybrid kits born after the first Hunt. When we arrived…" He shakes his head.

My mom closes her eyes. "When we arrived, Mathilda had already delivered one of the other kits herself. The woman was dead and the kit was near death. But neither cause was natural. Mathilda was covered in blood and scratches. The woman, Tressmay, had a knife sticking out of her chest. The baby was strangled and scratched, but still alive. We managed to save it, your father and I, but it was clear what had happened.

"Somehow, Tressmay figured out that Mathilda intended to take away her child. She fought back. Mathilda couldn't deliver the babies and contain the mothers, so she had us deliver the children. The women she…she killed them herself. To avoid such a result in the future, your father and I aborted the babies produced in subsequent Hunts because we feared the females would not survive."

"In this we did not lie," my father concludes, "But what we *omitted* was that their survival had nothing at all to do with the human female physiology. They are able to pass hybrid babies just fine. What we feared was their death by another means."

"And the kits were sold?" I'm shocked by the sound of my own voice. I sound like a killer. Like Krisxox right before he goes into battle. When he is most magnificent and most calm.

"We don't know. We must assume they were," my mother says.

"And Miari and Darro?"

My father and mother exchange a glance. My father reaches up and touches the faded blue edge of his yarmulke. "We have thought of this at length over the rotations. Your mother and I think that they were rejected, as offerings. Miari was born underweight and smaller than the others and Darro was the son of Tressmay. He was injured and recovering for several solars."

I nod and suddenly I'm standing, looking down at my parents. My voice is shaking with a silent rage and I try to remember what my father told me mere moments before.

"We will get through this together," I say. "But I need you to confess your crimes to the Va'Rakukanna. Kiki will forgive you even if the Tri-God may not. I...I doubt he will forgive me, either. I gave my body to the Voraxian male looking after me. He saved my life and I...lost myself. We are not married and have no intention to be."

My parents' faces are too wreathed in sadness, bitterness, and grief for them to truly hear me now. My mother just nods. "We still love you, Sheifala. The human is fallible in even its purest form."

"Yes. And I know one more fallible than most."

"Where are you going, Svera?" My father calls out to me before I'm even conscious that I've moved. I'm back at the door now, tea staining my abaya around the hips.

I wrench it open and step out into the light. "I'm going to crucify her."

10

Svera

"Mathilda!" I'm pounding on her door. I've never pounded on anyone's door before with my fist and I'm shocked by the sound.

Boom, boom, boom. "Mathilda!"

Mathilda's house is the highest on the hill, the largest *and likely storing all manner of secrets. I want to know all of them.*

"Mathilda, open the door!"

Suddenly, it swings open in front of me and I'm caught with my fist suspended in the air. "Svera," she coos and I jolt at the sound of her voice, so practiced and diplomatic.

"Mathilda, I…"

She cuts me off. "Svera. You're ahead of schedule. Come in, sweetheart. You look positively frightened, like you've just seen a ghost."

As she sweeps her arm back and ushers me inside, I realize that even though I know her face, I don't know this woman at all. Clean, smooth skin, long, locked grey hair. Her robe is made from the same nightshade leaves I just drank with my parents. Nightshade tea is expensive enough, but this robe… she should not have this. She shouldn't have her own *life*.

I catch myself at the thought. It's one I've never had before. A thought that I just shamed Krisxox for — that I rejected him for. I wonder where he is and if, perhaps, I shouldn't have asked him to accompany me. Mathilda is wearing an easy expression that I know I should not trust. She's up to something. But what? She is not so stupid as to think she can kill me with the entirety of Voraxia watching.

The soft click of her door latching sounds magnificent. "Do you have a message for me, advisor Svera? I heard the birth was a great success."

"Unlike so many others that came before." There. It's out. I said it.

I hold the paper towards her and she takes it from me. Her dark eyes flit over the page. Still, her serious, concerned expression never wavers. "Oh goodness. I see. You wish to know what an *oud* is? I'm sure this would not have come up in your dictionaries."

"I know what that word means and you shame us both by repeating it. What I want to know is where the hybrids are. Their location is the only thing that will save you."

She just nods at me and her eyes are kind. They have only ever been kind. So is her smile. She sweeps her long locks back over her right shoulder and wades deeper into her home, past the cooking area filled with foods I have never even seen before. And it's all been right here this whole time. What else is she hiding from us?

"Yes, of course, you know. You know quite a great deal, don't you?" She opens a door to her left and gestures for me to enter. From where I stand, I can't see where it leads. "You want to know what became of the hybrids? Come and see."

"So you don't deny that you bartered with Bo'Raku, knowing he would sell the babies to the Niahhorru."

"That is what he said he would do," she replies, again in confirmation. "But it is not what he did. He sold them to another bidder before the Niahhorru could get to them. They were not so organized as they are now. Rhorkanterannu had not yet risen to unite the pirates. I believe some of them went to the Skyth, while another of the younglings went to Sky, though the two are not to be confused." She smiles. "No human would want to end up with the Sky, or so I'm told."

I've read about the Sky. They specialize in creating bio-machinery and are said to be the best at grafting cybernetic enhancements onto their so-called patients, often against their will.

am disappointed that you don't see what I was doing, Svera. I am all that stands between us and the horrors of the outside universe."

"You're right. What need have we for more horrors when we already have you?"

Her smile falls and a muscle in her cheek ticks. "I don't expect you to understand. You're just a child, really."

"I understand well enough and I want the coordinates to the hybrids so they can be recovered."

She sighs and shakes her head softly and gestures again to the open door to her right. "All the answers you'll need are inside."

"You can't kill me, Mathilda. You know that, right? Krisxox of Voraxia is my Xiveri mate." My stomach clenches the moment I speak such a ghastly truth.

After the way I left him, I have the gall to claim him now? I wasn't even angry with him... Well, I was angry with him, but only because all I could think about were the hybrid kits and his hatred for them. I couldn't count on him to rise to anger with me on this and even if he did, I couldn't ensure my parents' lives against his desire to punish.

I don't trust him.

And to claim him now still feels wrong when the last time I saw him, he looked like he was about to pass on into the grave.

I've seen him zapped and slashed by the Niahhorru stunners and swords. I've seen his arm broken, his neck shackled, his back lashed, his body speared and poked and cut and bruised, but I've never seen him look hurt like he looked when I told him I would not marry him.

"That would explain the hair," she says slowly, carefully. She is a worshipper of the Tri-God, too, but not so devout as to wear the clothes or practice the rituals.

She reaches up and combs her fingers through her long locks. "I would not be so foolish to try to kill you."

I exhale and step forward, cautious as I reach the door. She backs away from it and gestures for me to walk down the stairs. She follows close behind and says nothing as we reach the bottom.

Neither do I.

I can't.

It…it's magnificent.

Long, rectangular basins are filled with newly formed crops, while lights hang suspended above them, shining down and bringing them to life. There are too many varieties to name. Off to the right stand huge cisterns that seem to be providing either water or fertilizer to the crops through clear, blue, and silver tubes that weave out of them and across the flat white floor.

To the left, there are a dozen additional tanks, most marked with names I can't read, though one distinctly says *geeran*, a type of meat that's common in Voraxia. One carcass could feed an entire colony on the family for a dozen solars and, judging by the size of that tank, it looks like Mathilda has hundreds of them.

"It's beautiful, isn't it?"

My jaw works, but my gaze has locked on the clear chamber at the far end of the room. I start to run towards it. "Deena?" I gasp.

I press my palms to the glass as soon as I reach it, looking for seams. "What has she done to you?"

"You shouldn't be here," she says, glancing over my shoulder.

She crosses her arms over her chest. It's full. Far fuller than any female's I've ever seen on the colony. She's rounder than any and why shouldn't she be? She's trapped in a cell with nothing but food to keep her company.

"Mathilda," I bark, feeling hot, feeling frantic. "She is your granddaughter! You're keeping her caged like a rat."

"But that's the problem, isn't it, advisor Svera? She *is* a rat. You see, this one has been snooping around my things for rotations. She knows as much as you do. Maybe even more. That I didn't kill her outright rotations ago was only a gift to her mother."

"Who you killed, too," Deena growls out behind me.

Mathilda's face doesn't change. Not even once. Ageless, not a wrinkle to be seen, I wonder if this woman has any emotions at all.

"Yes, my daughter was an unfortunate victim of the first Hunt. I thought she understood my way of thinking but, when the babe came, she tried to keep it and I couldn't have that. She also threatened to tell the colony about what I'd done should I try to take the kit from her, so I had to take action. Just like I am taking action now."

I look into Deena's heart-shaped face. Her locks are twisted just as tightly as her grandmothers, but are a deep brown tinted by red hues. Interestingly, her eyes are a bright, icy blue. They watch me now with pure flame. Even as she takes a step back on her twisted left leg and shakes her head only once.

"You really shouldn't have come. She's been planning all this for you for half a rotation. Since the pirates came for you and Miari the first time."

I turn and meet Mathilda's gaze with a trembling sort of hate. "You will not get away with this."

"Unfortunately for you, I will have to. I have no intention of being exiled or relinquishing my position."

I balk, "You have no position. You report to *me* and to Miari and to the Raku. The Council will be disbanded as soon as I send word."

I flip open my life drive and issue a series of quick commands only...the holographic images are all stuck.

"Jammer," Deena whispers through the glass at my back.

"Yes, according to your life drive, you never left your parents' house." I brace my shoulders as Mathilda smiles.

"You cannot kill me. You said so yourself."

"And I do not intend to." Just then, there is a soft beep. Mathilda lifts a hand to her right ear and presses against it. For a moment it looks like she's listening to someone speak to her, though I can't hear anything out loud, then she nods, lowers her hand, looks down at me and smiles.

"But I will not have to."

"What have you done?"

"Pirates," Deena whispers behind me. "They're here. Svera, you have to run."

The sound of footsteps gets louder and when I turn, I see two males descending down the stairs. Sons of Council members, they're each carrying weapons that I've never seen before.

"That isn't Voraxian technology," I whisper.

"Nox, it is not. And Svera," Mathilda curls one bony hand around my shoulder, gripping it tighter than a woman her age should have strength for. I wince as pain lances into me. "This is *my* world. That you think to take it from me is pointless. Just as pointless as it would be for you to try to run."

//

Krisxox

"I don't like lurkers, Krisxox."

I grunt and step into the healer's cabin. It hangs suspended and slightly apart from the others and, of all the buildings in Qath, it is the most protected. Li'Lemoria is the most useful of us. He's put bodies back together again too many times to count. Including mine. I'd have far more scars without him, though I never minded scars. Except for the one that lingers beneath my chest like a third heart that I don't want because it isn't the right kind.

The door slips shut behind me and Li'Lemoria stands to his full height. He is not an imposing male — he is too kind for that — but he is tall. He watches me now and allows a brief flash of blue to surface in his ridges, letting me know that though I am interrupting his work, he does not mind.

"I need to ask you about Xanaxana."

Blue again, more of it this time. "I would not proclaim to be knowledgeable in this area. Why don't you ask va Kaku? Or Lemoria? Or any number of happily mated pairs here in Qath?"

"Because I want to know how to sever a bond."

The color in his ridges dies. He falls back into his bowl-shaped seat and rubs his left knee. He also rubs the space between his two hearts. "That is…"

"This is all theoretical, of course. But if someone were Xiveri mated, could they break the bond?"

"In death."

I can't kill her and I won't kill me. "How else?"

He shakes his head. "There is no other way."

"There has to be."

"None have ever attempted to deny the Xiveri bond. None in recorded history that have felt it have been able to resist it at all."

"So it takes strength." Strength I can do.

Fuchsia colors his entire face. He doesn't understand. "I don't understand. Do you feel…"

"I don't feel anything, I just want you to confirm that — in theory — if one were strong enough to deny the bond for long enough, one could break it?"

"And I'm trying to tell you, I don't know what would happen because this is not something ever experimented with. It would be sacrosanct to even think to keep a pair apart. It could kill them."

I can't kill her. I'd die first. "But if one…" person, I almost said person… "If one being did not feel the bond, then they wouldn't die if it were broken."

"Krisxox, are you talking about a pair in particular?"

Nox. It doesn't matter who I'm talking about. I just want to know that it can be done."

"And I'm trying to tell you it can't *be. Xana and Xaneru do not make mistakes. Trying to deny the will of the universe could have egregious consequences."*

"Or it could have none."

His expression is ghastly. Ghostly. "I do not believe that this would be the case."

A rumbling beneath my chest fires my mind to life and rips the memory away. Where am I? I'm not on Qath. What happened? All I feel is pain.

I suck in a breath that tastes like pain and fills me up with it. Scorching heat touches my insides, then spreads to consume the outsides. I roar into whatever ground is beneath me.

What happened? I'm not in Li'Lemoria's cabin. I *did* resist the Xiveri bond, but only for as long as it took for her to feel it. Nox, when she wanted me, there was no question of what I would do to her. *Feast on everything.* I took her virginity and she looked so wounded afterward. I…tried to tell her, I'd take her for a mate, but then…then what? What happened next?

She said nox.

I passed out. I xoking fainted.

The Krisxox of Quadrant Four *fainted.*

"Well, this is a sight. Isn't it, my Okkari?"

My neck feels like it's been sawed off and sewn back together with barbed stitches when I turn to look over my shoulder at the pair walking towards me. The last xoking pair I want to see right now.

"Krisxox, your ridges," the Va'Rakukanna says, looking up at her mate in wonder. "Are his ridges supposed to be like that?"

"Verax…" I roar.

Pain.

It rips through me like a knife through the gut. I can tolerate any amount of pain — I have trained for it — but the sensation destroying my body from the inside out is pure, unfettered agony. I grab for my chest where I can feel my third heart, much larger now, too engorged to fit the space left for it, beating out an angry pulse.

I broke the bond. Nox, I didn't. Then what is this?

The answer comes to me after a second ripple of pain rages through my body. *Failure*, it says, and it speaks in a female's voice.

"Nox, I do not believe they are supposed to be like that. I don't think Krisxox has any control of them at all anymore."

I stagger to one knee and grab my ridged forehead with my left hand. I open my eyes and look at the carpeted floor where I can see a cascade of colors shining down from my face onto it. The backs of my arms aren't immune either and are blooming with color. I bet if I looked, my xoking xora would also be putting on a light show. *Xok! What is happening to me?*

"I believe he is being punished."

Punished?" The female asks.

"Punished by Xana for denying his bond."

"Nox! I didn't deny her. She is the one who denied *me*." The pain twisting in my gut twists tighter, harder. My xora shrivels, but my stones jerk beneath it, wanting release that I only get at the touch of one female. The one who says she hates me.

"Ah well, that explains it."

I turn to glare at the two of them, but Va'Raku watches me without a hint of emotion while his xoking queen hides her laughter behind her hand.

I try to turn my emotions off, but like a faucet with no valve, I can't. She steps past her mate and waves the hand she had pressed to her lips at me dismissively. The gesture would enrage me if she weren't one of the few humans I tolerate and I only tolerate her because of her fighting acumen. She's nothing like Svera. Hopeless in combat. *Hopeless because she is mine and I am unworthy.*

"Let your ridges run wild, Krisxox. You're not fooling anybody. We've all known for fifty solars that your Xanaxana is on the fritz for Svera."

Alright, perhaps I can feel rage towards this female, then. I start to stand, but she doesn't manage to look intimidated and Va'Raku makes no move to intercede. This deflates me.

"More than fifty. Since he first saw her on the transporter that took you off of your human colony, would be my guess."

"How long has she known?" I snarl, trying to tamp the colors in my ridges again and failing. What is this for a punishment? How long will it last? Why was it structured specifically to shame —

Shame.

An icy realization creeps up on me like frost before the thaw.

This is what Svera feels. *And I didn't care when it counted.* I failed her when I needed to wrap her in strength. I need to get to her now. If I get to her fast enough, maybe I can fix this...undo it, somehow... make her believe she's my...

"I'm not sure. I'd guess a while, though she's way too polite to say anything."

Anger. Towards Svera, this time. How *dare* she know that which I've totally failed at hiding. "You authorized her to find a new guardian," I hiss. "And you knew that she is my Xiv...Xiv..."

"Xiveri Mate. Hexa, we know. Svera is your Xiveri mate, but that doesn't mean that you're hers. For all we know, humans might have the ability to call the Xanaxana in a whole bunch of different Voraxians, and she can do a lot better than you."

"You xoking..."

"Krisxox," the dark rasp is immediate and sharp. Va'Raku steps up beside his female and slides his hand around the back of her neck. He levels me with a stare that I'm too xoking weak to repel right now. Because as she circles her arms around his waist and they step out onto the lift, I realize that I've lost something very precious to pride.

Time.

Half a rotation of it. Because Va'Raku is right. She was my Xiveri mate from the first moment I saw her on board that transporter. And if I'd been kind, I could have swayed her sooner. We could have been sharing laughter, clandestine looks and stupid little xoking kisses the way Va'Raku and his mate do now.

"It isn't possible," I say to her, but mostly to me.

"Maybe." She looks up into Va'Raku's eyes as she speaks, his jet black hair streaming over her skin like water, marred by just one flash of white. Drakesh heritage. Another hybrid. Is he, this male who I respect more than almost all others, truly so different than Svera? He holds Drakesh ancestry as well and is a product of inter-species mixing. Yet, he still holds his own planet, the largest in Voraxia and one of the wealthiest, one of the strongest too. He repelled a Drakesh invasion led by the former Bo'Raku. And now he's taken a human mate without any shame or hesitancy on his part.

From what I've heard, he even wooed *her*. As if she wasn't already his by right.

And now she looks up at him with total adoration. She holds him. *She holds him.* And he sweeps his hands into the cloud of her hair, pushing it back from her face.

And just before the doors close, Va'Rakukaltha says, "Hate fills the wound. Love erases it. Trust me on this before it festers." She points at my ridges and before I can shout at her and demand she tell me what the xok she's talking about, the doors shut with a ding.

There is a knock on my door. I lie on my sleeping pallet between two Drakesh females, their red skin glittering as their fingers trace the outlines of the muscles in my abdomen. They feel excellent against me, but they are simple breeding females that have agreed to accompany me on this voyage. We have already coupled many times, but I feel a surge of lust *and* adrenaline *— I've felt it ever since we landed on this wretched colony moon. It makes me want to take each of them again a dozen more times.*

Nox, it does not. It makes me want…something else. But I don't know what…

The knock on my door distracts me from the way their fingers lace together around my turgid xora. I shove them off and give whoever it is leave to enter. The door slides open soundlessly and Ga'Roth appears with his hand locked around the upper arm of the most shocking creature I have ever seen.

She is small. And her skin is not the proud, Drakesh red, or even the Voraxian blue — or any combination of the two. Her skin is a dark sandy color, much lighter than darkness, but much darker than the xamxin river. And her eyes — her huge, round eyes — they have different colors and though the colors are static, I can see at least three different shades shining at me in horror. She is terrified, this female, and she is not Drakesh and she is not Voraxian and she is the most beautiful creature I have ever seen.

It hits me — this wounded female who smells of blood and war and something dark and twisted and pulls me to her like she's aimed a grappling hook for my chest, fired and now, reels me in — she is my mate.

I order Ga'Roth to stop touching her, because she is naked and her naked body will take mine now. I order the two females to leave and never to return. And then we are alone. And I have the naked female cowering beneath me and my thoughts are firing with every effort at restraint because I know that this female is my Xiveri Mate.

But she isn't Drakesh.

She. is. not. Drakesh.

The realization tackles me from behind. I pull away only to be surprised when she also pulls away. Surprised and also deeply disappointed.

What has Xana done? As I snarl for the female to get the xok away from me and she disappears into the wet room, I sink to my knees, cover my forehead ridges with my hand, and I know...I know...

I am cursed.

And it does not stop me at all from grabbing my xora and pumping my seed onto the floor in bright blue bursts at the thought of the small, impure female in the other chamber, who was born mine from the start.

A female who I lost.

And now, I'm going to get her back.

I run onto the lift, power it down onto the scorching hot sands and charge through the colony's little village. People jump out of my way as I sprint, running so hard my full lungs buoy me all the way to Svera's parents' house, where my illegal tracker on her life drive says that she is. Though Raku told me to, I never removed it.

I bang on the door angrily only to remember that these are her sires and she cares for them deeply in a way I'd never cared for mine.

I straighten up, try to tame my hair into something...pleasant. I adjust the crude pressure of my xora in my kilt and try to calm the raging of my ridges, only for them to rage even harder.

The door swings open, revealing a man's wrinkled face. He has pale, peachy skin, a color I have never seen before except in fruit, and looks absolutely furious to see me.

What he says next I have no way of understanding, so I cut him off. "Svera," I bark.

"Bah," he grunts. He starts to shut the door on me, but I shove my boot in the doorway, blocking it.

"Svera," I say louder.

"No!" He shakes a finger at my nose in a way I don't like.

I snarl, "*Yess.*"

"No!"

"Yessss!"

"Habibi!" A woman steps up to the male's side and I know immediately that this female is Svera's mother, even if her skin is a little darker. Her hair is darker, too. I stare at it, feeling shame pool in my crotch, making my cock shrivel and my balls desiccate as I glance again to her male. *She's married. He did right by her.*

They speak in Human before the female turns to me. "My husband and I want you to know that you should be ashamed of yourself for what you did to our Svera. She is a good, pure woman, and you've defiled her before her god. We understand that you will not be seeking to marry her and…"

"I seek to *may'ree* her," I blurt.

The female blinks at me, stunned. Her hands go to the cross around her neck. "You…you do?"

"She will not have me. I…have not always been… I…I need…I just want to speak to her!"

Svera's female sire translates for the male and when she's finished the male lifts his finger and waggles it angrily at me again.

His female says, "My husband and I do not feel your intentions towards her are honorable. We do not give our blessing, though I'm not sure you even knew to ask for it."

Blessing? Ask? I recoil. "I should ask you?"

The female nods. "Hexa. In our Tri-God culture it is custom for the male to seek permission from the female's parents before pursuing her."

I scoff at this. "The Xana does not have time for this. The Xana is demanding."

"Xana. Hexa, we have read of this in Svera's manual." She exchanges more words with the male who shouts angrily back at me. "He says that he doesn't believe you. That a male who truly loved a female would always seek to do right by her."

I groan, exasperated. "That is what I am trying to do now."

The female shakes her head.

"*Pulayeez*. I…I am ashamed, but she did nothing wrong."

She and her husband enter into another short exchange before she says, "My husband says that he knows that. He tends to think Svera is perfect — "

"She is perfect." The words shoots out of me before I can catch them. I wince as I struggle to remain rooted and not tear down the xoking door.

"This is what all parents think of their children, but not mates." She shakes her head and speaks to me like she might a child. I am, ostensibly. I know nothing of humans and even less of mating. Like Svera, this is my first time. "We are meant to find flaws in our mates and love them anyway."

"You're right. Svera is a disaster. Now can I talk to her?"

"You are a stubborn male, aren't you?"

if by stubborn you mean that I do not accept failure, even my own, then you'd be right. I'm going to speak to Svera if I have to tear down your house."

The female laughs at my threat and the male nudges her until she explains what was said. He guffaws as he hears it and shakes his fist at me all over again.

"My husband says that if you're Svera's mate, then she has her work cut out for her."

That sounds dangerously like acknowledgement. I press my lips together, not wishing to bait them any further or lose the little ground that I have. "*Pulayeez.* I just need to see her. And I'd rather talk to her about what I mean to talk to her about — not why I tore down her house."

The female's mouth quirks. There's another exchange between her and her partner. Finally, she says, "You may speak to her with her consent, but you will not find her here. She is at Mathilda's house."

"Mathilda? She is treacherous. Svera would not go there alone."

I check my life drive again and, sure enough, Svera's tracker is active in her parents' home but...it's very stationary. Almost like...nox...could it be a ruse? *A jammer.* The technology exists, but I do not know how the humans would have gotten ahold of it. *Bo'Raku. Pirates...*

"Where?"

It's the highest home on the hill. I'm only telling you, because Svera told us that you were watching out for her and we fear that woman. Please make sure she stays safe. There are things we will be soon sharing with the Va'Raku and Va'Rakukanna that will make our family targeted."

I tense. "You have nothing to fear. You are sires to my mate. No harm will come to Svera and no harm will come to you." As soon as I say the words, some of the pain in my ridges lessens. I can breathe again. Deeply.

The female offers me a small smile, but it is full of sadness. "This is kind of you to say, but only the Tri-God can help us now." I'm about to cut in when she points past me, towards the colony's hill where new structures are being built.

"Go. Please," she says. "Make sure our daughter is safe."

"Until my last breath." I nod and switch my gaze to the male. "You are wrong. I *will* receive your permission. I am Krisxox of Voraxia and I do *not* lose."

Red rises in his face as the female translates, just like it does in Svera's, but before he can answer, I take off towards the houses sprouting from the hilltop.

I pound on the door to the largest structure for what feels like an eternity. No one answers. I'm about to break down the door when I get a sharp poke to the rear.

I growl and spin around, but there's nothing there. Nothing but a kit holding a sharp stick.

"What are you doing?" I shout at it, but it doesn't speak Drakesh or even Voraxian and just stares at me with globes for eyes and a smile on his face. He's not scared of me. He should be. But he isn't.

Instead, he just raises his stick again and pokes my thigh with it. I slap it away with a scowl and he stumbles a little to the side.

He says something to me in Human that sounds like a huff, then "eye."

What is this? A greeting? A warning? What? I don't have time for it as everything pulls together. Every muscle, every tendon, every xoking bone. I squeeze myself into oblivion, trying to will myself to not to explode as a sense of urgency causes the pain to resurface in me. Xana's punishment...

But then there's that xoking stick. He taps it to my abdomen and I reach out and try to grab it, but my left arm jerks when I see that he's pointing it again, this time, away.

"You know something?" I ask. He just giggles. I groan, exasperated. "Svera," I bark. "Mathilda."

He nods and my breath and pulse pick up. He points again with his stick and, when I still don't react, he starts to run at a bobbling little pace.

He runs to the crest of the hill, high enough for me to be able to see down the other side of it.

Xok.

Looking out over the bleak and lonely landscape, it's all dense, packed sand that's a slightly redder hue than Qath's golden brown forest floor, but unlike Qath, there is no vegetation here.

Just endless sand, interspersed only by rocks which form knobby, jagged hills some ways away, and the nightshade trees dispersed inelegantly among them.

That, and the glider.

At least, that's what it *should* be. But it isn't a glider like any I've ever seen before. Instead of a sleek silver floor, it's got no floor at all, but rubber wheels rolling underneath some rickety metal contraption. Clouds of black dust streak behind it as it races across the sand, heading to a destination unknown.

"Xok."

"Svera," the boy says to me, "Mathilda, Deena…" he says more that I don't understand, but we're interrupted by a female's shrill squawk.

"Mahmoud, gettaw awy fum heem!" A woman is racing up the road toward us.

I hitch my two thickest fingers in her direction. "Mahmoud, go."

He lifts his stick again and offers me a little wave and the strange thought crosses my mind as the little human kit starts down the hill at his awkward bobble…

I will make a warrior of him someday. A Voraxian *warrior.*

The pain in my body lessens again, becoming even fainter as I take that first step, and then tear across the landscape.

I've got two choices, but unfortunately, I don't realize it. I could go back and secure a glider of my own, but that doesn't occur to me until I'm halfway down the hill, racing for the shimmery side of the Droherion Dome. I won't be able to make it through, at least, I *shouldn't* be able to make it through.

But *shoulds* and *shouldn'ts* aren't working like they're supposed to.

There's a slit in the dome, like some giant shoved his hand into the side of the dome and ripped a chunk of it right out. *Mathilda.*

I tormented Svera with my hate and now, I've let her walk right into the sun.

The suns above feel like twin torches hanging too low in the insufferably bright white sky as I race, as I glide over the sands, following the tracks and the smoke that the putrid human glider leaves behind.

It's faster than I am, though. It shouldn't be, but there it is again, *shoulds* not operating in their proper order. Because it's gaining ground now, disappearing behind the dramatic screa outcrops that are fast approaching.

As I reach them, I think about charging ahead, but I can sense a strange energy emanating from the other side of the screa. I glance at the outcrop and then climb.

I scale the jagged edges of the screa boulders until I reach their peak. Crouched between two massive screa blocks that effectively conceal me from whatever is below, I look down at a Niahhorru battle transporter.

It sits among the sands, towering just beneath the highest screa point. Something of this size should *never* have been able to slip past the Voraxian defenses we have stationed around the human moon, but here it is, in living color.

Shouldn't. The word hits like a lightning stick to the skull — a sensation I've experienced before at the hands of Niahhorru pirates many times and most recently for Svera. *And I'd do it all over.*

I might just get that chance, I think glumly as I climb down towards the shimmery exterior of the Niahhorru transporter.

It pains me to admit it, but for as disorganized as they are, they're known for their technological prowess. Dealing as they do, they get ahold of all kinds of illegal weapons and technologies it takes rotations for our regulators to process.

With that access, and in view of this transporter unlike any I've ever seen, I'm not foolish enough to think that they don't have imaging and sensors enough to spot me, but no one comes. Maybe, I'll get lucky. Maybe this isn't a Niahhorru transporter sent here to steal my Xiveri mate from me. As if I weren't doing a good enough job of pushing her away already. Ha.

Xana is a wicked thing.

I drop onto the hard packed sand, feeling it shift uncertainly beneath the thick soles of my boots. The air is hot and I can hear voices now, not clearly, but close. The material of the ship must be something we don't have access to, because it's not *still*. Nox, as I make my way around all of its loose, folded edges, it feels like it's breathing beside me. Like a living organism.

It gives me the xoking creeps.

"...yookan tayck hurrn ow," says the voice.

They are the first words that I can make out and they are spoken in Human, a language I did not bother to learn... And now it puts me at a disadvantage on the battlefield and my Xiveri mate's life hangs in the balance. I grit my teeth, feeling flushed with a heat that is becoming just as familiar as the cascade of colors to my ridges that won't give me a xoking break.

The answer comes in Meero, a language I *do* know. It is the trading language. The language of the pirates. And as a familiar voice speaks, fire ripples behind my eyelids. *Rhorkanterannu*.

I shake my head, trying to focus through my rage and Xana's punishment. I'm not sure which is more vocal.

A second voice speaks, one that soothes that pain. *Svera, I'm coming.* "Mathilda is a traitor," she says. "She dishonors me. She dishonors *you.*"

A thwacking sound followed by Svera's nearly silent "oomph" makes my toes curl. I'm weaponless, but that doesn't matter. I am Krisxox. A strategist. I need to play this smart. I can't take down Rhorkanterannu, not unless he's alone and pirates never are.

A long moment of silence. I lift a foot off of the ground, but before I can take that next step, the sound of falling stones pulls my attention back and up to the left.

A human female is attempting to follow the path I took down the mountain. The sight of her there in her drab clothes shocks me. What shocks me even more is that she's staring straight at me as she moves in awkward little jerks. She's got a flush high in her cheeks and her heavy chest bounces with each abrupt lurch onto the next downward ledge.

I quickly assess her frame, finding it slightly taller than Svera's but remarkably less graceful…there. Her leg. It's bent at an unnatural angle, but does not slow her down too much as she makes her way to the sand mere paces behind me.

She waves at me, like I haven't been staring at her this whole time, and gestures for me in the human way by crooking her fingers again and again until I finally, begrudgingly, *painfully* relent and move closer to where she's standing.

The moment I'm within grabbing distance, she does. Lurching forward, one of her too-soft human hands catches my wrist and she starts to pull. I resist, but only because she's pulling me away from Svera. *Svera needs me and there's nothing in the xoking universe that could make me turn my back on her.* What about all the other times I've turned my back on her? Every solar that she's been living with me and I've rebuked, ridiculed or ignored her.

I stumble and it's that stumble that allows the small, soft creature to tug me around the ship — I'm not even sure that it's the *back* of the ship, the front or one of the sides — the construct is too fluid for that. She lifts up the long, coiled strands of her hair and presses against a small, black bead fitted into her ear canal. Then, with her hand still on my arm, she closes her eyes.

I rip my arm away, hating that this female is, for whatever xoking reason, touching my body — *a body that belongs to Svera* — and is wasting my xoking time…

Xok me.

The surface of the ship directly in front of her — in front of us — splits down a non-existent seam. A dark hole opens up in the middle of so much sunlight. Her eyes flutter open and she doesn't look the least bit surprised to see the ship cave to her demands — not like I am. I'm xoking stunned and I just stare at her for the first moment, but only just the one.

Xok me for underestimating her.

When she steps forward and looks over her shoulder at me with annoyance clear on her face, she leaves me no other choice but to follow her plan, and follow in her wake.

Xok me. I guess, we're taking a ride.

12

Svera

My head is pounding as I'm forced to my knees in front of the largest, most beautiful ship I've ever seen. It's nothing like the last Niahhorru ship Miari and I were stolen in. That was a hulky block of crudely constructed metal pieces that had aged for decades before I ever saw it. Or maybe centuries. Millenia.

This thing here looks like it was *poured* out of the darkest raincloud, spilled like a drop of ink among white sands. Looking at it, it seems to *shift*, becoming akin to the black mountains framing it. My eyes can't seem to contain its mercurial form. I blink again and again against it, and only find my voice when Deena, restrained behind me by two human guards I've known since childhood, finds hers.

"Don't do this, Rhork, don't do this…"

I pull in a deep breath and blink my eyes up at the males descending from the ship. The *Niahhorru* males. A shudder racks my body as I'm throttled into the past, into the arms of Nondah as he wrestles me to the ground and I fight for my life, ill-equipped as I am with just the smallest dagger to defend myself.

That wasn't all I had though. Then, I had Krisxox.

I blink quickly and try to harness my remaining strength but it's...hard. Memories are wicked things. They prick like needles with the ability to incapacitate. The ship *peels* open like two polar edges of a magnet repelling away from one another, all abrupt and sinewy, and the pirates descend. I feel like a child.

There are only three of them, this time, but that doesn't make me feel any better. The sight of their brutal forms makes my mouth dry.

I try to stand, thinking maybe I'll run, but there's a heavy weight on my arm keeping me grounded. Mathilda's hand clutches me brutally, even as she pitches her voice so syrupy sweet.

"So kind of you to join us, Rhorkanterannu. Please pardon the ramblings of my lunatic granddaughter. Though she wasn't ever the most enlightened conversationalist, she has been badly out of practice for quite some time."

"Locked up, chained and shackled by her own grandmother," I spit, though why I think he'd care is beyond me. In this case, the buyer is just as bad as the seller. Or nearly. Though, to my knowledge, he hasn't killed any human females.

Yet.

Rhorkanterannu snorts out of his broad nose. It is strangely human, like his mannerisms...but these are the only human things about him. He is, otherwise, the embodiment of carnage. Of *fight*. A battle to the death and, more importantly, its victor.

He wears scars across his plates like badges of pride, and that is almost all he wears except for the thick pant-like things hanging low enough on his hips to reveal deep V muscles carved into his abdomen. They are grey, his pants, and match his skin in both color and unpleasant-looking textures. They look hard and gritty. *Maybe because they need to be thick enough not to allow the many weapons that hang from his belt to rip through his plates or his skin beneath.* The thought makes me shudder. Why does a male like him who is already a living weapon need more weapons to defend himself? *Not to defend, to eradicate...*

His hairless, ridged pate catches the sun as he stares past me and Mathilda at whatever's directly behind me.

"Rhork," Deena says again, calling him a name that I have trouble placing until I remember that his *full* name is *Rhork*anterannu. *But why is Deena calling him Rhork, and why is she speaking to him with such familiarity?* "You can't take Svera."

Rhorkanterannu's expression betrays nothing. His stare is just pinned to Deena.

"*She* isn't willing, Rhork. Mathilda is trying to get rid of her for her own gain." I hear thrashing again and Rhorkanterannu goes dangerously still as Deena emits a pained gasp behind me.

His gaze narrows. Does everyone see how his lower right arm flits towards the blaster on his belt? It makes me feel like we are all very, very close to death. "I do not tolerate harm to females," he says and I haven't forgotten when he said something like that to me once before. Right before he slaughtered the male who wounded my cheek. I reach up and touch the scar.

Behind me, Deena laughs wildly, *sadistically*. "What are you planning to do to Svera if *not* harm her? You think she's going to enjoy going through a shekurr with you and your giant shroving cock?" It takes me until then — hearing her curse in Meero — to realize that she's been speaking entirely in Meero this whole time.

How? What...is going on here?

"*Enough,*" Mathilda shouts. Does she interrupt Deena now because she sees that Rhorkanterannu is clearly unsettled? His jaw ticks. So does a muscle in his thick neck, right along the column of his throat — one of the few vulnerable parts of him.

"Rhork, *please.* I'm asking you. I'm *telling* you. I'll do the shekurr. Take me instead..."

"No!" I shout at the same time that Mathilda leaves my side and I hear a loud, horrible *thwack*.

Rhorkanterannu draws his largest blaster so quickly I blink and see my entire life flash before my eyes. I'm dead. We all are. Because he moves more quickly than anyone I've ever seen.

Anyone except Krisxox.

But he doesn't fire.

"Those who harm females in my presence tend to lead very short, painful lives."

His eyes narrow. The hard plates of his lips peel back to reveal stone teeth. They're a strange color, his teeth. Like mother of pearl. Strange, only because they don't fit at all with the rest of him.

"Rhorkanterannu, your Grace…" Mathilda starts.

"I am a *Niahhorru pirate*. Not a pompous quadrant king. I am Rhorkanterannu and that's how you will address me. Now tell me why I shouldn't vaporize the head off your neck and leave the rest of you here for the khrui pod we spotted before landing. There were younglings among them. I'm sure they could use the fresh meat."

Behind me, Mathilda chokes and I feel a sick sense of satisfaction I'm unaccustomed to, hearing her suffer.

"Deena's words are obscene. She does not understand that a virgin's body is worth *more* in the eyes of any male. She is *also* a virgin. And she is also available, for the right price."

Nobody speaks.

Rhorkanterannu's gaze returns to Deena. In his expression, I can read nothing.

"Centare," he sneers — the Meero word for *no*. "I don't want her." Behind me, Deena makes a small sound right before Rhorkanterannu says, "She is defective. I could not even *give* her away at the slave auction. Release her. She is not even worth the ebo it would take to keep her fed."

Mathilda laughs and it's that laugh more than Rhorkanterannu's words that make me wince. I try to shrug out of Mathilda's iron grip, but it tightens. "As I suspected. Release her," she orders the guards.

With a tortured grunt, Deena breaks free of their hold. She looks at me and says, "I'm not going to let them get away with this."

"Go," I rasp. Before they change their minds! "Go!"

She shows Rhorkanterannu and his pirates her middle finger, turns and takes off running, her defective leg carrying her far and quickly.

Rhorkanterannu and Mathilda both watch her go. "Don't go far, Deena," Mathilda calls out in a light, cheery tone before turning back to Rhorkanterannu and clasping her hands together. "Shall we proceed, Rhorkanterannu? You are free to take her."

Rhorkanterannu hesitates for a long moment, staring Mathilda down, as if debating...debating...He still hasn't lowered his blaster.

Mathilda must sense her life hanging in the balance, because she says, "Don't forget, I am your only access to human females on this planet and only by taking this one will I be able to guarantee that access. Next time, for a much higher price..." Her voice trails off, as if in question.

"What is the price, Mathilda?" I say, but she doesn't answer.

Rhorkanterannu doesn't look at me at all, but his expression shifts, his plates moving microscopically even though he's hardly moved. He's just a wall.

Then he barks, "Get the female. Bring her on board."

The two pirates behind him come towards me and my stomach cramps. I feel sick, my brow breaking out in cold sweat. My palms get clammy as they carefully latch onto me and pick me up off of the ground with all eight of their arms. I'm nearly boneless as they carry me, and though I fought Nondah, it's memories of him now that keep me from fighting at all.

"Krisxox," I whisper, but I know he's far away now.

We reach a low ramp that ascends into the black, bowels of the ship. I dig the heels of my sandals into its slippery surface and scream, "What price is this, Mathilda? What price am I being sold for?"

I look over my shoulder and the last thing I see is Mathilda's sweet as sin smile as she says, "Nothing at all."

And then I'm dragged into the dark and my stomach lurches into my throat and I feel sick enough to vomit, but before I can, I fall unconscious.

13

Svera

I've felt this before. That's the thought that comes to me as I wake what feels like a rotation later. It must have only been moments because I'm still being dragged by the same males on what looks like the same ramp.

I blink away the fog in my head and swallow several times to keep my stomach under control as I fight to find the rest of my limbs. They're all restrained as I'm cradled by two males with eight arms between them.

I glance around. *Stars,* the transporter is huge. So much larger than it looked on the outside. My ears are popping and my sweat is making my arms slick beneath my torn, ash-covered abaya.

Ramps, like the one beneath me, crisscross over one another and none of them have railings. When I look down, my already fragile stomach does another precarious dance. There are Niahhorru everywhere.

Hundreds of them. Maybe more. They walk the railways, moving this way and that — all with purpose. Some wear more and less clothes than others. Some carry tools. And the canyon below me goes down so many levels.

The silver planks crisscrossing below me seem to come and go...their mechanics too hard to grasp. And *worse*, or perhaps, more *spectacular*, the walls of this ship aren't static. They're the same fluidity that I saw on the outside of the ship, occasionally parting in places to reveal a black sky full of billions of faraway stars. Then the windows shut, swallowing the universe back up before revealing it again in new windows that fold and unfold elsewhere, all around us. I feel faint trying to chart their course.

The two warriors hold me easily, so I just let my weak, stumbling legs go. It makes no difference. Two hands come to grip my waist, joining the ones on my arms. They lift me up so my feet don't even touch the sleek grey ground anymore. One of them calls ahead to Rhorkanterannu.

He's stopped halfway down this ramp that leads to a shimmery silver wall and is staring over his shoulder to the left. I follow his gaze to the exterior wall. It's parted again to reveal a taste of the universe. I can see our moon colony, just a speck of brown the size of a hand, then the size of a bean, then the size of a grain of rice, then nothing.

He must have used the machine again, the same one that transported thirty of his warriors onto Voraxia's surface without notice. He must have used it again, this time to transport an entire ship.

"Jump quadrants a dozen more times, until we're sure that the Voraxians will have no way to track us. We cannot make the same mistake we did before. And disable her life drive."

One of the pirates holding me fiddles with my left arm while the other lifts his hand up to his ear and begins speaking in low, rapid tones to absolutely no one, just like Mathilda did back in her home. *It must be some form of communicator...*

Rhorkanterannu resumes his pace just as the wall shifts again, gobbling up the sight of my home. Just like that, the threads of hope binding me to it all break.

I feel a surge of hysterics threatening to take completely control of my body, but I also feel... something else. A stinging in my chest wasn't there before that sits where Krisxox's hearts sit below my sternum. That odd pain is strangely *calming*.

Then, I'm hefted *through* the next wall because there are no doors and deposited alone with Rhorkanterannu into a long, rectangular room framed by three silver walls and one that's entirely transparent and has a beautiful view of rapidly shifting light. It stalls and those streaks of light become stars. The process repeats and I get dizzy trying to follow it, knowing that we must be entering some sort of near-light speed.

Instead, I turn my attention to the male I'm alone with and the room surrounding us. It's a plush, decadent room, full of bizarre things. Huge nets hang suspended at irregular intervals and, in the center of the room, stands a very weird looking podium. Aside from that, there isn't one single decoration on the walls, but the floor...oh my stars, the floor. It's covered in hand-woven carpets that look so human I would not be able to tell the difference.

"They are from the Eshmiri reavers. They operate frequently out of Kor and claimed to have located an asteroid filled with trash belonging to you humans. I do not know if they are real, but I felt compelled to purchase these. I found them beautiful."

I nod, distracted by a flash of green carpet among the many others. I push aside a net to get to it and pull it free of the overlapping rugs concealing it fully from view.

I hold it up to the lights shining muted overhead in shades of pink and yellow and run my fingers over the gold embroidered lettering.

"Allah alrahman el rahim," I whisper, turning to Rhorkanterannu, who is watching me now with a puzzled look.

"What does it mean?"

"No one knows the original translation, only the symbols." I offer him a smile, though it is shaky. "It means that my Iri-God has not forsaken me. I close my eyes, whisper a prayer, then say, "And it means that you have not been cheated by your reavers. This is a true carpet of the old world."

I start to set it down, but he says in a rough whisper, "Then it is yours."

I meet his gaze squarely and try to remember that I'm alone, but along the way, I learned something. I can stand up for myself against this male because I've done it already to Krisxox and there's nothing more frightening than going toe-to-toe with him.

Well. My gaze rakes Rhorkanterannu's wholly alien frame. Almost nothing. "I will not need it. I don't plan on staying long." I set the prayer mat down and turn to face him with my arms crossed. "Now, tell me what you want."

He chuckles under his breath and the sound is jarring. The overlapping waves of his voice make me feel like I'm adrift at sea and can't find the shore.

"I don't see what's funny," I try again, cautious with how I use my limited Meero. "I know that you won't force me to participate in the shekurr."

"What do you know of shekurr?" The swirling silver of his eyes changes all of a sudden, becoming more frantic.

"I know that it is a Niahhorru ceremony intended to produce kits. Because your birthing rates are so low, many males will seek to impregnate one female."

"That female is thus honored. If the shekurr is successful and she is able to bear a litter, then she has no shortage of fathers."

"Where I come from, the family has one father and one mother. We mate monogamously and for life."

Rhorkanterannu pulls in a breath so unexpected it makes me jump. His lips part to reveal those strange, shimmering teeth — some of which near the back look distinctly filed — and his lower left arm reaches up to cover his stomach.

"What?"

He shudders and abruptly turns towards the window. "That is a strange concept for a male like me." He crosses his upper set of arms over his chest and clasps the hands of his lower arms behind his back. He doesn't say more.

"So is the idea of a shekurr for me."

He sighs, "The Niahhorru have long lifespans, so we have a little time, but not much more of it. And while I have no interest in submitting an unwilling female to the shekurr, the survival of my species comes first. Sevrenn iahndru lat." Life must persist. The motto of the Niahhorru. One that makes me shiver more than his implication does, because I know that he believes in those words more than anything else. "So, I will force you to join the shekurr. You have a quarter span to prepare yourself."

He pivots on his heel and I'm wrapped up in the wind his huge body creates as he brushes past me and heads for the exit. My heart pounds rapidly. I can taste my heart in my mouth. I *thought* that Niahhorru honor would have prevented this. I *remember* the way he stood up for me against Nondah and the Niahhorru that couldn't control their mating lust. I remember the way he *slaughtered* the pirate who hurt me. I touch the scar on my cheek, feeling embarrassed, feeling confused. I know about Niahhorru honor. Or was that a lie, too?

"Fine." The word jerks out of my mouth, not wanting to come. "You can force me, then. When you hold me down with all four of your arms, will you feel proud then, your Grace?"

He rounds on me, coming towards me in an attack that I don't see coming. My hearts leap out of my chest, which simultaneously convulses. I fall back, landing on top of the prayer mat that I just set down.

Rhorkanterannu covers me with his body, planting all four of his hands on the floor and forcing me to lie back. He hovers his hips and chest off of me, but his knees brush the outsides of my calves when he sets them down, pinning my shift.

"You have studied well enough, little female, to know that we don't take kindly to insults. You've managed to insult me twice in one sentence in a language that is not your native one, so I will give you credit for this, but little female, I will not tolerate a third insult."

insults are all that I have," I say, chest heaving even though my throat is restricted at the back, like I'm fighting to get enough air.

His eyes flash, skein dropping down to cover them so quickly, it makes me flinch. I read that they mostly keep their eyes open, but that the skeins drop down when they're going into battle. Is that what this is?

Yes.

"Centare. You have something else."

His heat presses down on me and I'm forced back into memories of being overpowered. Of being hurt. I fight through them. "What?" My voice is a whisper. A breath.

"You have coordinates."

I blink while his skein slips back, revealing swirling silver eyes. He has a shallow brow bone and silver skin and at his hairline two large ridges stretch from his crown down the back of his head. In the valley between them, his spikes begin.

"How..." But he just lifts a brow in question. "That treacherous, evil, manipulative *snake* woman."

He chuckles and his breath smells like the frost of Nobu, winter clean and violently hungry. "Ontte," he says the Meero word for *yes*, "my thoughts as well."

Slowly, he picks himself up off of me and leaves me lying there where I am. "A satellite filled with humans left entirely unguarded and floating aimlessly through space? In *my* grey zone, no less? There was not a chance I believed that honorless wretch."

"What changed your mind?" I swallow many times, no less thirsty. No less disoriented. How could he know? If he doesn't know the coordinates because Mathilda wouldn't give them to him, then he's going to make me trade. I can feel it. The humans on Balesilha or my body.

But it belongs to Krisxox. I can't just give it away...

My hearts clench as I realize something quite funny. Ironic, really.

I miss him.

Not just because I feel safe, but because he feels steady. Even our fights are something known. Maybe because I always know they'll end in the same way. *With me melting and seething at the same time.*

"The Eshmiri."

Ah. "The asteroid," I whisper.

"Precisely. They did not just find carpets there, little advisor. They found humans."

"What?" The word slams out of me. I press a hand to my chest and sit up. "That can't be. You have humans?"

"Centare, I do not. I have seen human corpses. Hundreds of them. It took my pirates some time to put together the pieces, but when we succeeded, we came up with a rather interesting theory... The humans found by the Eshmiri were still cocooned in stasis chambers. Most of these chambers were broken and those that weren't stopped functioning tens of rotations ago. In our estimation, based on the amount of decay, almost a hundred.

"Why were they there? And why were sentient beings discarded alongside so much trash? It was almost as if they had been *intentionally* discarded. It could not have been by beings in any of the known quadrants, because any being, from the Oosa to the Eshmiri would have found use for such soft, productive creatures. So, we reasoned, a human did the deed. But why would another human intentionally discard its own kind?"

He pauses and I know he's asking me again and this time I actually have an answer. I wish I didn't. Because the fact that it comes more easily to me than it would have a rotation ago — even a solar ago — makes me feel like I've lost something very important.

My faith in people.

"They were a burden."

"They were a burden." Rhorkanterannu smiles and it is a chilling thing. He takes measured steps towards me, heavy footsteps dampened by the carpets, but still capable of making me flinch every time. "Ontte, Svera, they were a burden."

He reaches a hand down and I take it tentatively, let him help me up onto my feet. I dust off my shift as he walks away from me, pacing the space purposefully.

Who were they a burden to, my little advisor? And where are they now? I know that they are in the grey zone between the Fourth and Fifth Quadrants. I know that they are somewhere in my own territory, but I have searched the skies for them and they do not seem to want to be found."

His pacing brings him back to me and when he reaches me, he steps directly into my personal space, invading it, making me shiver involuntarily like my body is already programmed to know that he is a predator.

"Where are they?" He whispers.

"You'll have to cut them out of my thoughts."

I grit my teeth and flinch away from the pressure of his claws as they ever-so-gently scrape the side of my face, lingering over the faint scar I wear from our last interaction.

"Very brave, you are, little Svera, but you will give me the coordinates. You know what is at stake if you do not."

"You're a...bad male," I whisper.

He grins. "Unlike your sweet, darling Mathilda, I never claimed otherwise. Content yourself with that while you consider my offer. You have until I decide to come back for you and, when I come, I won't be alone. Thirty of my brothers will be with me and they've heard magical tales of human cunts. Whatever you decide, prepare yourself for it."

He's almost at the wall when the door appears before him. It seals itself shut after he leaves but, when I follow the path he took, no door appears for me.

I shiver, alone, and look around at the room. My eyes fall to the prayer mat and I shake a little as I spread it out in front of the window.

I pray, hoping Rhorkanterannu gives me time enough for this before the shekurr — he must know that there is no other option. I won't doom an entire satellite of humans to this fate just to save my own hide.

I'll perform shekurr.

And when I do, I'll think of Krisxox.

I exhale shakily, and then I start to undress.

14

Krisxox

The dark bowels of the ship — wherever we are — are difficult to maneuver. We don't travel in ducts, or in anything I can understand. There's just a black substance that sort of...moves away from us when we crawl, like some weird nonexistent foam or a blanket.

I'm xoking Krisxox of Quadrant Four but...I don't like this dark world, which occasionally — at the human's command — spits us out into a variety of rooms, some containing weapons' racks, others pirates' private quarters, food preparation units and stockpiles on stockpiles of storage. She, on the other hand, maneuvers it easily, not having a problem with the confined spaces at all.

We find a room that has unguarded access to escape pods. She points to one, but I grab her wrist. "Svera," I growl.

She rolls her eyes and begins speaking to me in Meero. Surprising. *Not the first surprising thing about this female.* Yeah. We'll get Svera then get our asses back here. I just wanted to know where they were."

She starts crawling again and I grunt after her in Meero, "Why are you helping me?"

"Because Svera doesn't deserve to be taken by that bastard or his thirty freaking friends."

Rage. It comes out in my speech. "Move xoking faster."

She rolls her eyes at me but the female does start moving faster.

A short while later, we're crawling nearly flat — no indication whatsoxokingever as to *why* — through the darkness, illuminated only by my ridges and their uncomfortable pressure — their light. *Her light.*

"Are we xoking there yet?" I hiss into the black.

Ahead of me, the female looks over her shoulder, her coils flicking at me like fluid Niahhorru spines. She raises a single finger to her lips, then points it straight down. A moment passes, then the darkness parts to reveal a flash of the world below. Eerie tech, not stuff we've developed yet, or traded for. Eerier still is this female's ability to control it. And she's *human.*

She lies on one side of the hole, flat on her stomach, while I approach from the opposite direction. I sidle up to the entrance, tense and ready to slaughter any Niahhorru in the room with Svera, should this be where she is. And it is.

But she's alone.

What is she doing? She's up against the window and there's a determined look to her now that makes my soul shrivel when she starts to take off her shift.

Nox. Nox. She isn't willingly preparing herself for shekurr, is she?

Rage. It comes again in different strokes. These are more weighted. I wait until she's completely bare and seated high up on the room's single podium, large enough for her to stretch out on comfortably. She plants her feet below her ass and spreads her thighs and then she...xok!

She's *touching* herself. I'm about to scream bloody murder at the sight before me — the xok is she thinking preparing herself for a Niahhorru invasion like this! — when all of a sudden, her determined expression parts to one of pleasure.

"Krisxox," she whispers. Her eyes are closed. She does not see me. "Krisxox," she says again and her back arches and next to me, the female claps a hand over her mouth.

I look up at her and raise a finger to my lips, then slap my palm over her eyes. I don't want her xoking watching this. This is *mine*. And it's doing strange, terrifying things to me.

The colors in my ridges pulse and surge, even as the painful punishment within calms. *Home.* The word comes to me then and makes me feel wretched and wonderful.

Home.

What am I doing? What have I done? I would risk losing *this* because she has the wrong bloodline? The words of my sires echo through my memories, recalling everything they've ever said about species that aren't Drakesh. *Disgusting. Unworthy. Impure. Fickle and stupid. Less than.* All words I feel like using against myself.

"Do not open your eyes," I snarl to the human beside me.

She makes an impatient sort of sound through the fingers that still cover her mouth and even though I can't make out the words, she's right. We don't have enough time. We *don't* have enough time, but I will make time enough for this. I can feel Xaneru wrap his arms around me in a loving embrace as I swing my feet into the opening and land on the floor below in a crouch.

The moment I land, Svera tenses and zippers her legs together. I storm towards her, knowing we're short on time and unwilling to waste a moment of it. I grab her ankles, drag her to the edge of the platform, spread her knees and step between them.

I grab her by the two thick woven pieces of her hair and wrench her up into a seat. "What were you thinking offering yourself up to the Niahhorru like this? This..." I hiss, reaching between us to cup her core in my palm. Its heat is scalding.

And mine.

"This is not yours to give. You belong to *me*."

Svera's eyes fly open. Black surrounded by green surrounded by golden brown. *Traces of the garden. Promises of what's to come...* The tension in my shoulders is hard to maintain. *I want to sink into those flowers.*

"What were you thinking, Svera?" I smooth my thickest finger over her cheek, reach up and touch the beads around her neck. "You thought I wouldn't come for you?"

A hysterical laugh bursts out of her right before she grabs the back of my head and wrenches me down to her mouth. I slant my lips over hers and fall into her taste.

"Xok," I whisper between us, knowing that this is what got us into trouble in the first place. But, like then, I'm not a decent or smart enough male to pull away from it.

Her tongue tangles with mine and I moan when she moves from my mouth to my jaw to my ear down my neck. She bites me hard enough that a nerve in my neck makes my right arm jerk. I wrap it around her back, pulling her even closer to me until the heat of her exposed core meets my abdomen. The pain of the Xanaxana releases little by little.

"I'm sorry I pushed you away," she whispers.

"You should be. You ran straight into danger." Against her feathery mouth, I snarl, "If I didn't know any better, I'd say you were trying to get captured given your success rate." Laughter shoots out of

Svera's mouth along with spittle. She wipes it off of my chest, but I don't care. "If it happens again, I'll have to punish you." I capture her hair in a fist and stroke her cheek with my own. "Don't try to run from me, again."

"If I'd been trying, I wouldn't be so grateful to see you now." She swallows many times and I pull back just enough to brush my lips over hers, without kissing. Just to feel their softness. Just to feel her heat. She is so warm.

I want to ravage her, enter her and explode into her again and again. After all, she's already on the sacrificial slab, ready to accept my offering.

"I just..." Her face turns pink and she bites her lower lip, drawing my attention to it. "I knew she couldn't kill me, but I didn't think she'd try anything like this. She must have been planning it for dozens of solars. And I walked right into her trap. But you found me. Somehow, you found me."

She shakes her head and I'm embarrassed by the way she looks up at me, then. Like she's in awe and I'm her hero. "How did you find me?"

"You have your human here to thank for that." I point up and back towards the hole where I left her. From here, I can see that the other human female has entirely disregarded my order and is waving down at us urgently. "We need to go."

I lean in and taste Svera's mouth one more time before pulling back, gathering her shift and wrenching it down over her head. I scoop her off the table and set her down, but she runs away from me a few feet and crouches down.

"What are you doing?" I hiss as she stands back up and folds a green carpet under her arm.

"What? He said I could have it."

I groan, "Unbelievable."

I quickly rush back to her human compatriot and grab Svera — and her xoking carpet — and lift her over my head.

"Deena?" Svera rasps, shocked as I help her up into the hole, Deena pulling on her hands to assist. They exchange in Human while I leap up into the darkness next to them.

With her unbelievable command over this ship, the female called Deena seals the hole shut beneath us and we continue through the darkness, back to the escape pods.

After a while of not being able to understand them, I bark at Svera to translate or switch to Meero — a language we somehow all speak together, despite being Krisxox of Voraxia and two human females with limited access to technology and even less knowledge of the quadrants than I have. *They persevere. They are resourceful. Clever. Brilliant, even.*

And this entire time, I underestimated them. *What have my sires ever done so clever as this?*

"How do you know Meero?" Svera says, switching to the language in question.

But Deena just shakes her head. "Not important." She keeps crawling and, abruptly, changes direction.

"How do you command the ship?" I hiss.

Deena hesitates long enough to turn back to face us. As my ridges shine bright, colors dance over the small silver bead in the center of her palm. She sticks it back in her ear and lifts her hair for me to look, but the bead is deep inside of her head and I can't see it now.

"It's a Niahhorru token. I stole one from Mathilda a while back. Much more advanced than the life drives Voraxians use, it locks in with other tokens and can act as a communicator. The ship is made out of the same material. It's a giant token itself. So, I can communicate with it."

Xok. "This device — is it worn by all Niahhorru?" If so, then we'd be easily detected.

She shakes her head. "Not all. Just a few. Rhork definitely wears one."

Xok. "Has he detected us?"

"I don't think so. I commanded the token to shield itself. I think I managed to scramble the communicator. We should be good."

And then Svera asks a single question I hadn't considered. "Have you...been able to communicate with Rhorkanterannu before this?"

Deena winces as if struck and doesn't answer. She just keeps crawling and, after another two turns, finally says, "I didn't...have anyone else to talk to. And I didn't think...He forced you into shekurr down there, didn't he? That's why you were naked on the table."

Svera nods and rage rips down my spine, showering the whole world in red from my ridges. "Ontte. He was trying to force my hand. What he really wants are the coordinates to an unguarded human satellite. Mathilda told him I had them."

Deena's face shutters and she closes her eyes for longer than a standard blink. I wonder what she's thinking and why her expression looks so pained as she says, "So he could steal and do shekurr with a bunch of other humans."

"Everyone knows this," I hiss, "The male is ruthless in his attempt to rebuild the Niahhorru race. Now let's keep going."

Deena hiccups, covers her mouth with the back of her hand. Then the floor just beyond her peels open. "We're here."

I edge up next to her and scan the space for threats. Finding none, I glance at her and confess something I never thought I would to a human. "I owe you. Profoundly. You were brave to do this."

And they're dismissed just as quickly. "Whatever," she mutters, face hardening. There is something going on here that I can't interpret. Something to do with Rhorkanterannu and this female, but right now I don't care to uncover it.

"We should split up," she says.

"What? Centare!" Svera scoots up until she's in between Deena and I. We lay on our stomachs shoulder-to-shoulder-to-shoulder.

Deena grits her teeth and points through the opening into the well-lit room beneath us. Huge doorways are marked by glowing Meero symbols demarcating which pods are stocked, fueled and operational.

"I'll take the first pod. You need to be ready in that one there," she says, pointing to another. "When you feel the ship start to accelerate and give chase, detach. Don't activate power though until the Niahhorru are out of range. I'm hoping that they'll be so distracted chasing me that they won't go after y'all — even if they realize another pod detached, maybe they'll assume it was me creating a diversion."

I nod. It isn't a foolproof plan, but it's the one I would have come up with. I feel a strange color touch my ridges as I look at the human called Deena. "Are you a battle strategist?"

Deena gives me a strange look in return and opens her mouth. It is Svera however, who says, "Ontte, she is." She's grinning at the female, even as she shakes her head and places her hand on Deena's shoulder. "Deena, it is a good plan, but I can't let you do this for us."

"I'm not asking, Svera."

"Khorkanterannu will catch up to you and what will he do when he realizes you don't have the coordinates? He will take you in shekurr..."

Deena tightens. Her eyes close and her lips purse. "Centare, he won't. He said so already. I'm defective." She gestures at her left leg. Defective? Strange. Like Voraxians, the Niahhorru view scars as marks of pride. It shows she has suffered and survived. "He won't perform shekurr." Svera's still shaking her head, but Deena grabs her arm with force enough to make my hackles rise.

"Svera! Listen to me. Get into the pod. Go back to the colony and *crush* Mathilda. She can't be allowed to get away with all the crap she's done. Who knows what she has planned next."

That does seem to sway Svera somewhat. She tries again to protest, but Deena shakes her even harder. "Svera, I can't fight her! Nobody would listen to me. Mathilda's painted me as some spoiled colony brat. I mean, look at me."

She points down to her body and I don't understand, then grabs the flesh of her belly and gives it a strange tug.

"She made me like this so everyone would think I was a spoiled, rotten princess. Why do you think she didn't care if I ran back to alert the colony? She knows that no one will listen to me. Please. I'm begging you.

"If you knew half the shit she did to me, I'd... you'd...I *can't* know that she's out there. *I want her* crushed. I don't care if you have to kill her. I don't care if you have to shoot her into space. I just want to know that she can't hurt anybody anymore and I can't make that happen. I need you to do that. I can do this. I can handle Rhork."

Svera stares at Deena. Tension threads the darkness. It is not in Svera's nature to leave her humans behind. Nox, it is not in Svera's nature to leave *anyone* behind, human, Voraxian or otherwise. She offered to be rutted by a dozen Niahhorru to save the lives of humans who she has never met, who she may not even be able to find.

"Take the coordinates," she says finally.

"Centare. That's not gonna happen." She starts to move down into the room, but Svera holds her back.

"If you're caught, you need a backup. You don't know what could happen. What if Rhorkanterannu changes his mind? What if he *doesn't* change his mind, decides you are defective and instead of keeping you or releasing you, decides to sell you? He could sell you to the Sky where they'd cut you open and graft bio-mechanical parts to your body to try to turn you into a soldier or an assassin. You could be sold to the Oosa who would use you for pleasure and possibly kill you in the process. You don't know what would happen and you need to have some form of backup. For all we know, the humans are well equipped and capable of defending themselves against Rhorkanterannu should he try to attack."

Deena scoffs. "You'd have given him the coordinates yourself if you really thought that."

"Deena, *please.*"

"Both of you, *pulayeez.* We're wasting time."

"I agree," Deena huffs, dragging her body towards the hole.

Svera grabs her arm. "I'm not getting into that pod without giving you the coordinates."

"Augh! You are so annoying."

I huff, "Tell me about it."

"Deena," Svera says, voice cold and unwavering. And then she beings to repeat the coordinates over and over until Deena is able to recite them back to her from memory.

"Satisfied?" Deena says.

Svera smiles and in Human answers, "Yes."

"Give Mathilda hell," Deena replies just before entering into the first escape pod.

"Use the coordinates if you have to," Svera reminds her.

"I won't, but whatever." Deena starts into her pod with lopsided gait, but I don't doubt for a moment as she retreats that the Niahhorru pirates have finally met a worthy adversary.

"Deena," I call. She stops in the center of the four seats, choosing the largest one with the control panel embedded in the arm. "The moment you detach, warp into another sector." These escape pods can't move faster than the speed of light, but they can get close to it. Khorkanterannu's ship will be able to immobilize yours the moment they lock on. You can't let them lock on. Keep warping until you lose him. We'll do the same."

With a serious look on her face, she nods jerkily. "Got it." She doesn't say anything else, or offer any thanks.

I feel the edge of my mouth jerk up. "Stay safe," I tell her.

"Yeah, yeah. Whatever." The door to her pod slams shut between us and she begins to detach without warning.

I rush Svera into the pod we'll be commandeering and steer her to one of the seats. Four of them sit facing in towards one another. Meanwhile, the fabric of this ship is built by the same material as the Niahhorru mothership. It is one single window, relatively circular, with black matter appearing and disappearing across the transparent body. The stars are visible all around us, as is Deena's escape pod detaching, and then floating into space.

The rumbling of our own pod detaching has Svera muttering prayers again. I take the seat across from her and type the coordinates to the human colony into the armrest.

I wait to warp, wanting to make sure that the ship does indeed chase Deena and that Deena does, in fact, manage to warp herself.

Svera stares in the direction I do and we both sit, tense, watching the infinitely larger ship power to speed as it chases the tiny pod into the starlight, until even the ship the size of an asteroid — or possibly a small moon — eventually winks out of sight.

They're gone.

Svera's safe.

I exhale.

I fire on power and set course for home. *Home? Why would I think that?* And as our escape pod finally begins to move, Svera rips her eyes away from the view pane and looks at me. Finally. *Maybe for the first time.*

My skin feels *prickly* every place her stare touches. And it isn't a *stare,* really, because nothing about her is ever exactly what it should be. Because *shoulds* don't exist anymore in my vocabulary.

Twitching underneath the weight of her silence, I unlock the belt strapping me into my seat and stand. "You owe me, Svera."

She jerks, eyes narrowing. "For what?"

"For sacrificing yourself for humans — *again.*"

She balks, "And I owe you for this?"

"Hexa." I prowl towards her. It only takes two strides to bring me to her knees.

"And what is it that you want?"

I take the rolled carpet in her lap and pull it aside, noting the way her thighs are clenched tight beneath it. "*May'ree* me."

203

She quiets, her jaw goes slack. I brace my either hand on either arm of her seat and lean in, undaunted to by the rejection I expect to hear. I know that I deserve it. But it will not stop me from asking again and again and again.

"You don't want to marry me," she says as I lean in towards her, mouth separated from hers by a single hesitation, not more than that.

I kiss her tenderly. "Don't tell me what I want." I kiss her again.

"You really want to marry me?"

"More than I want my second heart."

Her eyes blaze when she opens them. She licks her lips and her chest hitches. "Oh stars…I think…" Her gaze flicks to my ridges and I tense when she leans in, bites my pectoral where my plates meet more sensitive skin.

The sensation ripples like electricity through my right side, making me stiffen awkwardly. I wrench her hips out of her seat, picking her up and carrying her to the nearest wall of the transporter. Against the vastness of space, I rub her against my body. She feels so xoking good. *Mine.* And she's safe and she's alive.

"*May'ree* me, Svera," I breathe against her neck, rutting her through our clothes.

I hike her shift up and she mewls as her wet lips come in contact with my skin. I lower her down until she's separated from my xora by nothing more than my kilt.

"I will consider it," she says, bloodthirsty little thing.

I laugh and grind more forcefully against her, watch her eyes roll back into her skull. "You will *may'ree* me. I *will* be your *house'band*."

"You don't...even have...my parents' permission."

"I will get it," I snarl. "I am Krisxox of Voraxia."

"And I am a human."

"Hexa. A human who took me to the garden and butchered me among the flowers. Whatever I have to do to be yours, I will do it."

She moans, loud and deep. "Krisxox, please take me."

I laugh darkly at that. "After what happened last time? Nox."

Her eyes fly open and she mewls. "You...you won't?"

"I have felt your shame." I reach up and touch my ridges. "I won't rut you again until you are my *whiff*."

"Wife," she whispers. "What do you know of it?"

"I know of it." I grab her breast, drag my ridged tongue up the length of her neck. "I know that *whiff* and *house'band* share this *lawv* for one another."

"And what...what do you know of love?"

"It is the garden, Svera." My stones are tight against my body, desperate with the need to release all over this female. I lower her to the floor, wrench up her shift, exposing her beautiful body to me.

I release my kilt and watch her eyes flare, but instead of covering her, I lower my mouth to her nipples, worshipping each dark brown peak in turn. Then I move lower still.

I bite and suck my way down her skin and as I move, I say, "It is not the fire in the desert, but the desert itself. It's not the bright flare of the supernova, but space. It is forever, without change. A constant. It is *heimo*."

She gasps as I reach her most sensitive skin, just below her curls. I pull up on them, then devour her. She shrieks loud and long as I rub my ridges up and over her most sensitive nub. Nectar from her hot slit spills out onto my chin and I lap at it, spearing her deep with my tongue when her shivering begins.

She grabs onto my hair like it's the last thing anchoring her to this pod and I taste her and suck her and lick her until she breaks apart.

She comes for me and I feel like a god.

Her core clenches around my tongue as I slowly retract it from her body. She moans and kicks out with her right leg, the motion involuntary.

"Krisxox," she begs, she pleads.

I sit up and wrench my kilt out of the way, then drop forward onto one hand. The other grabs my xora at its base and pumps one, two, three and a dozen more times.

I empty myself all over Svera's body, covering her tits with blue, making sure to claim those pert nipples with my seed. I cover her stomach from rib to rib, her chest, her sternum. I want her weighted down by it and for the moment, she is. Arms spread out to either side, lips parted like she wants nothing more than for me to bring my xora to her mouth. The thought makes me wild and more seed comes. I shift forward and, with her shift bunched all the way up around her neck, I skip over it and aim for her mouth.

A shot of blue wets her lips and her cheek. She blinks rapidly and then the little bloodthirsty thing shocks me.

She wraps her arms around my ass and wrenches me forward, leaving my xora nowhere else to go but inside her mouth. She takes me into her wet entrance and the nerves up and down my shaft explode simultaneously.

"Aughwah!" I roar, unleashing a garbled shout as her heat creates a vacuum around me. She sucks and I collapse forward onto one elbow, unable to control the way my hips shudder and plunge forward, in and out of her.

"Xok!" I roar. Followed by, "*May'ree* me, Svera!"

She chuckles with my xora still inside of her and the vibration makes my toes clench in my boots. Why are we still xoking wearing our shoes?

I collapse onto the side of her, pulling out of her slowly. My muscles are all still firing, but I can't move.

Time passes, not a lot of it, but enough for me to beg her one more time. "*May'ree* me. *Pulayeez.*"

She sits up and licks the blue off of her lips. She glances down at her chest and the blue spattered across it and then the filthy, *filthy* human drags one finger across her nipple, removing the blue, and sucks that finger into her mouth.

"You taste good," she whispers.

"Xok, Svera. I need you."

"Then take me." She reaches down and smears the blue in her lower curls down...down. She spears two fingers inside and rolls onto her knees. She reaches for my xora, but I grab her wrist.

Shakily, I hack out, "I can't. It is against the Tri-God."

"I...wasn't angry with you before," she says slowly. "I was angry with...with everything. And Krisxox, I am sorry to tell you, but this is against the Tri-God, too." She gestures down to the blue all over her as she whips her shift off of her neck and lets it flutter down onto the floor beside me.

"We did not rut," I contest.

"Hexa, but it's still against the Tri-God."

"Xok me," I growl, sitting up.

I touch the side of her face and look down at her mouth. "*Pulayeez*, Svera."

But she redirects. "Did you read the manual? You quoted the words that I wrote about love, about heimo. Do you know what it means?"

Hexa. It means *nome* in your ancient Human tongue. And of course, I read your manual," I say after a beat. "I memorized it."

She watches my eyes and jerks back. Then she hits me. She *hits* me, striking her hand over my cheek. It doesn't hurt, but it is still shocking. "What was that for?"

"For being such a brute. For telling me these things now when I am trying so hard to hate you."

"Good luck. You're not capable of hate. This is how I know I will *may'ree* you."

She rolls her eyes and shoves on my shoulder. I yield until she pushes me back onto the floor and swings one leg over me. She sets her sopping wet core down over my xora and slides over the ridges lining my erection.

"Svera." I pick her up by the hips, holding her off of me. "Not until..."

"You *owe* me."

"The xok I do."

She glares and leans forward, pinning my shoulders beneath her much smaller hands. I let her. "You have been rude and uncivil to me every single solar since I met you. If I want to rut you now, then that is my right."

Xok. "Your god..."

"My god..." She huffs and sits up and it's a perfect agony. She rubs her face, smearing blue across her cheek. "My Tri-God is a confusing one. My parents…" She shakes her head and slides off of me and it's a perfect torture. "The females that died in the first Hunt had no trouble passing the kits. Mathilda sold them to Bo'Raku who then sold them to someone else — not to the Niahhorru. Then Mathilda killed the human mothers.

"Subsequent births that came out of the Hunt would have been possible, too, but my parents, seeking to save any females from that fate, aborted those kits. They told everyone that the first round of hybrids and mothers died in childbirth because they were afraid of Mathilda. The only reason Miari and Darro weren't sold is because they were considered defective at birth."

She sighs while shock parts my lust and desire. Not parts. *Shatters.* "So, when you ask me about my Tri-God now, I'm not sure how to answer. He is a cruel being if he allowed all this to happen to us. And I am done with cruelty for now."

She touches my ridges, which still shine with color. I'm no longer certain if Xana is still punishing me, or if I've simply lost what little control I had and am making up for lost time, screaming my colors for her to see. I don't feel pain anymore, not like I did. Now all I feel is sadness.

I shake my head. "This is…unforgiveable."

She winces. "My parents were only doing…"

"Nox. Not your parents. Your parents are heroes. They saved countless female lives. But Mathilda…" I growl. You were right to accuse me of enjoying punishment because I will skin her alive happily."

I grab her wrist as she picks at her lower lip and pull her body back to where it was on top of mine. "But Mathilda is not here and for now, we will not think of this. For now, we will think only of the garden."

I lift her hips and position my erection below her entrance. "If you are sure, then I will take you there."

"What about marrying me?" She questions with one brow lifted. Her braids drape over her stained breasts, frizzy and frazzled in places. I reach up and yank the ties binding them. Quickly, I comb my claws through them until her hair spreads in golden brown waves across both her shoulders. She looks heaven-sent, a gift straight from her god and mine.

"I will. That is not a question."

"We'll see." And just as I'm about to accuse her of her own form of cruelty, she lowers herself onto me.

We release shared moans, our breaths mixing as she collapses forward, catching herself on my chest. I move her arms out to the side so that I can feel her breasts against me as I piston up into her. Her warmth is pure ecstasy. I release muttered curses as she releases muttered prayers.

"Take your pleasure, bloodthirsty female."

She is unsure as she starts to move, switching her hips back and forth. Eventually, she finds a position she likes, one where she can rub her soft nub and curls against my body as I arch into her.

Her back curves. She thrusts her breasts out and xok, does she look lovely. She starts to whimper as her first orgasm builds.

I'm panting, thighs clenched, whole body strained as I fight to keep my own orgasm contained. "Don't retreat from it," I say. "Follow me."

She doesn't know what I mean, but her body does and soon, our movements have matched into a steady pulse. The beat sounds like the drums of my own heart. I know, looking up at her face, that she feels it. The Xanaxana is settling. The Xanaxana is claiming. It's running wild. The pain of Xana's punishment has all but released and I know that this means my Xiveri mate's own shame is receding, if only for now.

"That's it..."

"Krisxox," she whines. Her mouth opens and her body begins to tremble. Her insides tighten around my xora and just as she releases and I release right there with her, I hear the first warning beep.

I roar into her hair as my hips lift and her whole body pitches. I catch her against my chest, strapping her to me with my arms as she screams into the plates covering my right pectoral. Her nectar and my seed slide down the length of my shaft to wet my stones as she tightens around me convulsively.

I shout her name. She whimpers mine.

The beeping gets louder and more frequent, intervals closing in on one another. I roll over and my hips keep me from getting up. They're pinning hers and slapping against her, my balls swatting her ass with each thrust.

I empty into her again and again, muttering curses as well as her name. The moment I've finished, I pull out of her even though it causes us both to buckle.

I struggle over to the control chair and check the screen. "Xok."

"What is it, Krisxox?" Svera says dazedly.

"Put your shift on. Take this." I limp over to her, feeling like a madman as I rip open the weapons' cache built into the floor. I hand her a short dagger, too scared to let her use a blaster or anything else more dangerous.

"Verax."

"Our thrusters have been disabled and there's an incoming Eshmiri ship."

"Eshmiri?"

"Pirates, like the Niahhorru but uh…different."

Her face falls, turns bright red and then a horrible white. "Can't we…should we… You're going to fight?"

I'm going to try. But Eshmiri aren't like the Niahhorru who at least fight with some semblance of honor. The Eshmiri are maniacs and will likely use disablers as soon as they get the doors open.

The entire ship shakes and rumbles. Svera nearly falls, but manages to catch herself on the back of a chair just in time.

I strap on my kilt and start mounting weapons to my frame.

Svera shakes her head, snapping out of it. "Nox. Nox, nox, nox." She drops her dagger and grabs her stupid carpet instead. "You think fighting is the only way." She reaches me and covers my hand with hers. In my fist, I hold a grenade.

The Eshmiri ship reels us in, but I don't break her gaze, preferring to watch her straighten instead and smooth down her skirts, like she isn't completely covered in my seed and like we aren't trapped in this universe-forsaken transporter, me, about to be sold.

"What are you going to do, talk them to death?" I balk and meet her gaze. It's even and cool. It gives me the chills. Me. Krisxox. Ten times her size, I'm suddenly caught in her shadow. And not for the first time.

"Precisely. I'm going to negotiate."

15

Svera

Krisxox is still staring at me like I've gone completely mad when the doors to our escape pod are pried open to reveal a small battalion of Eshmiri reavers standing in a square tunnel brandishing all manner of fantastical weapon.

I've read about Eshmiri and seen their holo-images, but I'm still startled by the sight of them. They stand shorter than I do, but their torsos are built like barrels and their legs are short stumps. Their arms are thick with muscles big enough to carry the weapons they hold and they are *armed*. I thought Krisxox looked lethal, but these little creatures look positively mad. Especially because they're all *smiling*.

Their faces are mostly eyes and tiny, round mouths full of tiny razors for teeth that sit where a chin should. They don't have noses, but apparently have gills behind the stiff flaps of the large ears that lie flat against their round, compressed skulls. Those gills filter in all types of air, making it possible for them to survive up to half a solar in deep space without any oxygen. At least, this is what the reports say. I hope not to have to test it.

They regard me curiously, even as they jump and scream in their own high-pitched war cry. It's enough to make anyone run away screaming.

But I don't run. Not even as Krisxox grabs my arm and tries to pull me back. "Xok, Svera!" He shouts, lifting a blaster and pointing it at the first male who lifts his own long staff. It's got a spear affixed to the end of it and I know that if it hits Krisxox even once, we're completely doomed. It'll paralyze him, leaving me to deal with them alone.

"You really are going to deserve punishment after this," he hisses, but I don't let that deter me as I take another step towards the Eshmiri, hold up both my hands and scream, "Stop!"

The Eshmiri look between one another. There must be at least twenty of them all crowded in the doorway, but there are more in the dark shaft of the derelict ship behind them.

We should have prepared for this. Eshmiri are known to glom onto the underbellies of Niahhorru war ships and raid any incoming and outgoing transporters, picking off the smaller trading vessels — or escape pods just like this one. Their technology is said to specialize in cloaking shields, which allows them to remain undetected by even the most advanced fleets.

"Svera…" Krisxox growls. I can see the flash of his blaster beside my head. A massive thing, he trains it on the Eshmiri holding the disabler pointed at my head.

"Look. We are outnumbered and well aware that you intend to take us to sell us," I explain to them in Meero.

They all look between one another. Or at least, most do. The rest just stare at me, nod and smile.

I exhale, shaky as I continue, "We are ready to surrender…"

"The xok we are…"

"We are ready to surrender," I say, louder now. "But we have some conditions. You will sell us, ontte?"

They all nod, smiling wider, now — some are even giggling. "We want to choose who you sell us to."

Their leadership structure is much of a mystery to the Voraxians, so I don't know where to train my gaze as the Eshmiri speak all at once and seemingly not to one another. I can't make out their hushed words.

Finally, two of them shout contradictory things at me in Meero. "Why would we do that?" And, "We want drink!"

I latch onto the latter. "Ontte, excellent idea. Why don't you all come onboard and we'll make you some nice tea." I don't even know if they have tea on this escape pod. "Then we can decide together where you'll sell us. If you don't do this now, then unfortunately, we will have to fight you. My Xiveri mate here is the Krisxox of Voraxia, their strongest fighter. You will kill us and he will kill many of you if we fight now, and then you won't be able to sell us at all. It will be a losing scenario for us all. Now come."

I step forward against Krisxox's snarled orders, and reach for the Eshmiri holding the disabler. I gently push the tip aside and watch as his eyes widen even larger to consume almost his entire head. Cautiously, I place my hand on his shoulder.

"Come," I repeat. "Let's work this out together."

I manage to get all of the Eshmiri inside our escape pod. They cover the entire visible area of the floor. I also manage to find some sort of black drink encased in tubes shaped like vials and dispense them among the Eshmiri gathered. They giggle gleefully as they drink.

Krisxox stands against one wall. He refuses to take a seat or lower his weapon, but the Eshmiri don't seem to mind. They're shouting and speaking amongst themselves in Eshmiri, a high pitched language that sounds like laughter and makes me smile inappropriately whenever I hear it.

Perhaps it's just the fact that I'm sitting in a seat negotiating with my captors while drinking a black syrup from a small vial that tastes like burned garbage or the fact that, as I do all of these things, I'm completely covered in blue seed beneath my shift, or that, I've finally realized that the male glowering around at everything against the far wall is, in fact, my Xiveri mate.

"So," I say with a smile, looking around at this uh...odd bunch. The Eshmiri are wrapped up in scraps of leather and cloth. Some of the colors are matte and familiar, while others shine with iridescence and others vibrate, as if charged. They also all appear *male* and I have to remind myself that they aren't actually male at all. The Eshmiri only have one gender. Babies are grown in cocoons when multiple Eshmiri get together and...couple.

"How do you feel about selling us back to the Voraxians? We are highly valued members of the society and they will pay an enormous sum to have us returned."

"How much?" One of the Eshmiri pips.

"At least..." I glance at Krisxox. He holds up three fingers. "Three million credits."

Whispering erupts, more laughter, too. A disagreement between two Eshmiri is settled when one of them punches the other in the jaw. That one laughs as he falls back into the Eshmiri sitting next to him.

"We would make more selling them to the Niahhorru. They'd give us a ship!"

"We could give you a ship," I interrupt.

"Bah. Not like the Niannorru."

More murmured agreement. My heart starts to pound. If they won't sell us to the Voraxians, then who?

More names are flung back and forth, some I'm familiar with. Some I'm not. "What about Igmora? She'd take the female for a lot of credits. Or even Kintarr."

They all *ooohh* at that. "Bah," one of them shouts, "She only likes babies, remember? She likes to raise them from birth. She wouldn't take this one. It's not a kit."

More assent.

"What about the Oosa?" I know Reoran personally. If we could get sold to the Oosa, I'm sure they'd trade with Voraxia to return us. I'd convince her.

"The Oosa. Hmm…"

"Ontte, the Oosa would trade us a lot." They seem to be considering the Oosa and my heart beats faster in hope.

"Wait!" One of them shouts, "What about the Sky?"

"Oh ontte, the Sky!"

"Nox," I shout. "We won't go to the Sky willingly."

They make sad, disappointed sounds at that. "What about Evernor?" One of them says.

There seems to be tentative agreement over this when Krisxox interjects. "Evernor. We want to go to Evernor."

There's laughter at this, some applause. Eventually, there seems to be wide agreement that Evernor is the destination we'll be traveling to.

"Evernor, then." The Eshmiri seated at my feet stands and pats the top of my head. "You will go to Evernor." The Eshmiri smiles down at me with its sharp, frightening teeth and nods and all of the Eshmiri stand with it.

Without another word of protest, they start backing out of our ship — pod. So stunned that this actually *worked*, I give them a wave. They start murmuring again at the gesture, giggle loudly and then wave back, using both of their short, muscular arms. I offer a final, confused grin as the door seals itself shut between us, blocking the sight of them out.

"What's Evernor?" I say, turning to Krisxox, but he's already closed the distance between us by half.

He scoops me up off my feet, one strong arm cupping my rear, the other winding into my hair. His lips find mine and he kisses me so hard, I feel it in my toes. His mouth tastes like lemon and sugar, the bitterness eased by something sweet. His tongue is covered with ridges and it scrapes the roof of my mouth, pressing against my tongue, lapping at my lips. He kisses me like someone who has practiced a thousand times before, studied every manual, read all my thoughts and knows exactly how I want to be kissed.

Maybe he wasn't lying when he said he practiced for me.

Just as I start to lose my breath, he breaks the kiss on a wild, raucous laugh. I'm struck by the sound. A beautiful melody, it must be the language of the stars.

"Verax," I say.

"I can't believe that xoking worked." He smiles at me. Brushes my cheek. "You're incredible."

My hearts flutter with pride. "Thank you."

"*May'ree* me."

My mouth parts and my stomach lurches. I correct quickly and whisper, "Maybe."

He kisses my forehead, all sweet and tender. "I'll take it, but only for now."

He starts to retreat from me, returning to some of the weapons he dropped on the ground. The Eshmiri left behind a thin sword and he inspects it, then hands it to me, forcing me to wrap one hand around it.

"What are you doing?"

But instead of answering me, he says, "You are the garden. Proud, fiery, bloodthirsty and sweet. And you ruined me, Svera. You ruined me before I even knew who you were. You ruined me the first time I looked into your eyes and saw stars. You're pure light and better than me in every way and you make me want to be part of that light, to rise up beyond my heritage and be *everything* you deserve, even though I know I never can be because you deserve the universe. But it won't stop me from trying. I'm not a decent enough male for that, but I'm your male. Your mate. And I will *may'ree* you. You will call me *house-band* and I will call you *whiff*."

I grin up at him and shake my head. "Husband," I say. "Wife."

"That's what I said."

"Nox." I laugh. "It isn't."

He grunts and opens his mouth, but the ship is suddenly lurching along at a violent, jerky pace. I grab hold of his arm to stabilize myself. "Where are we going, Krisxox? What's Evernor? Are they allies?"

"It's not a species. It's a place."

"A...friendly place?"

He grins in a way that unsettles me.

"Krisxox..."

"Your way got us this far, now it's time for mine." He takes my hand, the one holding the sword, and lifts it up high. "Now, we fight."

16

Krisxox

"Krisxox, explain to me again why in the comets you thought this was a good idea." Her voice is tight and furious as she hugs close to my side and watches the waving Eshmiri fool appear in the broken doorway of our transporter, beckoning us out with an infallible grin.

Svera has the gall to smile at the creature and wave back as she follows tight behind me out of the transporter into the pit, onto the black-and-red-sand battlefield.

The Eshmiri giggles loudly when she waves and snaps all its fingers. Eshmiri are each born with different numbers of fingers. This one has eleven of them strung across two hands and it waggles them gleefully.

Stupid, smug little bastards.

Svera just smiles and waves back.

I roll my eyes at the both of them. Because the Oosa would never have sold you back to the Voraxians. Reoran has been talking at length to Raku about buying a human off of him. He hasn't mentioned it to you humans because he didn't want to frighten you, but Reoran is obsessed with the Rakukanna and wants a hybrid for her collection.

"The Sky would kill you or sell you and take me for parts, turning me into some mindless assassin.

"The Voraxians can't offer what the Eshmiri want — more than credits, they want access to Niahhorru technology or Kintarr. We have neither in abundance.

"If we fight our way out of Evernor, we'll win a percentage of the credits and be set free. Those are the rules. We only have to win one battle."

Svera huffs and clutches her sword and her carpet to her chest. In her hands, both are equally deadly. "You keep saying *we,* but I don't remember signing on to fight anyone."

I just shrug, feeling strangely light as the smell of her smoky skin guides me into the light, through the gates, and around the perimeter of the arena.

The arena is ringed by low, metal walls that stack high to provide seating for the spectators. There are thousands of them.

My mind is calm and steady, the Xanaxana running like a smooth current, powerful and disruptive, but no longer destructive. I can breathe. The tingling in my skin is just that. Tingling. It's no longer the powerful gnashing bite of Xana's punishment, or the cutting talons of my own Xaneru being ripped away. Xaneru is settled. Xana is satisfied. My body glows with a light that I feel reverberating through every inch of my being.

She's mine.

Somewhere back in the past half solar, something changed for her. I can feel it pulsing through me, in the way her fingertips touch the strap of one of my weapons, like she knows now that she has that right. Like she knows she owns me, and that she should never be scared.

I want to hold her hand, but my hands are full of weapons, so I content myself with her touch. I inhale... And exhale.

"You're a mighty warrior," I whisper. "You'll do just fine."

She grunts at that.

I make my way to the opposite side of the arena from the gate and turn to face it. "Behind me," I tell her and she doesn't question the order I give her. "Not too close to the arena wall."

I don't need an eager spectator reaching down behind me and grabbing her. I can fight whatever opponent they send through that gate, but I can't fight ten thousand bloodthirsty spectators all at once.

I grab her by the front of her shift and yank her up against my spine and away from the raging crowd gathered on the nearest blocks of seats.

They froth and shout and roar, holding up paper credits, metal chips, plastic canisters, and digital pads for the Eshmiri to come around and collect in their floating hover stands. Each time the xoking Eshmiri come to this section of the stands, they look down at Svera and wave at her.

Stupid little cusses.

And Svera waves back.

"Focus," I bark, and I might have laughed if the stakes weren't so high. Literally.

The bet that hangs suspended from the biodome high above our heads, trapping in breathable air, is in the millions and beside it are a host of non-monetary prizes the Eshmiri are likely more eager to take. Weapons from Quadrant Eight. Even a Niahhorru stealth ship. A rare animal from Quadrant Two. The golden hair of a Quadrant One prince that is said to be magical.

I snort at that and ready myself as I stare at the arena's only gate. The spectators here must know already who I'll be fighting, given their bets and their excitement. Maybe there's a favorite. Will it be Niahhorru? That'd be a challenge, but not one I'd mind. Will it be an Oosa? I frown at that. I don't want to fight an Oosa. They're too hard to kill and they fight savagely when a sexual object that they want is on the line, and there will be no doubt that they will want her. She's a liability in here with me, but I wouldn't have her anywhere else. I need to see her at all times.

I shake off the heat attacking my bones. The air is hot beneath the dome. The asteroid Evernor is caught in the gravitational pull of a lonely moon. There is no nearby sun in the grey zone, so it's dark, but the fires from the city thriving in the tunnels beneath our feet are hot and make the surface temperature heat.

The gates start to crank open. "You ready, Svera?"

"Nox."

I chuckle. "Where's your sword?"

"With my prayer mat."

"Maybe put the rug down for now."

"Can I put the sword down, too?"

"Nox. Hold onto that. Just try not to stab me with it."

"I make no promises."

I laugh but…not for long. Because when the gates are fully open my opponent walks into the arena.

And there are eighteen of them.

"Krisxox!" Svera grabs the strap of my blaster. "You said this was the safest option! This doesn't look safe!"

She might be right about that. "It's a derby," I tell her.

"What does that mean?"

"What it looks like. I'll have to fight all of them at once." No wonder the bets are so high. No wonder the species are so mixed. A small thimble of fear enters my bloodstream but just as quickly, I banish it. I have no choice but to win. There is no alternative.

"Don't worry. This will be easy."

"You're lying."

Hexa, I am. "Nox, I'm not."

"There are Oosa," she hisses. "Aren't they almost impossible to kill?"

"Nox, easy," I lie again.

She beats a fist lamely on my back and I hear shuffling behind me. When I glance to my right, I see she's holding the sword in both her hands. She's put the prayer mat behind her. She glances up at me.

"Your way, huh?"

I nod. "My way."

She huffs, "My way is so much better."

My eyes lock on the two Oosa rolling into the space, still wrapped in fusion chains. *Just my xoking luck.* Apart from these two, the Niahhorru, the Avmar — a long, reptilian creature with an impossible-to-crack carapace and eight long, taloned legs — and the Egama — a one-eyed giant with plates covering most of his bare, moss-colored skin — are the obvious standouts.

But there's also a pack of four death hounds, a flying Kato and a robotic, fanged Tevalope that looks like it was engineered by the Sky that would be a danger to underestimate.

The rest are creatures that look as if they were brought in here specifically for punishment, because they are too skinny and ill-equipped to pose a threat.

What's your plan, oh mighty battle strategist?"

I laugh at that. *Laugh.* At a time like this. "Since when did you get so bloodthirsty?"

She doesn't look up at me as she says, "Since I found out I'd been blessed with a Xiveri mate and for whatever outrageous reason, that mate happens to be you."

My heart explodes. Just the one. And it feels so xoking beautiful. "You're beautiful," I tell her. "*May'ree* me."

She glances up at me like I've lost my mind. "Have you lost your mind?"

Hexa, every piece of it. "*Yess.*"

She opens her mouth, but before she can tell me she's thrilled to be my wife, a giddy xoking Eshmiri floats into the center of the ring while the opponents are lead around its perimeter by their chains. The Tevalope on my left. The death hounds on my right. At least neither will be interested in Svera.

The shrill voice of the Eshmiri projects through the dome, translations fluttering in about a thousand different tongues through the various translators worn by the spectators. They are all fists and thrashing tentacles and skin in as many shades as there are colors in the universe.

I don't know what he says, but I can see the attention of the spectators shift to me and my Xiveri mate. I pull her a little further forward, away from the spectators throwing things at us.

"Krisxox," she whispers at my back as the Eshmiri continues to prattle on. "What is he saying?"

"Nothing."

"Is it bad? It sounds bad. This looks bad," she whispers.

I huff out laugh, still feeling buoyed. "Faith, Svera."

"Verax."

"Isn't that what your Tri-God teaches you?"

I don't dare break my concentration, not even for the draw of looking at her and crushing my mouth to her lips. She hesitates, then says softly, "Hexa."

"Then have faith in your god. He will not allow me to fail you. And neither will mine. Whether or not you believe in her, Xana has fought on your side this entire time."

The buzzer sounds. The thunk of chains releasing follows moments after. The pack of death hounds splits — half the pack lunging for the Tevalope while the other two descend on the thin creature to their other side and tearing the thing to pieces.

"I'm not so sure about the Tri-God right now," Svera whispers as I step forward and brace my feet and watch the giant launch into a sprint, heading straight for me. "But I have faith in you."

17

Krisxox

A flare of light. A flash of green. The giant dives into the ground as I unleash the full spray of canon fire at his chest. His fist flails out and in order to avoid its strike, I step into the acidic spray of the Tevalope, which has pieces of death hound dripping from the twin fangs jutting from the roof of its maw. I let the heat scald me as I sprint up the back of the fallen giant's left leg and plunge my sword through his neck.

His arm is stretched forward, hand closed around Svera's feet. She stabs down with her sword, missing by a mile. *Hexa, the carpet would be more useful to her.*

I round his form and kick his gruesomely large hand away from her. I grab the sword in her hand and stab through his wrist…

…blood wets my entire right side as I transfer my sword to my left hand. The Oosa won't die and the Niahhorru won't give up. He comes at me again, but the Oosa blocks his path and engages him, leaving me to deal with the Oosa to my left.

It comes at me in a gelatinous blue mass, its lust for Svera radiating through it in sharp colors as it squeals its delight. The tip of my sword does little against its flesh as I cut into it again and again and again, exhausting myself. *That's what they want. Their strategy...* I jump back, revolving around the thing and forcing it to give chase.

To my right, the Niahhorru screams and I look over just as the Oosa slides on top of him, muffling his cries, suffocating him as it slides its amorphous shape into his nostrils, mouth and eye-sockets, aiming for his brain. *Nox, this will not be my end and it xoking won't be Svera's.*

A flash of pain lights up my spine and I spin and kick out at the Avmar, whose long, sharp forearm is steeped in my blood. A lot of it. I feel nothing of pain. All I feel is the terrified pounding of Svera's heart underneath my sternum. Her fragrant smoke, that woodsy euphoria, is all I can taste...

...the Avmar rears up onto its four hind-legs and I stab upward, catching the thing in between two joints. I have him...but I'm too focused that I don't notice the Oosa until he slings into me, knocking me off of my feet.

The Avmar takes that to its advantage and brings its foreleg down sharply to pierce my shoulder. A scream sets my entire world on fire because I know that it's Svera's and it's getting *louder*.

"Nox!" I roar as the sight of Svera's glowing hair flames into view over the sight of the Oosa's body. Though they have no eyes, I can sense its delight as it starts to shift its attention towards her and I can't move. And she's coming closer. And she has no xoking weapon — she's holding her carpet!

It's rolled up in her hands and she uses it like a bat, swatting at the Oosa. The thing rears up and squeals in confusion, but when Svera swats at it again, shouting obscenities I didn't even know she knew, it backs away.

I would have laughed if the Avmar hadn't taken my distraction to its advantage. It comes down again, piercing me in the stomach. I roar and see my sword's hilt still protruding from its leg. I force myself up, through the agony, and grab hold of it. When I wrench back, I tear the Avmar's front leg apart at the joint. It screeches its terrible screech and rears back, pulling its leg free of my gut and giving me the space I need to switch around onto one knee and use both hands to stab up into its belly where the carapace does not reach.

The scream that tears out of it is enough to make me stagger. It rips its second limb out of my shoulder, taking my body with it and I'm flying over the sand as it falls. I can't stay down and am up again, though my vision is starting to blur and darkness is beginning to encroach.

On my feet, two holes decorate my body that are so wide I can feel the hot air pass straight through me. And still, I see the Oosa reflected blue in Svera's eyes as she throws her carpet over its gelatinous form. It screeches its frustration as it tries to pull her into its body and I waver as I start towards it...

...Svera has her carpet in her hands again and is swatting at the Oosa, but it's backed her against the arena wall and that same xoking tentacled spectator has reached down from the stands and grabbed her by the hair.

She flails, drops her carpet — her only defense — and kicks with her legs. I try to tell Svera to run, but my jaw isn't working.

Suddenly, one of the thin creatures I discounted slices through the tentacle, spilling bright orange blood everywhere. While the tentacle flails and the owner it belongs to shrieks its agony, Svera's savior shoves her back so hard it knocks her off her feet. The creature is hardly larger than she is, cloaked from head to toe in black. I can't see what species it is, but I'm surprised when it calls out to me in Meero.

"Throw me your grenade!"

The voice is rough and the sword arm rougher as it stabs into the Oosa with a thin, whetted blade. It pierces the gelatinous husk of the creature, but does little damage...then I understand. I free the grenade from the grip on my wrist and toss it. The hooded figure snatches it from the air, then shoves it deep into the Oosa's core next to its small glowing heart.

The explosion sends blue matter flying. It slashes over me, tasting like the ocean...

...there is only this. Only blue. Svera's behind me, shouting my name. I'm afraid for her, but the cloaked figure that has remained largely out of the fray up to now has shown itself...*capable*...and seems to be fighting for her, too.

The two of us revolve around the remaining Oosa, striking, cutting it down...but it's smart. It won't let us get close enough after it saw what happened to the other one...

...I spin and slash. The Oosa hurtles towards me, but I jump out of its path...the cloaked figure is limping worse than it was, but it, too, narrowly manages to avoid the Oosa's strike.

And then I realize with horror that it wasn't aiming for us.

Svera stands near the edge of the arena wall holding her carpet in one hand, her thin sword in the other. She's staring at me, but I can't get to her fast enough.

"Run," I start to say, but the voice of the hooded warrior is louder than mine is.

"Oosa," comes the rugged shout. "You want a female?"

The figure rips away its hood and yanks down on its black mask, revealing a face as brown as many of the human faces I have seen on Svera's colony. It contrasts violently against hair as white as any Drakesh's — as white as mine. Cut short against her head, the white cloud forms rings and rings of curls.

When the female turns and looks at me, I see that her eyes aren't like Svera's, but they aren't like mine. Those eyes are just as white as that hair until all at once, they shift, becoming black. Unsettling, this creature. This *hybrid*.

She is female.

She is human.

She is Drakesh.

She is split in parts, equal or perhaps, unequal.

She is saving my Xiveri mate.

And she's saving my life.

She unwinds her cloak from around her body and exposes a shape that is reminiscent of Svera's — full chest mounds, a slit covered in fur, though hers is colored black where Svera's matches the color of her hair.

The Oosa hesitates, then changes course as the hybrid begins to back away. Her gaze flashes to me, that bright white and that hard black. She needs me to save her. And she is human. And I shouldn't want to.

But *shoulds* have only ever held me back.

I roar a battle cry as I charge the Oosa, spearing its flesh with my blade. I run it through and ordinarily, this would do nothing if I didn't suddenly have the idea to kill as the Oosa kill.

I'll kill it from the inside.

I thrust my arms into its gelatinous blue body, following the line of my sword. There is resistance, but I fight my shoulders inside. Beneath me — *around me* — the Oosa rolls away from the female and tries to attack me, but every move it makes only helps further my cause. I'm inside of the thing up to the shoulders, blue jelly squeezing me from every direction, tickling my arms, suffocating my mouth and nose, getting into my wounds.

I slash and fight and I keep slashing and I keep fighting until I see red. Until I no longer see blue. And when I come to, I'm wavering on my knees and the Oosa lies in thousands of pieces around me.

The spectators are on their feet and the Eshmiri announcer hovers on his platform a few paces above my head. He is saying something to me — nox, not to me, to the hooded female. And she is saying something to him, but I can't hear them. All I can hear is Svera's reply as the hooded female clutches her arm and demands why she won't leave me.

"He is my Xiveri Mate," she cries and I waste to the side with a smile.

"*Whiff,*" I croak. "She is my *whiff.*" And then the lights dim and agony gives to numbness and the heat simmers down until I'm shaking and cold and, above all else, satisfied.

18

Svera

"You're a human, huh?" The female plops down across from me. A cracked plastic seat squeals under her weight. It looks like it's seen better days, but then again, so has the frayed pillow visibly losing its stuffing at her back, the shoes she wears, which are scuffed beyond recognition and have leather patches sewn over the toes, and the entire rest of the ship surrounding us.

Like the last Eshmiri ship I saw — the only other Eshmiri ship I've ever seen — this one is all blocks soldered haphazardly together. Metal slats and planks cover the floor and rattle beneath my heel, which is beating frantically against the metal below.

I only have one shoe on — my other sandal broke somewhere back in that arena — and the floor is cold. My nipples are stiff, still crusted in blue seed, while the orange blood of that tentacled thing and the blue gel of the Oosa wet the rest of me. All of it, an unwelcome experience.

I dab a bit of the prayer rug in my lap to my forehead, trying to wipe off some of the slime. "I am," I answer the female in Meero. "And you appear to be human as well."

"Ha! Appearing human is what I'm best at," she crows. Her lips curve up in a smile that would have made the colony boys wild. Then they'd have looked into her eyes and run screaming the other direction. She wears her colors in there. *Fascinating.* Beautiful. Deadly.

"You were sold by a human traitor to a Voraxian traitor. The former Bo'Raku."

"Don't know who that is or what you're talking about, but I'm quite familiar with traitors. Go on."

This is why I'm here. Why she convinced the Eshmiri that she should get to claim both me and Krisxox as battle prizes. It helped that she speaks fluent Eshmiri — or maybe, even, that she knew them? They seemed familiar with one another, all laughter and smiles.

Then again, that's been the entirety of my experience with Eshmiri, to date.

"And your mother…" As of yet, I have no guesses as to which female that might have been. "…was killed. I'm so sorry…"

"Don't be," she snaps, cutting me off. "I have a mother. Well, not a mother, per se, more like fourteen fathers, but still. They treated me right."

I blink at her, surprised, and for the first time since she brought me and carried Krisxox on board her ship and we took flight off of that asteroid, my foot stops shaking. Silence. I didn't realize I'd been rattling the floor boards so loudly. She looks down at my leg then and grins. She hasn't stopped grinning. Her eyes are still bright white, betraying no color.

"You…are an Eshmiri reaver?"

"And proud of it."

"How did you end up in the derby?"

"I wasn't on the fighting list. I was a spectator. I snuck into the fray after I was sure your guy could kill that bug thing. Ugck." She shudders. "I hate those creepy crawlies. And after I realized you were human. Eshmiri have all heard of your kind — everyone in the fourth and fifth quadrants knows about the new species discovered by the Voraxians and the Niahhorru — they just don't know what you look like. But I knew you were like me. I haven't seen anybody else with skin so soft."

She rifles around in a metal bin next to her yellow seat, tossing aside wires and broken bits of things I can't name, until she finds a bottle. She pulls the cork out with her teeth and takes a long swallow.

"That hits the spot," she says with a long sigh. "Want some?"

it's alcoholic. I can smell it from here. I shake my head. "Centare. Centare, thank you…"

I glance over my shoulder again at the door barely hanging on its hinges. There's lots of small rooms aboard this ship — some large enough to accommodate humans of Ashmara's size, but most small enough to comfortably house a few Eshmiri. The only cabin large enough to accommodate Krisxox was a storage unit they threw a few boxes out of and plopped a rickety pallet down into.

I'm terrified at the thought of the pain he's in. I can feel it echoing all over me, as light as a breeze, but one that burns me everywhere and fills me with sick dread. *I want him to live.* I want it more than I've ever wanted anything.

"Ashmara," she says.

"What?"

"Ashmara," she repeats. "And who are you?"

I swallow hard. "I'm Svera."

"Svera." She rolls the word around on her tongue while her eyes assess me. Does she see me sweating? Because I'm still sweating, even though it's an ice box in here. I flinch with the urge to glance over my shoulder again, seeking out Krisxox, but only after I've determined what she wants from me.

Or what she'll do to us.

"You scared, Svera?"

Yes, petrified. My hesitation makes her laugh. She kicks her legs up over the beat up arm of the loveseat and rests her head against its lumpy, curved back. "You shouldn't be scared of me, human. I'm taking you back home." She takes another long swig from her bottle.

Somewhere in the recesses of her ship, the Eshmiri reavers on board drop something — a box of tools? At the sound of metal crashing, she shouts something so loud and tumultuous, I don't catch all of it. Whatever she said sounded like an order, but is met by the trilling Eshmiri laughter I'm familiar with now. She laughs with them, throaty and full.

"You...you are?" My fingers tighten in the carpet, squeezing it.

"Ontte, you can relax."

I don't. Not even close. "Thank you," I say. "You will be rewarded..."

She cuts me off. "Not in it for the reward. Plus, I got to collect a little of your winnings since they declared the match a stalemate."

"A stalemate? But you won. Or Krisxox did."

"I cheated and the rules say that you have to be able to walk out of the ring in order to qualify as the winner. Technically, *you* won the derby," she snorts. "But the Eshmiri weren't exactly eager to hand winnings over to a little female who fought with a carpet." She laughs. "Brilliant, by the way."

I feel myself redden. "So then, what is your plan for us?"

I'm not gonna get you that close. I'll send you down in a shooter. You'll be fine."

"If you'd like, you could come with us to the human colony. Meet some of the others. You'd be welcomed there with open arms."

Something flashes across her expression and she closes her eyes. *Keeping me out.* She takes a calming breath and when she opens her eyes there is no color in them. *But something tells me there might have been.* Her easy, rakish smile returns, revealing a mouth full of straight, white teeth.

"Centare. I'm alright." She makes a clicking sound in the right side of her mouth and winks at me. "Thanks though, heelee."

"Heelee?"

"It's a bug. The good kind though," she amends with a shrug. "They eat the rust off the metal parts of my ship."

I glance around and whisper before I can sensor myself, "Perhaps you need a few more of them."

"Watch your mouth there, heelee," she says, but she's laughing. "This beast's a trooper. She's weathered countless storms and she'll get you back to your moon colony's coordinates, but I'm not gonna land there. I'm an Eshmiri reaver. I don't need any Voraxian heat."

"The colony is a haven for humans. You may even be related to Voraxia's queen. We could test your DNA..."

"Centare!" She bangs her fist hard on the table between us. It makes me jump. "I said centare. I just want to get you back home. You and your warrior." She takes another swig. "Where'd you find him, anyway? He's an Evernor champion if I've ever seen one. I haven't ever seen anything that fights like he does."

"He's the Krisxox of Voraxia."

"That would explain it." She nods, upending the bottle down her throat and when she looks back up at me, her spooky eyes are half-lidded. "Well, tell him if he ever wants to make a killing, the fighting pits are always happy to have him back."

I shudder visibly and she sees it and laughs. "You, on the other hand, better stick close to that one. He tore an Oosa alive from the inside and you don't have so much as a drop of blood on you." She looks me over, gaze sweeping my frame before landing on my carpet, where I've been rubbing my hands. "Well, alright. You don't have any of *your own* blood on you." My abaya is covered in blood. All of it Krisxox's.

Tears prick the backs of my eyes and my hearts yank in my chest. I feel...unsteady. Shaky. Broken. *I just want to go to him.*

"Hey! Don't do that. Warriors don't cry."

"I didn't say I was one," I stammer, fists clenching over my knees. "I won't ever be and I don't want to be." I sound downright teary now. Maybe the solar's events catching up to me. "I want to live in a universe where beings use reason to communicate with one another, not their swords or their fists."

She shakes her head at me, but there's a softening around her mouth that reminds me of a faraway word — *compassion*. Then it's gone just as quickly. "Then you picked the wrong universe. Tell me when you find the one you're dreaming of."

She shoves the cork back in the bottle, shaking the little bit that's left of it up against the flickering yellow light overhead.

"Or maybe, the right male picked you to help you get through this one."

"Hexa." I sniff, getting ahold of myself. "He did."

"Lucky you." She cocks her head. "Go on. I can see you itching to get back to him."

I stand without hesitating. "Thank you for saving us."

She empties her flask and tosses the bottle back in the metal box. It lands with a distinct clink and a loud rattle. *There are more bottles in there.* She settles back against her loveseat. It's lumpy and brown in most places, red in others. The color combination is disconcerting against the blood that covers both of us. Neither of us have bathed. On this decrepit transporter, I'm not even certain bathing is possible.

"You know, I can't decide if you're completely hopeless or kind of sweet."

"You should meet Krisxox when he wakes. I'm sure he'd agree with you."

She rolls her strange eyes just as a dash of green crosses them. If her colors are anything like Voraxian colors, then that would mean she's amused.

"That so?"

"Ontte. And here. If you ever want to know more about humans, I wrote a manual. You should have access to it."

I flip open my life drive and draw up a scan of the manual. She glances it over, then pulls a small black box out of the left pocket of the leather Eshmiri vest she put on as soon as she shed the robe she'd been wearing earlier. Paired with patchwork leather pants, she truly does look Eshmiri in everything but skin.

But I suppose skin never changed the soul beneath it. Beneath that skin, we get to be whoever we want to be and if she tells me she's Eshmiri, then she is.

"Yeah alright, I'll take a look." The black box releases a wave of energy that I feel in the hairs that lift on my forearm. A laser shoots out of it, performs a quick scan, then is gone.

She slips it back into her vest and as I make my way to the door to Krisxox's chamber, I say, "Thank you for saving his life."

"Whatever. I'm just giving y'all a lift. I was heading to that side of the grey zone, anyway."

I don't believe her for a moment, and in that moment, I hesitate. "Where have you been, Ashmara?"

She leans back and pulls her hood all the way up over her head to cover her wild eyes. "Everywhere."

"And you truly do not wish to return home with us?"

"*Heelee*, there's no such thing as home." Her full lips quirk up in one corner.

"You're wrong, you know. There is home. Perhaps it isn't with us, but the stars will lead you home and you'll know it when you find it."

"Go, heelee. You're starting to annoy me."

I smile a little trepidatiously at that. She is a formidable female and I owe her a lot and I'm still not sure she won't chuck us out of an airlock if I say something wrong so I just nod and leave her to her box and bottles and slip into the storage room.

My stomach punches down into my toes at the sight of Krisxox on the thin, dirty mat on the floor. Metal boxes are tottering high all the way to the low ceiling — a ceiling so low Krisxox would have to bend in order to stand upright — and the path between them and Krisxox's mat is narrow.

I yank the door shut behind me and squeeze onto the mat on Krisxox's right side. His chest looks gruesome and the entire room still smells like burning flesh from when his wounds were cauterized.

Using the prayer mat for a pillow, I lay down beside him and look up at his face. His right shoulder is a heaping mass of black fabric, none of which looks sterile, but that the Eshmiri assured me were safe. But his expression looks oddly peaceful.

I place my hand on his chest, reassured by its rise and fall. His plates are scratched badly and he sports two grisly bruises on his face and neck, which blacken his skin.

I touch his chin, stroke his ridges, kiss the outside of his arm. "Hexa, Krisxox," I whisper out loud, even though the only one that can hear me now is the Tri-God. "I will marry you."

19

Krisxox

Pain. I feel it, then I don't. My warrior's training understands pain, every curve, every crest, every trough. I've been trained from the time I was a youngling and first knew that I was destined to be Voraxia's greatest warrior on how to keep it at bay. The only painful chasm I couldn't cross was what Xana gave and now she's satisfied, so there is no need for pain anymore.

I take the dark web of agony spread across my body and I carefully tie it into little knots, then move those knots into a little box where I let them live only in two places — a small patch of skin in my gut on the left side and in my right shoulder. Then I come to life.

I open my eyes and scan the world surrounding me — caging me — for a weapon. There are pocked metal crates everywhere and I see a syringe the length of my hand sticking out of one. There's a weapon already. On the count of three, I'll reach for it, then I'll tear the walls of this prison down until I find her. She needs me. I felt that while I slept. That she needed me and I couldn't get to her. *Failure*. I failed her...

I suck in a breath that fills me to the soles of my feet.

I let the bursts of exquisite pain flare, but I don't let them own me.

"Krisxox?" The small sigh comes from somewhere close. Very close.

I try to say her name, but my jaw feels like it's been wired shut and my tongue doesn't obey my commands. All I manage is a weak grunt, but the reaction is immediate.

Her hand. I feel it there on my abdomen in scorching heat. All five alien fingers.

I swallow but my mouth and throat are so xoking dry. "Here," she says. She sits up and I know my eyes are open when I see her face.

If this were a dream, she'd be clean and free of the blue and orange goop that covers her. The sight of her all mangled like this nearly makes me laugh. Never have I seen her less dignified.

"Are you laughing at me?" She says, managing to look stricken, and that only makes everything worse.

I start to cough. She whispers a prayer to her Tri-God and quickly brings a rusted metal cannister to my lips. "Instead of teasing me, you should focus on healing. Here, drink this. Don't try to speak. The heavens only know you'll just shoot yourself in the foot anyway — it's a human expression. I'm not sure it translates."

I choke on some of this substance she calls water. "It's awful, isn't it?" Hexa, and the only reason I know it's water at all is because she says it is, and she's too foolish to lie to me.

"Augh," I sputter, choking more of it down and Svera laughs and everything is okay. There's a hard bed under me, sweat covering my front, a hard wiry blanket lying over my hips. I'm naked beneath it, but for the first time since my xora met Svera, it doesn't rise to the challenge.

"Where are we? Are you safe?" I croak when she pulls the can away from my lips. Water dribbles down my cheeks and she dabs at it with something soft.

Her expression softens then and I try to reach up and touch some blue on her cheek — more likely Oosa than my dried seed — but I can't move my arms.

"You're safe and I'm safe. We're on board an Eshmiri reaver ship, but it's operated by a human. A *hybrid*. She was one of the original kits that Mathilda sold, but whatever happened next, she ended up in the hands of a horde of Eshmiri. They raised her and she considers herself Eshmiri now. She's taking us back to the human moon and sending us down in a shooter of some kind, but she won't join us. She's doing this just because she's got some honor."

I grunt. "And credits. How much did she win?"

I shrug. "I'm not sure, but I doubt she'll see those credits. Or if she does, I have no idea where she's hiding them." Svera glances around and wrinkles her nose. "This place...could use improvement."

"Bloodthirsty," I say with a light chuckle.

She smiles down at me again and brushes her hair behind her ear. She looks perfect. Like a xoking dream.

"*May'ree* me," I grunt.

She bites her bottom lip. "I think we have more pressing matters to worry about than this."

"Nothing matters. *May'ree* me."

She shakes her head and laughs. "It's kind of hard to say nox to you now, isn't it?"

"Hexa." My heart beats faster. "That's why I asked."

"Oh, Krisxox," she rubs her face and then she arches over me. Mouth near my mouth, her warm breath fans over me as she whispers, "Of course, I'll marry you. I love you."

Xok. Xok! She...she...verax! "You...*lawv* me?"

"Hexa, I do." She ends abruptly and I...I can't speak.

She frowns, "Now, aren't you going to tell me something?"

I don't know what she means, but her cheeks get more and more pink beneath the filth covering her the longer I stay quiet.

"Verax," I finally blurt.

She pounds her fist on my chest very lightly, but the pressure is intense. I groan and she jumps out of her skin. "Oh, I'm so sorry. Are you alright?"

"Nox," I say on a grunt. "But I don't give a xok about that. What should I say?"

"That you love me, too." And now I understand her redness. She is *nervous* that she may care more than I do.

I laugh. I laugh and it sends bullets cascading through me. "Oyff," I moan. Svera is busy dabbing some green cloth to my forehead and gently stroking my hair.

It calms me, settles me, even if the pain still tries to break free of my hold. "Svera, of course I xoking *lawv* you."

"No need to curse."

I grunt, trying to control my laughter, my bones. "Come here. I need to taste you."

"I probably don't taste very good."

"Let me be the judge."

She arches over me and painfully gently, presses her lips to mine. She tastes just like she always tastes, like a poison that's going to take me to the afterlife. I try to lift up and deepen the kiss, but I'm pretty xoking immobile and Svera, with her skinny little arms, is easily able to hold me down.

"Xok," I roar when she pulls back too soon. "Come back here. I'm not finished." My xora is starting to stir at the scent of her slit. Her arousal is potent. The air is thick with it.

"You need to sleep."

"You are my *whiff* now. I can kiss you when I like."

She narrows her eyes. "You are sorely mistaken, Krisxox — "

"Anand," I blurt.

She freezes. "Verax."

"Anand. I want you to call me this. Or *houseband*."

"Anand," she whispers. She leans back in and kisses me, a reward for my sacrifice. "It's a beautiful name."

"*Houseband* is beautiful, too."

"Husband."

"That's what I said."

She laughs and collapses onto her side at mine and stares up at me while I struggle to stare down at her. Whenever I try, shooting pain fires down my neck.

"Relax, *house-band*," she says, saying the word in the same tone I use.

"I suppose I could use a lesson in Human."

"My brother, Ibra, has signed on to teach some of the Voraxians that have asked. A lot of the humans think the life drives and the translator mites are strange, so Voraxians are meeting them in the middle. I think Tur'Roth even wanted to take classes from Ibra."

Bloodthirsty. I heave out a breath and it tastes like fire as I spit, "Do not mention that male again."

She chuckles beside me. *Bloodthirsty.* "Whatever happened to him? You didn't...harm him, did you?"

"Nox. I just told him what I should have told you long ago. That you are my Xiveri mate. He respected this." And ran off like a coward. Why I don't tell her that is beyond me, but I don't.

"Xhivey," she says, fingers tracing a pattern over my arm all the way down to my fingers. She laces her five fingers through my six. "I'm glad he knows. In truth, I did not care for him. I tried, but I was often distracted by a male with scarred red skin and hair as white as the sky. A male who moves so quickly shadows would be jealous and who fights like a battle god.

"A male who draws terrible and wonderful things out of me. Who makes me question everything. Right and wrong. Good and evil. Who makes me feel in ways I've never felt. I feel twice the woman I was and it's because of you. Because fighting you makes me feel strong. Because having you at my back makes me feel invincible." She kisses my shoulder. "You fought so beautifully for me on Evernor."

"And I'd do it all over." Her words fill me like a well overrun. I am so deeply, profoundly grateful.

And then she flicks my rib cage, making wince. "Nox. Never again. Your way is the absolute worst."

I laugh and it just about kills me. Choking through the pain, I say, "I saw you out there. You looked like you were having a great time, fighting that Oosa with your rug."

"It was working," she huffs.

I grin. "Hexa. It was. But next time, you might not be so lucky so please, when I hand you two objects, please choose the pointy one."

"We'll see."

I growl, "I'm your *huzzabend* now. You have to do what I say."

She flicks me again and picks herself up so I can see her glaring down at my face. "You are sorely in need of education about the role of a husband."

"Maybe a punishment is in order."

Her expression catches. She bites her lip. "I'm not sure I like your punishments."

"Nox? Maybe *you* are in need of education about the role of a *huzzabend*. Come here. Sit on my face."

"*Verax*," she balks.

"Lift your shift and sit on my mouth. I want to taste you. An orgasm might kill me, right now, but I can give you one. It'll be my punishment."

"I..."

"Move, Svera," I order and she swallows hard, staring at me agog before finally, she starts to crawl.

She maneuvers careful around me in a way I wish she didn't have to be, but I'm still not myself. There are still pieces in there put together wrong, or broken entirely. *Xok if I care.*

"Sit on my mouth. There," I coo as she spreads her knees around my head and lowers herself hesitantly. She lifts her shift up around her waist and holds it so I can see everything up to her ribs.

"Like this?" She asks shakily.

"Just like this. Lower."

"Are you sure?" Her wet, weeping slit hovers directly over my mouth.

"Lower."

She lowers herself until I'm able to latch onto her lower lips, spearing her with my tongue before I give her another chance to back out.

She gasps my name — Anand — and it's a beautiful sound. I laugh, "Do you enjoy the duties of a *huzzaband*?"

"Husband," she whispers, lost as she is in the garden.

"That's what I said." I spear my tongue deep inside of her and she jerks forward, catching herself on a metal crate. Its contents rattle, just like the desire in my gut and the *lawv* in my heart. "Do you?"

"Hexa," she breathes as her body begins to tremble. "I do. And I cannot wait to marry you."

20

Krisxox

I look at the cramped, rusted inside of the shooter and then at hybrid, Ashmara, then back at the shooter again.

"This will work," I say, and it isn't a question.

She just rolls her eyes and shrugs. "It'll work."

"If this doesn't work and *anything* happens to Svera, I will hunt the cosmos until I find you and dismember you."

"Krisxox," Svera says disapprovingly at my back.

Ashmara just grins lopsidedly and crosses her arms over her chest. "If this doesn't work, then you'll have a hard time resurrecting yourself to enact your revenge."

"Don't underestimate me. I'm *extremely* hard to kill."

She cocks a brow in that way that humans often do. I wonder if she even realizes how many

mannerisms of theirs she has, despite having been raised entirely Eshmiri.

"It'll work," she says, a little more stonily this time, and I edge clumsily inside.

The space is cramped. The two seats that occupy eighty percent of the space are bolted to every side of the square shooter, leaving only a small path to get to them.

Everything here is built for Eshmiri proportions, so Svera has no trouble buckling herself — and her stupid rug — into one of the seats, while I struggle painfully into the narrow chair.

It's metal, covered in thick padding, but it does little to cushion the ragged wounds in my torso. More importantly, will it be enough to break our fall?

I open my mouth and glance at Ashmara, but she only rolls her eyes. "It'll work," she says again and then the door hisses shut between us.

I glance at Svera. "I don't think I like your hybrid friend."

Svera just smiles and kicks her feet. "Friend," she answers.

"Vrent," I repeat.

"Furr-end," she says.

"Vur." I try the first part, then when Svera nods encouragingly, I continue, "End."

"Xhivey," she says, kicking her feet even harder.

"Vur-end."

She's smiling now, a little too widely. I can see the slight gap between her two front teeth. Xok, she's beautiful. It's not fair. I never stood a chance, did I?

"Hexa, but quicker. Friend. No space between the first syllable and the second."

"Vriend."

"Perfect. Exactly perfect."

I shake my head as the shooter detaches. "I xoking *lawv* you."

Svera giggles and wraps her arms around the rug she's got fixed to her chest. "I really love you, too."

And then we're cruising. And then we're *falling*. The turbulence in the shooter is jarring and forces me to cry out, "I *really* loathe your hybrid!"

My filthy white hair is whipping around my head just as Svera's matted curls whip around hers. It's been three solars and we've been no closer to a wash room than when we started. Ashmara, the despicable cretin, didn't wish to waste the water on us. The most we got from her were a few cans of rust-water and a couple protein bars that tasted like shit.

And now, *this*.

"Xoking Ashmara!" I roar as the shooter bangs through space, like we're hitting a thousand asteroids on our way to the surface.

There's no window or view pane. Just black and rust-colored metal.

Over the sound of chaos, Svera shouts, "Xoking Ashmara!"

I close my eyes and clench my teeth and pray to the God that watches over Svera that we'll get out of...

Whoosh! Bang. Clang. Thump.

Suddenly the ground that we were supposed to meet is repelled away from us and we're shot back into space. *Thrusters.* That was Ashmara's big plan? Thrusters?!

She called it a shooter for a xoking reason and I vow that I will kill her the next time I see her. The thrusters are the only thing we've got to break our fall, but the violence of our change in momentum is enough to break Svera's xoking neck. I scream her name as she vomits to the side of her seat. Her head is held back against the metal curve of the chair by the velocity with which we fall, but when we land, I pray. All I can do is pray.

My eyes slam shut as we make impact. I keep my jaw clenched so I don't bite off my tongue. I hold every screaming muscle in my body together so tight, I can feel the wound in my stomach reopen. Agony slices every inch of me until finally, it all splinters apart as the front half of the ship explodes open.

Pieces of metal go flying and I roar out my rage. "Xoking Ashmara!" A single piece of shrapnel could slice Svera's throat. Just like the shrapnel that finds my right thigh in three places and my stomach near the wound.

Fine. I'll take all of it, just please let her keep her xoking neck! The pain radiating through mine is unbearable and I feel my own stomach turn with the desire to purge.

"Aaugh!" I roar, trying to fight back the desire to close my eyes and keep them shut and sleep. *She needs me.* She needs me.

Smoke and burning metal waft in through the open sides of the shooter. Xoking Ashmara. Evil xoking hybrid. But beneath that, I smell sand. I triple checked her coordinates. We're here. We made it.

"Svera," I croak, but her hair blocks my view of her face. And then my gaze drops and everything inside of me turns to the sand I scent on the breeze.

Past the curtain of her hair, a huge piece of metal protrudes from where her chest should be. Xok. Nox. Nox, nox, nox.

Panic claws angrily up my chest and I reach for the straps holding me against the chair and quickly break them. My feet thump down onto mashed metal and sand.

I buckle, catching myself on a piece of metal so hot it scalds me instantly. I jerk my hand back and kick it, but that hurts just as bad because the xoking female and her Eshmiri band of goons took my boots — along with thirty thousand credits. Enough to buy at least another half dozen of these cursed death traps.

I curse under my breath as I wade through the wreckage, burning myself half a dozen more times by the time I make it to Svera's body hanging limp overhead, looking frighteningly like a corpse.

She's just low enough for me to reach her feet, but not low enough for me to reach the straps binding her and the metal…Everything in me stills.

There is a piece of metal sticking out of her. Is she…

Nox. Nox nox nox nox *nox!*

I glance around, looking for something that isn't going to flay the skin off my feet to stand on. Seeing nothing that matches that description, I look up, push the pain radiating through me into little cubes and swallow them, then I jump.

I bury my claws in the outsides of Svera's chair and climb until I'm high enough to be able to pound my claws into the back of her chair and grip the outer edges of her seat between my knees. I hold on so hard I hurt, but it's nothing compared to the sight of the blood dripping from her nose and the metal sticking out of her chest.

"Svera," I hiss, panicked, Xanaxana in my chest doing something strange. Flipping and expanding. Becoming too much to take. "Svera!"

"Mhm," comes her small, shattered whisper. The pain of hearing it is only matched by my relief. How is she…she shouldn't be breathing.

"Svera." My muscles are shaking now and my xoking left leg is threatening to give out on me. I glance down, catching sight of the metal sticking out of my skin and plates. I'll be fine. Nothing that won't heal. The only thing that won't is my xoking Xaheru if Svera isn't okay.

I canvas her body with my gaze, having a hard time making out what's new blood and what's old blood. Her once tan shift is now some other color. A lot of colors. *All* the colors. She's still got blue Oosa blood embedded near the neckline and my copper blood eating up most of her sleeves. A few droplets of her own horribly bright red blood stain the front of her tunic, between her breasts, but now with the angle, they drip off of her perfect upper lip onto me. And I can't do anything about it. Not with her strapped into her upside-down seat and me, suspended like a spider below her. I'm scared to move her, though. Scared... just scared.

"Svera, can you breathe?"

"I..." She coughs abruptly. "I'm fine. Are...are you okay?"

She blinks and her eyelids flutter. Her eyes open, but they're distant and unfocused. Still, she smiles and breathes, "Anand."

I grin at her but it doesn't feel like pleasure. It feels like insanity. "How...how are you..." I look down at the metal sticking out of her chest. Right over her heart. It should have killed her. Should have... The only thing between her and the metal is her...

"Rug," I choke, all mangled and wild. I take hold of the metal piece in one hand and when I yank it free, the rolled up carpet covering her chest flops forward.

I touch her breast.

"Krisxox," she mumbles.

I shush her and feel for damage, finding none. Then I reach for the folded carpet and pick up one edge and find it broken on the first two layers, but by the third, it's back to being intact.

I meet her gaze, aghast. "There *is* a god."

She just smiles back. "I told you."

"Xok." I wrench the rug out from around her and hang it over my shoulder, determined to worship it. "Come on. Grab my neck."

She does and I manage to lower us down somewhat safely and together, we stumble out into the light.

Underneath the sun, in the shooter's graveyard, I make it twenty paces past the last flaming piece of metal before collapsing on the hard, packed sands. Rocks dig into my knees and Svera's breathing is thin and ragged when she rolls onto her back.

I collapse forward, flinging onto my back beside her. We lay there for a long time. So long that I'm fully baked by the sun when I next wake to Svera's light touch on my face. I open my eyes.

"Remind me never to trust a pirate again, no matter the species," she grumbles, wavering where she sits.

I laugh and reach for her, touch the wild tufts of her hair. "Xoking Ashmara."

At least we're alive, though you..." She just squints down at me and wipes her face, smearing blood and vomit across her cheek. "Your injuries look bad. We need to get you to Lemoria."

I nod. There's no denying that.

"How far do you think we are from the colony?"

I shrug, too dead to move. "Xok if I know."

"Don't give up on me now. Not when we've made it this far."

"Never."

She tilts her head, blocking out the light of one sun but not the other. Her skin is pink all over and when I reach up to touch her forehead, she winces.

"What is this?" I ask.

"Verax."

"The color."

"Which one?"

"Pink. You're pink all over."

"Burn, probably."

"Burn?"

"Hexa, sunburn."

"You can burn in just the sun?" I sit up abruptly. My head spins and I feel my stomach lurch, trying to give up its contents.

"Anand," she starts and I lose myself to the way she says my name.

Then I remember. "You're burning alive."

"Nox, it's not like that."

"Come on."

Anand:

"Svera, I am your *huzzaband*, you have to do what I say."

I chuckle at the rage that spreads across her cheeks, turning the pink to a bright fuchsia. "You *are* going to need punishing."

"I look forward to it." I wink at her and she tenses, but it isn't arousal this time. It's surprise. *Relief.*

"Look. I think…are those gliders?"

I twist to face the direction she's pointing and exhale, "Thank the xoking stars."

"Thank the Tri-God."

"Hexa. Especially him."

"And Xana," she says, lips quirked.

I nod, smiling back. "Hexa. Her, too."

We're rescued by a group of xcleranx sent to investigate as soon as the shooter hit the colony's atmosphere and, as the glider powers silently across the dunes, I make the xcleranx find a cloth that Svera can use to shield her sensitive skin from the suns.

"Do you need me to help you fix it so you can conceal your hair?" I ask her as the human settlement appears on the horizon, many squat buildings in the center, the magnificent tower of the birthing center to the left of the jumble, a few prominent dust-colored houses to the right.

"I told you, Anand. I've already been had. I don't need to wear the scarf anymore."

I huff at that. "Because you are *may'ree* now."

She lifts a brow. "You do know we're not *actually* married yet, right? There is a ceremony involved."

I huff again. "Fine. You don't need to wear the scarf, but you will call me *huzzaband*."

"In private," she says under her breath. "My parents will think it an insult if you don't have their permission first. But don't worry, I'll talk to them."

"*I* will talk to them."

She gives me a skeptical look. "Maybe I better do it."

"Nox. I will do it. Have faith in me."

She opens her mouth to answer — *argue* — but the glider below our feet begins to power down and she falls into me. I grab hold of the railing for support and as Svera clings to me, I know I cannot fall. It might be the only reason I don't as we finally come to a complete stop and step down in front of a crowd of gathered humans and Voraxians.

"Svera!" The Va'Rakukanna's voice is louder than the others and she is first to approach. She surges towards us, breaking free of the crowd, her mate at her back. For the first time since I have known him, his emotions slip and his ridges flare bright white. Even his mate looks aghast.

"Stars! What happened to you? Svera, are you alright?"

Svera's weight sinks into my arms and I catch her as she starts to fall. "Oof," she breathes. "I'm alright. It's Krisxox Lemoria needs to see."

"Holy comets, what in the xok happened to you two?"

Before Svera can answer, another chorus of her name sounds and I'm left staring at the faces of the ones I know created her. And here I am before them, completely xoking naked. I take a step bringing me to Svera's side and that alone causes the female leading the two males to stop dead in her tracks. Her eyes expand, canvassing my naked body in a way that makes me grit my teeth. I realize in that moment that I have absolutely no idea how to greet a human. If our last interaction was any indication, I better figure it out *fast*.

I place my hand to my chest in the traditional Voraxian greeting and bow low. "It is an honor to return your daughter to you," I growl, sounding half-crazed with pain.

"Mom." Svera breaks the silence and stiffly ambles forward, letting the female and the two males come around her and swarm her in their embrace. Va'Raku comes to my side and attempts to engage me, but I have attention only for her and her kin who she has this *lawv* for.

They speak to her in Human but, it isn't long before her father turns his gaze to me. He approaches me with water in his eyes and, while I clutch my stomach in an attempt to keep my organs all inside, he comes to a stop directly before me.

forward, takes my shoulders in each of his thin hands and kisses my either cheek.

He says something to me that I don't understand. I look to the female behind him. "He says that you have our permission," she covers her mouth with her hands and nods. "You have our permission, Krisxox."

"Thank you," I heave, and it's that final breath that pulls the last of my strength out of me.

Va'Raku catches me, but it hurts everywhere. He starts issuing orders rapidly and soon, I'm being lowered onto a hovering stretcher and rushed over the sands, my Xiveri mate on the stretcher by my side.

21

Svera

Two solars pass and somehow Krisxox is released from Lemoria's care before I am. It might be that he makes the most surly patient in universal history, but Lemoria insists that it's because of my concussion. *Xoking Ashmara…*

As Krisxox would say. The thought isn't mine and he hasn't rubbed off on me. Of course.

Krisxox hovers over my side until Lemoria forces Va'Raku and Kiki to shove him out of the chamber and make space for my parents and brother to enter. I'm embarrassed to see them, but when they come in with unshed tears in their eyes — all of them — all my father says is, "We are so grateful to the Tri-God that he brought you home."

I smile, sure, but not as sure as I once was that the Tri-God had everything to do with it. Xana and Xaneru played their own roles. And Krisxox, Ashmara and Deena should also be mentioned.

Determination.

Pride.

Bravery.

"And mated, no less," my brother adds. He crosses his arms over his chest, looking irritated.

I laugh and feel heat touch the tops of my cheeks. "I..." I swallow. "Yes, he is my Xiveri mate, but that is only the Voraxian recognition. We're still not married but, with your permission, we would like to be."

I reach my hand up and tuck my rat's nest behind my ear. It's stiff in places, crusted with gunk I don't even want to think about.

"And he has it," Ibra huffs. "I didn't believe our parents would ever find a male they thought worthy of you, but this?" He gestures at my body, covered in a lush fur and the holo monitors beeping on the wall behind me. "He is worthy and I would be honored to officiate the wedding."

"So much planning to be done!" My mom is near giddy. She's beaming ear to ear.

My father raises his hands. "We have time. First, time for healing. Then discussions of plans and officiants can be made later. And this is all contingent on Svera truly wanting the male. Do you, sheifala?"

To this, I grin. My face is so hot. I laugh with the relief that sags out of me. "I love him. He is a disaster, but I love every part of him."

My mom claps and my brother and father both grin. "He said much the same of you when we ran into him earlier."

"More like, when he hunted us down," Ibra says with a chuckle. "He asked me to teach him our Human language and to educate him on the Tri-God. Did he tell you he wants to be baptized?"

I shake my head, crying in earnest now. "Oh, sheifala." My mom comes and rubs my shoulder. It's bruised. So is every other part of me. Including my weary hearts.

My mom smiles, her eyes welling with tears as she takes my hand and brushes the backs of her fingers across my cheek, smudging away one of a million dirty spots with her thumb. "As far as we and the congregation are concerned, you are already wed, Svera. There is no reason to feel ashamed." She touches the top of my head, then immediately makes a face. "Though perhaps a bath is in order."

I laugh. Tears come to my eyes as I do. "You aren't disappointed that I...didn't manage to stay true to the Tri-God?"

"After what we have done, how could we be?" My father says.

I don't like that and open my mouth to tell him that two sins don't create a virtue, but my mom speaks first. "You were wedded in Voraxian law before you consummated your marriage. From what we have heard from Kiki and Miari, the biological bond is strong. It would have been unnatural for you not to consummate it." My brother chokes on his next cough and my father's cheeks turn a deep red. He looks anywhere but at my face. So awkward, I can't help but laugh again.

My mom swats my dad on the shoulder, forcing him to turn towards the bed. He says, "You were not ruined, sheifala. We could not be prouder of you. We just wanted to make sure that you were certain about him for your mate and, if you two would still like to be married under the Tri-God's faith, your husband. After all, he is a male of some *intensity*."

I bark out a laugh, but it's my mom who says, "I believe Svera will have need of that intensity, given her role."

"It's true," I agree. "He is the kind of male I'll need at my side if I'm to continue working to protect the humans."

"Because you need someone to protect you," my father says and he removes a kerchief from his pocket and dabs it to his brow. He looks momentarily a decade older. "We thought we lost you, sheifala. And Krisxox brought you back to us."

I nod. "He will always bring me back to you."

"If for no other reason than that, we gave him our blessing should he, of course, have yours first."

"He does. I would not have anyone else. He is my mate — my Xiveri mate — and I'll be proud to have him for my husband."

My mom starts to clap again. "Perfect. This is excellent news, sheifala. But for now, how are you feeling? Nauseous. Hungry. Dizzy?"

I shake my head. "Lemoria and Ki'Lemoria corrected the concussion, but she told me I might still experience some lingering symptoms for the next couple solars. She says that I'm alright to go home, but she's asked you to monitor me... She said that she gave you all some medical equipment to take with you?"

"Yes, we've got it," my brother says, holding up a large box that's translucent white. "We're ready to take you home."

I smile. "I'm ready to go home."

"We're ready to bring you home. And Svera." My father clears his throat. He brushes his fingers through his light brown hair. I got his hair and his eyes, but my grandmother always said that I got my mother's heart. "We have spent much time with Lemoria over these past solars and we told her everything about the births."

I tense. "So, they know about the hybrids?"

My parents nod. "Yes. They know about the hybrids and the Council and Mathilda and the deals she brokered with beings off-planet. We were surprised that they believed us so easily, but we had to do something when you disappeared. We were sure that Mathilda was responsible when she told us that you'd been kidnapped."

My mom nods, and then picks up where my dad left off. "Miari and Raku had the other members of the Antikythera Council arrested two solars ago and the Council itself disbanded. Unfortunately, Mathilda, Harold, and Jopard were missing."

The two Council members' sons who detained Deena and me. I tense at the memory and my thoughts flit to Deena. Shame hits me that this is the first moment I've even had to panic about her. *Where is she?*

Then my mother says, "They haven't been found since."

"What?!" My chest burns.

My parents look glum as they say, "Jaxal is leading patrols across the moon, but so far, they haven't found them."

"Where could they have gone?"

"We don't know."

"Who is in charge now?"

"There has been chaos. The humans are frightened to be under Voraxian rule. It is...too reminiscent of the Hunt."

My brother and dad nod. Ibra says, "They still don't trust Miari, even after all she's done for us. And they're downright frightened of Kiki now that they've seen her training with the Voraxian soldiers. She's a terrifying specimen..."

He makes a face and even though we're only one rotation apart in age, looking at him feels like looking in a mirror. We could have been twins.

"I'll speak to the Kaku and Kakukanna, Va'Kaku and Va'Rakukanna and help them find an interim solution until they decide who should take over."

My parents and brother exchange a look I can't interpret. My brother opens his mouth, but my mom cuts in, "That would be lovely. Until then, let's get you cleaned up. And should we plan to have Krisxox staying with us as well?"

"Oh, um, I don't know."

She nods. "It's not a problem. We can decide later."

She comes and touches my hair and I say, "Mom? Dad? I want you to know that the hybrid who helped us out of the fighting pit was one of the babies Mathilda sold."

My parents both pale at that. "And..." My dad licks his lips. "How was she?"

I grin as a spasm ripples up my right side, then say through clenched teeth, "I think she's doing just fine."

22

Svera

Miari comes to see me when I'm steeped in my second bath. The water is even hotter this time and actually appears clear-ish, unlike my first bath which was rendered muddy on my first dip.

She has her kit in her arms.

I squeal as she edges herself into the bathroom and squats beside the basin. "No, no, don't get up. Dora and I just wanted to come by to see you."

"Dora," I say, pulling myself into a seat and reaching for the bundle. I stroke the back of my finger down Dora's soft-as-down cheek. She is a perfect combination of Miari and Raku, her skin a perfect shade of purple, reminiscent of Va'Raku's tone, only lighter. Her hair is a few wisps of dark fluff and when she yawns, a little pink tongue peeks out with a little bump dotting its center. Her first ridge. I wonder if she'll have more of them.

I beam down at the kit, feeling emotion well in my body as I wonder if Anand really has changed so much that he could one day learn to love a hybrid. Ours.

"How is she doing?"

"Wonderfully."

"How are you and Raku doing?"

"Perfect. Minus the fact that my best friend went missing the day I gave birth, I've been great." She rolls her eyes and shakes out her wavy hair, mouth turning down into a pout. "Your parents confessed about the hybrids. They wanted to be punished, but from what I understand, they were heroes. They saved a bunch of lives."

I nod, feeling guilty. "Yes. I should have told them that. I was ashamed that they could do something like that, but I know now that they did what they thought was best. And it was."

"And you...you say you met one of the hybrids?"

I nod, huffing out a laugh. "She was something."

"Tell me."

So I do. I tell her everything.

She and Kiki share dinner with me and my family that lunar. Conversation veers towards the Council and who will take over for them, but Miari and Kiki tell me that a proposal is in the works and that they'd like to share it with me when I'm fully healed — a proposal put forward by Krisxox.

I let them evade plans for now. I'm not a xub'Raku, so I know that there are things that they may wish to keep close to the breast, it just...hurts my feelings a little. I wonder if Miari's questioning my ability to act as her advisor, and it keeps me up all lunar. Well, it's part of the reason I can't sleep. After spending the last three — or was it four? — lunars sleeping with Anand's warmth and strength and scent at my side, I find that I can't sleep without it.

Operating on tea and determination alone when Kiki comes to pick me up the next solar to take me to Miari and Raku's house, I'm xoking pissed off. Oh my... I'm *very* upset. There, that's better.

Anand made all these bold pronouncements, asked me to marry him, and then vanished. Poof! He must know I've been released from Lemoria's care this past solar, but he hasn't come to my parents' house to see me. I vow that, the moment we're finished here, I'm going to find him and give him the punishment he deserves.

"You alright?" Kiki whispers under her breath so low that Va'Raku on her other side can't hear her.

I grunt and pull the veil I carry with me higher over my hair to shield my face. I don't wear the veil anymore but, right now, I need something to keep the sun from burning my skin even more.

The suns are blazing and for all of Lemoria's technology, she doesn't have a thing to solve their cruel grip on the lighter shades of skin among the

humans, like mine, Ibia's and my dad's so, I'm
to coating my skin in the aloe from the mixture my
parents make from the sticky desert weeds that crop
up everywhere.

Lemoria found the substance fascinating and has
been working with my parents to manufacture more
and improve it so that it not only soothes burns, but
actually reverses their effect.

"What's wrong?"

I shake my head.

"Krisxox?" she asks.

"No," I lie. "Well, a little. Mostly, I'm just worried
about the Council."

Kiki stops dead in her tracks and slaps a hand
over her chest. "Oh, my stars. Universe strike me
down now! Did Svera just tell her first *lie*?"

My lips twitch, even as fire comes to my cheeks
that does nothing for my burn but make it itch.
"Kiki…"

"Heaven forbid," she says. She laughs and loops
her arm through mine. "I think your time away from
us changed you."

"Your time away from us changed you."

She smiles and her gaze flashes to the male on her
left. "Yes, it did. And I have you to thank for getting
me through it. That call we had meant everything to
me. Thank you, Svera."

...deep into my lungs, smelling sand and earth on the wind. "You don't need to thank me for anything. We're family."

She bends over and knocks her forehead into mine. "I love you."

"I love you, too."

"And Krisxox is a maniac, but whatever change you might have gone through when you were gone, I think his was more profound."

I think of the language, the baptism, that he asked my parents for my hand. Why he hasn't shown up to see me is a mystery, but perhaps...Anand is still around.

"Have you seen him?"

She laughs, the cloud of her hair moving around her face, making her look angelic. I'm struck sometimes by how beautiful she is and I can tell Va'Raku is thinking the same thing, judging by the deep blue and purple swirling in his ridges.

His gaze hits mine and he straightens, his colors shutting off all at once, but not before I catch a fleeting shade of embarrassment. I smile broader, glad that Kiki doesn't notice our interaction.

"Have I ever..."

I frown. "What's that supposed to mean?"

She rolls her eyes. "It's been two solars since he fled Lemoria and he's still badly injured, but he's already been to see me and Miari a dozen times each and he's called three different meetings with Raka and Va'Raku and boy, has he got *plans*."

My frown deepens. "Why wouldn't he share them with me?"

Kiki's smile grows disproportionately and, as I watch her face, the tiled awning above Miari's front door casts a shadow over her expression. She reaches for the knob made of pink metal. "I think I should hold my answer to that one. Come on, Svera."

There's a buzzing energy about her and I still can't get over the fact that this is the same female who didn't speak for over two rotations. This is the same female who fought because she wanted to die, not to kill. This is the same female who I saw fall so hard, and who now looks around at the world as if she's on top of it. As if everything is beautiful and perfect.

Her aura buoys me and I forget that I'm irritated as we step into the house. It doesn't smell like a center for hardened warriors to come together and make battle plans. No, it smells like baked cane-and-root bread.

Kiki's favorite.

"Stars, bless you. Miari, is this cane-and-root bread?" Kiki drifts to the kitchen on the left. Without waiting for Miari to answer, she bends over the bread tray and inhales deeply.

"It is, indeed," Miari says, coming down the long hallway in a dress that swishes in shades of cream around her feet.

"I know." She winks at me and her teeth flash white in her red face and I look around at the xub'Raku gathered on the right side of the room and I can't fathom that these are truly the same creatures that convene in such austerity in the war room of Illyria.

The presence of the kit has changed *everything*.

Dora's currently in the arms of Xa'Raku and, even though the ruler of Thrax is known to be Raku's closest advisor, Raku still hovers over her shoulder, looking absolutely stressed.

"Careful," he mutters when Xa'Raku holds the kit out towards Islu'Raku, who takes the baby from her and shows her off to Xhen'Raku, who coos and strokes the side of her soft, purple cheek.

"Careful," he barks again. "You haven't blunted your claws."

"I blunted them, Raku," Xhen'Raku mutters. "Calm down."

Raku just grunts when Xa'Raku laughs. She sees me then and calls my name. "Svera! We are so pleased you're here and well. Please come. Sit."

So different than the war room.

Eventually all of the xub'Raku take their seats around an enormous, raw wooden table. I sit between Miari and Xhen'Raku who eventually offers the baby to me when she sees me staring. Raku, who is on Xhen'Raku's other side, looks like he's going to lose his mind that the baby is being taken further away from him, but when I offer Dora back, Miari grabs both of Raku's hands, shoves them in his lap and waves Dora away.

"She's family," is all Miari says. "Calm down."

"Your calm will drive me to madness," Raku growls back, leaning into Miari's lips when she tilts her face towards his. His shoulders sag as she smiles. She kisses him. He returns it so deeply, I feel a flush rise up inside my stomach and an urge to see Anand. I frown at the thought of him. If he's been scheduling so many meetings, why isn't he here now?

"This is only a convening of the xub'Raku," Kiki says, and I panic for a moment that I asked for him out loud. But no, she's merely opening this strange, disjointed, utterly human version of a war room meeting.

And then I register her words. "Apologies. Should I wait outside for you to open the meeting to civilians?"

"Nox," Raku answers, pulling away from his female, even as he crushes her to his side. He leans back against the pillows stacked behind him. They line the room and cover the floor. The pillow beneath me is crushed catacat silk and is a soothing balm against the burned skin on my legs, which feels stretched way too tight.

He takes a breath, then exhales and the room is silent. *Ah. Here...this is the war room.* I tense, knowing that I'm not in the right place, but I don't dare disgrace myself by interrupting the Raku when he begins.

The only sounds for the first moment are the subtle rustling of two females called Kuana and Kuaku. Both are warriors-in-training on Nobu, but also act as Kiki's helpers. It is, in Nobu culture, a highly revered position.

They distribute cups of nightshade tea among the xub'Raku gathered. It's good and complements the cane-and-root bread, but it doesn't beat my mother's. Nothing does.

"The events that have transpired have been told to us by the Krisxox of Voraxia, however, before we begin, I would like to hear a retelling from you, Svera."

I nod. "Of course."

I begin with the moment of Dora's birth and look down at the baby as I speak of her, listening to the way she snores like a tiny old woman. It brings a smile to my face that spreads around the room, even though I can sense that these powerful beings aren't accustomed to it.

Eventually, I explain what happened to me and to Krisxox, our rescue at the hands of the hybrid, and what I learned from my parents and from Mathilda and Deena directly. There is silence after I speak, broken up only by Dora's growls, which turn into mewls. I pass her back to Miari whose breasts are already bared. She lifts the baby to one of them, drawing a gasp from Xa Raku, who flushes with bright, bright embarrassment.

"My respects, Rakukanna. It is merely a magical thing to behold, the feeding. It is not a thing we Voraxian females are biologically built to do." With tough nipples and flat chests, Voraxians feed their babies mashed food from the first solar. Meanwhile, Dora's been responding quite well to Miari's milk.

God is great.

Miari smiles in response and looks down at her kit, suckling softly. "I just wish it weren't so painful."

"My parents have balm for that. I'll fetch some for you after we close our meeting," I tell her.

"Thank you. That would be such a relief." She looks like she means it. I can see the tired pouches beneath her eyes and the slightly frazzled way she watches me. She is sleepy, like all new mothers are. Her status changes nothing.

"You are a warrior," Kiki says from across the circle.

Miari makes a face at that — a tight-lipped smile and a lowering of the lashes. "Thanks, Ki... Va'Rakukanna."

Kiki tips her head forward. It's what she whispered to Miari all throughout the birth. She *is* a warrior. And I'm so proud of her.

Raku clears his throat, his arm tightening around his mate and kit. "For what you have done for my

Rakukanna and what you have done for your people, I thank you, Svera.

"We have been in deep discussion since we learned of Mathilda's treason and since she vanished. We have debated at length on how to establish governance for this colony. Our initial thinking was to fold the colony into Cxrian and, once a new Bo'Raku is chosen, leave the governance of this moon colony to him or her."

Oh comets, that is a horrible idea! I bite my lips together, but my whole body still jerks.

Raku tips his head forward and smiles. "Judging by your expression, I sense that this is not the choice you would make for your people."

"Nox," I blurt. "It is not." Over my dead body.

Raku's lips twitch at that and for a moment, I worry I've offended him. "It is with equal horror that your kin regarded me when I made this suggestion before them. And it was then that my Rakukanna and I determined that this would not be an acceptable solution.

"The acceptable solution however, was obvious. It only took Krisxox to suggest it the solar he returned you to us."

Raku levels me with a stare. A hard stare full of meaning. "Xok," I whisper, cupping my hands over my mouth. Both Miari and Kiki burst out laughing at that.

Light chuckles make their way around the room as I look around at all these people gathered. These xub'Raku gathered.

"You don't mean..." My chest clenches. All my aches disappear. Or maybe they ignite. I feel like I'm running screaming, falling face-first over a cliff.

And that Anand is at the bottom, making sure I'm alright.

He suggested this.

My body starts to pound, a pulse quickening within me that I know spells doom...

"Hexa," Raku says. "My Rakukanna and I would like to appoint you as Hu'Raku. You will be equal to all other xub'Raku and will govern the human moon colony as an independent, semi-autonomous planet within the Voraxian federation. You will report to no one other than myself and my Rakukanna. She will advise you on your budgets while Xhen'Raku will continue to oversee the protection of the colony until we have equipped you with your own xcleranx. Hu'Raka will be responsible for selecting said xcleranx and will do so from the new warriors he trains from the base established here."

My face twists in confusion. Kiki is the one who says, "She doesn't know about that yet, Raku. I had plans to show her the grounds after this meeting."

"Then it will be done," Raku replies.

Boom. Boom. Boom.

My hearts are clenching. My thighs are pressed together tight. My palms are sweating. "Hu'Raka?" I stammer. It takes me two tries and I flush, unused to being so inarticulate.

Miari nods, passing Dora off to Raku who places the baby easily on his shoulder. Dora looks impossibly small beneath his hands, which are entirely clawless and tender as he burps her.

"Of course. Raka are the male equivalent of Rakukanna. Krisxox would take your title. He has already accepted it."

He's already accepted the title.

"He's only waiting for you."

He's only waiting for me.

Boom boom boom BOOM.

Oh no. The Xanaxana...*I can feel her revenge coming for me.*

I shiver all over as that bloodthirsty heat blooms between my hips and quickly, I reach for my tea and concentrate hard on its cold taste now that I've let it sit.

I squeeze my eyes shut and think of the cold plains of Nobu and Tur'Roth lashing Krisxox and that horrible oversized insect stabbing him once and then again. I think of Ashmara and falling from the sky in that horrible box and none it makes any difference to the surge of fire that wets me below the waist.

My lower lips clench and I groan. My hand knocks over the tea and all the males in the room stand up abruptly and start to move away.

Miari and Kiki share a confused look while Islu'Raku clears his throat and moves jerkily towards the door. "If it is no problem, I will take my leave..." He quickly paces out of the room while Va'Raku grabs Kiki by the arm and whispers in her ear.

Her eyes widen and that's when it happens.

I burst into flame. *"Xok!"*

"Xok," Raku curses, lunging up onto his feet. He grabs Miari and starts to tug her down the hall while his ridges flare in deep lavender.

Kiki hurries to my side while and whispers in my ear, "Let's get you out of here."

"Take me to Krisxox. Please."

"Comets, come on."

She wrenches me up onto my feet and pulls me towards the front door.

"You are dismissed," Raku barks over his shoulder from the hall where he continues to glow lavender. Just before he disappears and right before my whole body buckles, I shout, "I accept the position of Hu'Raku."

"Thank the stars for that," Miari shouts.

Kiki laughs and drags me back outside under the sun. An arrow is loosed through my stomach and it's aimed at Krisxox, a male once so full of hate, just as Kiki was.

Perhaps, there is no such thing as hate, only gardens not yet tended to.

Every place I step, a flower grows as Xana finally grants my Xaneru peace and settles my soul.

The Xanaxana is complete. Or, it will be. I just need him.

"Krisxox," I call and I know he will come for me.

He always does.

23

Hu'Raka

The human called Jaxal and I find ourselves in mirrored positions. He hated Voraxians until his Xanaxana shone for the Nobu female, Lisbel. I hated everyone until Xana punched me in the face and knocked me down, bloodying me in a battle I was too stupid to surrender. Until now.

"Take over," I tell him while I move to the youngest fighters training here. They are kits themselves, but they spent all solar watching me at the perimeter of the training grounds and, since I trained as a kit, too, why not let them?

Jaxal gives me a firm nod, then shouts, "Drugh!" He punches his left fist forward, then ducks and sweeps his training staff around.

I've been showing him a new defensive move for the past two solars — since I first cleared this space just outside of the Droherion Dome and claimed it for our training grounds — and he has mostly mastered it, so I feel confident in his ability to teach the other fifty hunters gathered here. Thirty of them are human. Twenty of them are my disciples. Among those, half are Drakesh, though I weeded out the ones like Vendra, who I thought might pose harm to the humans. I won't tolerate that insolence and I won't stand for that threat, not when it means my Xiveri mate's wellbeing or her happiness.

The soldiers mirror his movements — even mine, who likely never thought they'd ever see a human training captain in their lifetimes. They better get xoking used to it. *I* better get used to it. Because neither did I.

I move to the edge of the dome where the younger fighters train. I keep them positioned here in case we are attacked by any of this moon colony's creatures. They will be able to step inside courtesy of the life drives they have embedded in their wrists.

For now, I approach the boy called Mahmoud and take his stick from him. I hand him a training staff that's blunt on both ends and sturdier than his stick was. I show him and the other kits how to hold their new weapons and I'm not at all surprised that there are more female kits here than males.

These human females are savage, in my experience. Bloodthirsty. Every single one of them. *One more than most...*

"Krisxox..."

I tense and look up, but the sands are empty except for my warriors. Empty, except for the aching burn in my chest. Empty, except for my wounds, that are struggling to heal with how I push my body.

Empty, except for the solitary heart in my chest, which beats, beats, beats.

"Krisxox!"

My breath catches in my throat and gusts out of me on a moan. I'm running now, feeling like I've lost my xoking mind as I issue orders to the warriors in training and enter the dome.

I won't be back for the rest of the solar. Perhaps the next. Or the next one...

"What happened?" I roar as the Va'Rakukanna carries most of Svera's weight. Svera reaches for me, her hand like a claw as she grabs onto my shoulder. And then I understand.

"Xok," I curse as the scent of her arousal washes over me like a tidal wave. "Xok..."

"Uhm...Yeah, so we'll leave you two to it then!" The Va'Rakukanna shouts over her shoulder. She is already running back to the Va'Raku stationed a dozen paces away. When she reaches him, she launches herself into his arms and his ridges explode in a dark purple lust as he carries her back towards the settlement.

I'm breathing hard, panting. My xora is tight in my battle kilt, fighting against it and her shift. Svera wraps her arms around my neck and tries to get her legs around my hips, but her shift is too narrow.

"Anand," she gasps. "I need you. Please…"

Her chest is heaving. Her eyes are bright and watery and I can feel the tension radiating throughout her back and arms. Her inner thighs are trembling.

"Xok. Is it the…"

She nods. "My Xanaxana. I think…I think this might be the final bond."

I'm running. Racing through the dense colony streets. "What caused this?" I ask as I run.

"Hu'Raka…" she says on every jolting step. I try to keep my body as centered as possible so as not to jostle her when I run.

I beam. "Hu'Raka? Does this mean you accepted your title?"

"Hexa. But only because you accepted yours. You will take the title of a human?"

"Have you lost your xoking mind? Of course. My Xiveri mate is human and she's xub'Raku of Voraxia. I must."

"Augheh," she squeals, her thighs clenching together tighter. I reach my hand below her ass, feeling for a wetness that I find. My wounds all tear just a little, but Lemoria welded me back together more than fine enough for this. *Nothing could keep me from sating her Xiveri bond now.*

"Where are we going?" She says, voice twisted and strained as she pulls herself even closer to me, rubbing her breasts up and down my plated chest. "We can't go to my parents' house!" She yelps when I head down the dusty lane towards it.

Adobe houses sit on one side of the road, tin shacks on the other. The tin shacks need to be *gone*. I hate the sight of them and I know Raku hates the sight of them. That is where his Rakukanna once lived, so exposed and derelict, unprotected by the elements. I don't like the adobe homes much better, but they at least have a natural insulation that protects against the bone-cold lunars and the scorching solars.

I pass by Svera's house on the right and approach the next home in the row. "This is not your parents' house."

"Verax…"

"This is my house." I kick open the front door and wade into the space. "It belonged to a human family…"

"Hexa, of course. This was Sansar and her family's home. Where…"

"They are in Mathilda's former home now. I moved them and took this one."

"Why didn't you take Mathilda's house?" She asks me from her back, looking up at me as I lay her down on the divan in the back room. It isn't anything so comfortable as the nest I had made for her in Qath, but it will do.

The burned, broken and mangled prayer mat hangs on the wall by the only window. Svera is staring at it, her chest heaving even harder the longer she stares.

"God," she whispers.

"Hexa," I answer. "I moved here because that house was too far from you." I remove my kilt and her gaze immediately drops to my xora.

She puffs out a breath and pulls the veil away that she'd been using for the sun. Before it can flutter to the ground completely, I snatch it up. "The first thing your Raka will do for you is bring some xoking trees onto this cursed rock. I will not see you hurting because you're pink."

She blinks, confused, then her lips tilt up into a smile. "But I thought you liked my pink parts."

Her shift slides up her thighs to reveal the brown and pink flower seated at the juncture of her legs. I grab hold of my xora, trying to wrangle it into submission, but precum weeps onto its tip, begging to be sucked.

"Anand, please…"

"Hexa, Svera," I say, pumping my xora hard. "What do you need?"

"Take me to the garden."

My ridges explode with color. I can see it in the low light of the room, whose darkness is only dispersed by the sole window. It overlooks the emptiness of this red and brown world, a quiet desolation exploding with life. Such a contradiction. Just like my Svera, spread wide on the mat in front of me, infecting everything with her scent, her salty, sweet arousal, her ruthlessness.

I growl, "And here I was thinking your god was not a believer in these kinds of filthy things."

Svera swallows. She doesn't break my gaze. "My god believes in doing the most good and the least harm. That everything is alright so long as you don't hurt anyone. And that you should treat others as you wish to be treated."

"And this is how you wish others would treat you?"

She hesitates, sensing the threat in my words. She must, because I do mean them as a threat. "Hexa." She spreads her legs just a little wider and says, "I do."

"Take off your shift."

She doesn't hesitate, whipping it over her head to reveal a body I have fantasized about these past lunars sleeping here alone, wishing…just wishing…

I drop to my knees between her legs as a savage desire grips the back of my legs and shoots up my spine. I line myself up with her entrance as I reach up and wrap my fist around her slender neck.

I meet her gaze and just before I punch into her brutally, shoving past her too-tight barrier, slick now with her arousal and my need, I rasp, "No one treats you like this but me. No one worships you like I do. You are mine, Svera. Mine to protect, mine to mate. And I vow to you that I will spend every solar for the rest of my existence showing you how wrong I was denying you in the first place." I swallow, stilling for just a breath. "*I lawv you.*"

She smiles up at me and scores her nails down my chest, but just as she opens her mouth to say whatever it was she was going to say, I slide home, rutting deep.

"Xok me," she curses to the ceiling.

I bark out a laugh as she clenches around me, making me dizzy. I lave my tongue up the column of her neck, squeeze her breast, twist her nipple, wait for her small body to adjust to my xora's girth.

"I plan to."

As I start to move, thrusting in and out of her, my white hair spills onto the dark colors below her, a fabric that's the same dusty brown-red hue as everything else on this moon — a moon that needs a name because this moon will be my home — I think about colors and contradictions. Red, brown, peach, purple, blue. Useless, all of it. All that matters is this.

I touch my hand to her chest where her one heart beats and I know everything I need to know about her. What I saw in that first glance, right at the very beginning.

An imperfection that matches my own.

She fills in all my raw and broken bits.

And I fill in hers.

Like this we are whole.

"Svera," I choke as a debilitating rush of this *lawv* cracks over my head like an egg. Like I'm the egg and

301

everything inside tumbles out in a sudden rush. My ridges illuminate her face. Her eyes dance with their light.

"Harder!" She gasps, holding onto my neck.

She is close, spiraling, spiraling... I change the angle again, dropping further forward onto her body and rotating my hips against hers in a wavelike motion so that my abdomen presses against her sensitive *clit* every time I thrust. I run my hands up and down her body and she does the same to mine.

"I can't hold out much longer, Svera," I grit. "You ruin me."

She meets my gaze with a bloodthirsty grin and whispers, "There is no such thing. There is only the garden."

We come apart together again and again. The entire lunar is spent sating Xana's final act of total ruination. It's only as the light of another of Cxrian's moons filters in through the solitary window and illuminates the prayer rug hanging on the wall, still covered in gunk and goop and blood, that Svera finally exhales contentedly. Dreamily.

I lean down and kiss the top of her head, hugging her close. "You must still be hurting," I say quietly.

"Nox," she exhales against my chest. "Everything is perfect in the garden."

"Xhivey." Then she flicks me.

"What was that for?"

"For keeping me out of the garden these past two solars. Why did you leave?"

"I knew where you were," I grumble.

"But I didn't know where you were. And I wanted to be here." She places her small hand between my two hearts, where hers has a home.

I tell her the truth of it. "I wanted to woo you."

"Wanted?"

"Turns out I'd rather rut you, instead."

Her head falls back on her neck and she laughs loud and hard. "Xhivey. Then from this moment, we'll never part."

"Never. Here in the garden, I am home."

"Me, too. Though I do still expect to be wooed."

"And rutted?"

"And rutted."

I chuckle. "I guess I have my work cut out for me, then."

"You do. It's all part of being a husband."

I grin and look down at her, meeting her gaze. "In this case, *whiff*, I'm honored." I stroke her hair away from her face.

Sometime later, when I'm awake still watching her and her eyes begin to close, I whisper, "You know, I think I have an idea for your human colony's name."

"Verax." Sleepily, she licks her lips.

I lean down and kiss them and say, "I think you should call it Heimo."

Sixty solars later...

24

Hu'Raku

The wind is hot, even though the lunar is upon us and the second sun has just begun to set. I stand on the crest of the hill, looking out away from the colony, towards the shards of black screa hills where the khrui roam. They keep to their side of the colony, we keep to ours, even though there is no more dome. We don't need it. Not with the new warriors-in-training that have come to live here to be near to the Hu'Raka — who still acts as Krisxox. Raku has not yet authorized a suitable replacement because there is no one better, despite Anand's pleas to the contrary. Secretly, he knows there is no one better, either.

"What arg yow zinking about, my whiff?" Comes Anand's slow drawl. His accent is still something of legends, but his Human is progressing…

Sort of.

My brother teaches Krisxox Human early every solar before first prayer. My brother, mother, father and I take first prayer together while Krisxox cooks us first meal. He is an extraordinary cook.

From there, I begin my duties as Hu'Raku. It's all budgets and numbers and organizing harvests. Construction of the biodome that allows us to diversify our crops and tilling the soil colony soil have been top priorities. Already some, but not all, species of trees we've tried to plant have taken.

We haven't had any luck with werros, but some of the spindlier, sturdier Arabat trees have succeeded and are now lush, providing humidity and shade. Anand still shakes his fist up at the suns whenever I get the slightest bit red, but it's a start.

There are also houses to construct, tearing down the old colony homes that are unsafe, repurposing the adobe homes into an "old" city center where shops and cafes can be found now in abundance.

It's a lot of work and I wouldn't trade a moment of it. Especially not the part where I seek the council of my friends and my Hu'Raka and come home in the lunar after a long day to Anand.

I grin and shake my head as he snakes his arm around my shoulders, pulling me into the wall of his chest. He bends down, searching for the same thing he always is. My lips.

As he offers his, I return his kiss in full, winding my arms around his neck, pulling him closer and closer as the breeze pulls around us. Anand pulls back just enough to look down at me and his expression turns all tender in a way I hate because these days I'm sensitive to every turn of his emotions and the result is always the same. He looks at me and has wonder in his ridges, flashing in all shades, while tears prick the backs of my eyes.

He scowls and pulls me in for another hug while I laugh. "I can't help it. This was such an emotional solar."

"It was," he breathes into my hair. "It is the day you became mine. Truly mine."

I breathe in his scent. Sugar and heat. Like caramel roasting over a fire. "Our wedding day."

He tenses when I say that. "I still can't believe it."

"Verax. That you're married to a human *and* baptized to the Tri-God? That was your idea, mind you. I was perfectly fine *not* getting married in the Tri-God center for worship…"

"Nox. Nox…" He tilts my chin up to his and I let him kiss me as much as he wants. "Of course not. Just that I get to call you my *whiff*. I like this word. There is something…bloodthirsty about it."

"Wife."

"That's what I said."

I wrap my arms around his neck. "I am not so bloodthirsty."

"That's not what I saw. When we found Mathilda, you had her exiled to Kor."

I wince at that. "It was better than killing her."

"She'll be eaten alive there." He speaks with glee.

I poke his shoulder — his left shoulder, since the scar on his right shoulder still looks like painful. "You shouldn't be so happy about that."

"I'm xoking thrilled," he says and though it isn't exactly within the teachings of the Tri-God…

Who the xok cares?

The Tri-God is forgiving.

"You are a glutton for punishment."

"Of course I am. And Mathilda deserves worse for what she did to you and the other females."

"And what she did to Deena." I wince, wondering where Deena is. If she made it out of the clutches of the Niahhorru. If she's safe.

Krisxox swears to me that she's a smart female and that they've sent word to all far reaches of all quadrants to remain alerted for her presence, but so far…nothing. I just hope, if she didn't return here, that she took the coordinates I sent her and found the other humans. They will take care of her. I know they will.

"Return to me, my *whiff*."

"Wife."

"And I am your *huzzbend*."

I grin and laugh all over again. "Hexa, you're my husband."

"Say it again."

"Husband."

"Huzzbend."

"Exactly right."

He smirks at that and runs his hand up the back of my dress. White with long sleeves and a train that is already red and brown from the spans of dancing we did.

Miari and Kiki organized almost everything and everything went so beautifully, I'd do it all again if I could. Hundreds were in attendance, transported in from all of the planets of Quadrant Four.

"I loved confessing my vows to you this solar."

He smiles down at me, ridges turning slightly yellow in sheepishness. "Hexa." He licks his lips. "I liked that part."

"I liked when you talked about love. About heimo. It is a perfect name for this place."

"I told you, I'm always right." I elbow him in the stomach and he laughs.

I grin. "I just can't believe we made it back here." I look out over the sands, the huge pavilion where people are still dancing, Voraxian, human and Drakesh. "And now we're back where we started."

"Nox, my Xiveri," Anand says, sliding his palm over my stomach where two little hearts of our coming twins beat. "I don't think we are."

Continue the journey and be…

Taken to Kor

Deena's not planning on getting caught by the space pirate Rhorkanterannu. She's planning on getting nice and homey with the humans on the Balehilsa satellite. But…what if it's better to stick with the monster she knows?

Taken to Kor: An Alien Pirate Romance
Xiveri Mates Book 5 (Deena and Rhork)

Available in paperback anywhere online books are sold or on Amazon in ebook

1

Deena

"Hello?"

"Interesting."

That's the reply. In a voice as dark as it is deep, a chill blasts through me that has nothing to do with the frigid temperature down here and everything to do with the intonation. He didn't expect me, and I know who he is. He doesn't know who I am yet, and he has no reason to. I'm nobody.

But he's curious.

I know I should take the little bead I found out of my ear, but I don't. I'm too starved for any sort of human interaction at all to care. Well, human or... otherwise.

"Um...hi."

"Hmm," he says and it's almost a sigh. "You know who I am."

What? How does he know that? Can he read my mind through this thing! Shit! I don't know the technology. This is the first time I've ever opened up the communication channel. What if he knows what I'm thinking and he knows that I stole this and what if he tells Mathilda and I get caught?

I laugh at that. It's more like a snort. What could she do to me that she hasn't done already? Kill me?

Well, she could do that.

"So um…" I clear my throat because my voice is all gravelly and hoarse. "How do you figure that?"

"You have this device and I can read its identifier. I know who once owned it since I gave it to her, but you aren't her, and since you haven't asked me who I am, I have to assume that you know already who I am and that you stole it. Now why don't you identify yourself so we can make this conversation a little less one sided."

He sounds so at ease, like nothing in the world could ever unsettle him. Like he's planned all this. Like he's seen every eventuality and in every scenario, he comes out on top.

I swallow hard and stare a hole through the ceiling. I'm lying flat on my bed, but my mouth is dry, so I sit up and grab the bottle of water Mathilda slipped into my cell last night. She hasn't been by since and it's been a day. I guess she assumed the one meal she gave me would be enough.

I um... am stuttering again. I can't figure out what to say. I had only half expected this to work since I only got this piece of technology to work for me a solar ago. Or has it been two? More? Who knows. Down here in this cage, time is irrelevant. "I don't think you need my name."

"Fine. Then tell me what you want."

"I um..."

"Um... I'm beginning to think this is a word of some significance in your language because it doesn't translate to mine. Either that, or you didn't expect your communication to be received and now you're completely stumped."

Shit. He can read my mind. I reach up to my ear as I chug what's left in my water bottle. Water dribbles down my chin. I wipe it off with the back of my hand and cross one arm over my stomach.

I should take the earpiece out and smash it into shards, but I don't do that either. Partly, because I'm not sure I'll be able to smash it but mostly because if I do, this will be the end of my lifeline. The last being I might have a chance to talk to except for Mathilda. *And I'd rather skin her than make conversation.* Only that isn't true, is it? I'm too terrified of her to do anything.

"Yeah, you're right," I confess.

He doesn't respond right away and I find that kind of funny. I chuckle. "What? Are you stumped now?"

"A little."

I don't answer. I don't know what to say. "I…"

"What are you looking at right now?"

The question is unexpected. Unexpected, but smart. I look through the clear walls of my cell at the rows and rows of food my *grandmother* has been hiding down here from the rest of the colony. From me. When I broke the lock and came down here the first time and discovered it was my undoing. That was when she locked me up. She couldn't have me spilling the beans, and I would have because the colony hasn't seen beans in rotations. People are starving topside and my grandmother, the conniving bitch, has been hoarding supplies away for herself this whole time. And that's the least troublesome thing she's been doing.

I could tell him that I'm looking at rows of vegetables growing underneath solar lights, but then he'd know right away where I am and I don't know what he knows yet. Maybe he's the one that gave her all of this. Maybe he's on her side. Maybe he already told her that I have her device and that I'm speaking to him when I shouldn't be. Maybe they're in cahoots. Cahoots. That's a funny word. I always thought so.

"Water."

"Water," he repeats. "Interesting. Is this water for drinking or water for swimming?"

"There's water for swimming?"

Again, he hesitates. "There is. Vast quantities of it."

Incredible. I don't even know how to picture it. "Really? Where? Is it in big tanks?"

"Many different places. Not in tanks, at least, not the kind I'm speaking of. This kind appears in nature, but not on little moons like yours."

I swallow. So he knows where I am, but not who I am. That computes. "You...have you...um..."

"I've decided I don't like this *um* word. Use another."

My lips quirk. I'm smiling. Wow. When was the last time I smiled? I frown then, unable to remember it. "Well, mister, I'm not the best conversationalist. I don't exactly get a lot of practice."

"Is that so?" He grumbles, voice sounding a lot like a growl. It's sexy. *Sexy.* Ha. I've *never* used that word before to describe anything, but here I am just smiling away and having a jolly good time talking to the one creature in all the galaxies I shouldn't be.

I reach for my water bottle. It's empty. Shit. I don't know when I'll get another. I glance at the bucket in the corner. The two buckets. One for pee one for...everything else. If Mathilda doesn't come back soon, I guess piss will be my drink of choice.

"No. I don't talk to many people."

"Humans," he answers. "You don't talk to many humans."

"Right."

"But you are human."

"And you're not."

"Centare," he answers, "I'm not.

"Centare," I repeat. "What language is that?"

"Meero. The language of the Niahhorru."

I swallow hard, thoughts firing too fast to capture them all. I blurt out the most random one of all. "Will you teach me?"

He laughs. *Laughs.* It sounds strange because it isn't translated, so it's just his raw voice. It sounds like overlapping waves and I find it oddly soothing. My shoulders relax down my back. I close my eyes, just listening to his laugh repeat itself, like he's speaking through a tunnel and I'm the only one at the other end. It's nice. Even if he is the enemy. Because everyone is an enemy. I don't know one person that's actually good. Maybe my mom. She was good, at least from what I can remember. But maybe I'm remembering wrong. I was just a kid when she was taken from me. My dad, even though he had the same dark skin most colony people do, succumbed to the sun plague just after I was born. I never knew him.

"I only have a mutinous planet of pirates to manage, but of course, I have no problem taking time out of my busy solars to teach you Meero."

"Okay, good."

"But you will have to give me something to call you by."

I chew on my bottom lip, gnawing it to shreds. "Deena," I finally answer.

"Deena," he repeats in his strange brogue. I like the way it sounds when he speaks it. Like he's savoring it.

"And...what's your name?" I stutter.

"Deena, you already know my name. I suspect, you already know quite a bit about me."

"You're trying to steal women."

"I'm trying to save a species."

"It's still stealing. You tried to take Miari and Svera."

"Perhaps that is only because I hadn't met you first."

My chest tightens. I imagine him wanting me. I shouldn't want that, but I do. I'd be willing to do a lot for a little attention at the moment. It's only been a few solars since I've been stuck in this cell, but it feels like a lifetime.

"Rhorkanneteru," I whisper.

He laughs again, this time a little shorter. "Rhorkanterannu."

"Rhorkanterannu," I repeat. "It's too long."

"All Niahhorru have long names. At least, all Niahhorru of worth."

"I still say it's too long. You could make it shorter. Just the end part, or the beginning."

"What would you call me then?"

I reach for my water bottle again, then again, lower my hand. I cross my arms over my chest and lie back on my bed, staring up at the ceiling, imagining it a lunar sky full of stars. "How about Rhork?"

There's a long silence after I say that. Then, "Interesting."

And that is the first time I ever met Rhork.

Two hundred solars later...

2

Deena

My whole body is jittery. It has been since I boarded the Niahhorru battle transporter, helped rescue Svera and managed to escape. Now, I'm in the escape pod staring blankly at the control pad built into the armrest on one of the four chairs in this tiny little thing.

I got it to jump space, like Krisxox told me too. That was good advice. Without it, I'm pretty sure I'd have been caught right away. But now the control pad is flashing at me in bright blue, asking me for coordinates to my destination because I'm apparently low on energy, or fuel or whatever. That's what I think the yellow blinking light means, anyway.

Coordinates.

My mind goes completely and utterly blank.

And then I start to laugh. I laugh long and hard and so crazily, I'm forced to remember every single time Mathilda, my dearest grandmother, told me that I was insane. Mental. Mad. A madwoman. A lunatic. I feel it, then. I feel all of it.

Because I don't know the coordinates to take me back to the human colony. I don't know *any* coordinates *except for the ones Rhork wants more than anything else in the universe.*

I gnaw on my bottom lip, tearing it to pieces as my fingers hover over the controls. Finally, the warning signs get louder and I fidget in my chair. What are my options? I could sit here and die, or I could go there and try to find the humans. Maybe start a new freaking life.

Yeah. That'd be good.

My fingers are jerky and hesitant as I input the coordinates I *do* know. The only ones I know because they're the only ones ever given to me. Svera told me to use them only if I was in a bind, but now I'm kind of in a pretty massive bind, so I throw them in and strap myself into the control chair and brace as the ship jolts, changing sectors again and returning me back to the grey zone between Quadrants Four and Five, not too far from where I disembarked the Niahhorru mothership in the first place.

I'm headed to the satellite that Rhork's been trying to get to all along. That's why he took Svera and not me. It has nothing to do with the fact that I'm defective. He just wanted the coordinates…

I stare at my leg, which is twisted out to the side, and frown.

I am defective.

I just…Rhork and I have talked every single solar since I first got that little communicator from Mathilda.

"You nosey little Cretan!" She hits me so hard my lower lip breaks and I taste blood the moment I hit the floor. The carpet is hard and scratchy under my palms, but there's something smooth among the threads, something soft. I wrap my fist around it at the same time that my grandmother wraps my locks up in her fist and lifts me up by them. She's stronger than she looks as she drags me, kicking and shrieking, down the hall, down the stairs into the basement.

I've been down here before. I broke the lock. That's what started this whole mess.

I'm so dazed I don't realize where I am or where I'm going until I'm on the floor and a door is sealed before me. It's glass, or something like glass. Something harder because it doesn't break — I spend the next few solars trying. Realizing it's pointless on the ninth solar, I eventually turn to the little device. I try to use it in all kinds of weird ways and eventually make it work on accident. I'm sleeping with it underneath my pillow when I first hear the static. I listen closer…and closer…and closer…and then the thing crawls into my ear canal.

I scream when it lodges itself deep inside my head and I try to shake it out. But then I hear something. I think I do anyway. It sounds like someone speaking very far away. It sounds like a man's voice. A male's anyway, because I know it can't be human. I think how wonderful it would be to actually talk to someone and then all at once, the connection sharpens, becoming clear. All other sounds drown out and I'm left listening to someone who I know can hear me.

"Hello?" I say.

Then comes the reply. "Interesting."

I frown. Defective. I don't know why it bothers me so much to be called that by him and I sigh, shake my head, put it out of my thoughts. He's just as bad as Mathilda and the things…the horrible things he was getting ready to do to Svera…

My muscles all firm up at the thought and I get up, out of my seat and pace around the small escape pod. I locate the weapons stashed in a cubby in the middle of the floor and quickly scan through them. I find a sword and pull it out, slash it around a few times aimlessly. I've never held a sword before. I chuck it aside and duel an imaginary opponent with a spear. At least, I thought it was a spear until it starts vibrating on one end and then a giant bolt fires out of one end. I scream and drop it back into the cubby.

I'm not stupid enough to try any of the blasters, or the glowing purple balls that sit in a glass case. Eventually, I get bored of the weapons and try some of the other floor panels. Eventually, one of them opens.

Food! I shriek with glee at the sight of the tubes of black liquid and the clear packages wrapped around a brown mushy substance.

Since the packages look kind of like someone pooped into bags, I go for the tubes first.

"Aguheaaaeeey!" I choke and have a hard time recovering my breath. The taste is like someone beat a fish to death with a bag of garbage and then liquified both with battery acid. It tastes bad. Like...real bad.

The taste claws up the back of my throat and enters my brain and I immediately chuck the black liquid away and opt instead for a bag of crap which helps. "Huh." Tastes like peppermint. A little like cantaloupe.

I eat three more of the bags of poop and look down at my stomach when I'm finished. I feel full and right now, in just a tee shirt that stopped fitting me half a rotation ago, it shows. I frown again. My stomach is full and my breasts are even fuller. Monster jugs, they sit heavy on my chest and sometimes, even make my back hurt. One would think that my giant bottom would have canceled out the weight, but I guess it just doesn't work that way.

Too bad.

I didn't always used to look like this. Just...after Mathilda put me in the basement. Food was the only thing I had to occupy my time. I didn't realize that I'd gain weight. Nobody on the colony ever gained weight, so why should I? But I did and I think it wouldn't bother me so much if it weren't so hard to run. Scaling those black rocks on the colony in order to gain access to this ship had been harder than I think it would have been when I was smaller. But maybe I was just terrified.

I'm still terrified.

As I walk around the eerily transparent edge of the escape pod, I stare out at the vastness and magnificence of space. Faraway stars blink like beacons to massive ships. Though, in a way, I guess planets are kind of like ships transporting millions of people through the enormity of space. I smile at that, feeling my cheeks redden for no reason at all.

I press my palm to the edge of the pod and whatever black material that periodically flares up over the transparency appears beneath my palms, like it's trying to communicate.

"What are you trying to say, little buddy?" I ask it, but it just darts away and doesn't respond.

I'm used to things not responding so I just shrug and don't let it bug me and continue to count out loud the number of asteroids and shooting stars I see. "Eight...nine...eleven...thirty-three..." The shooting stars are hard to make out because the asteroids are starting to bunch together.

Are they even asteroids? I don't know. They're big blocks of black and brown rock, some the size of this escape pod or smaller, but most, huge, hungry things. Still, the escape pod, maneuvers around them easily and I wonder what's causing it. Sensors? Sight? Is this thing alive? Can it see? Can it feel?

"If you can feel me, sorry for throwing around your weapons." I hold up my hands as I stare around at the transparent walls and the space beyond them. Cautiously, I return all the weapons to their cache and hum a song I made up as I do.

"Do you like music?" I ask the pod.

Crazy person! Yeah, maybe. But since I figured out how to disable the Meero communicator I wear in my ear before I boarded the ship so that Rhork can't find me, I know that I'm back to where I started. Alone. Alone in the emptiness of space. Or is space empty, really? Maybe it's full. Think of all the life floating through it. Me, just a solitary little pinpoint among the trillions.

"Oh right, you don't speak Human." Duh. "Do you like music?" I ask the pod again in Meero.

It still doesn't respond. "Humph. Maybe you just don't have experience with it." I open my mouth and sing it the only song I ever wrote in Meero, "Droganeene nene erro, wa da rogar tre hodona." I'm belting the words out now. It's a song about a plant. Lacking some er…inspiration when I was down in that cell under my sweet old gramma's house, I only thought up songs about the things directly in front of me.

"If you lift your green leaves up to the sun," or in the basement plants' case, the sun lamps mounted above them — but who's really counting? Then you'll grow big and strong...Ahh!" I scream as the entire escape pod lurches to an alarming stop.

My whole body sails, arms pinwheeling in the air. I'm headed straight for the clear wall on my left and, because it's clear, I'm caught off guard when I hit it. Luckily, I managed to bring my arm around to cover my head. Unluckily, I hit my elbow on the wall.

"Augh!" I writhe in a funny sort of agony as my funny bone sends jitters all up and down my left side. "You stupid shroving wall!" I kick my feet on the floor, hoping to dispel the sensation when a hard voice cuts into the quiet.

"Deena, are you alright?"

I jerk at the unexpected sound. "Shrov!" I curse in Meero and quickly scratch at my ear until I get the communicator out. I stare at it in my palm, completely and totally agog. Agog. I always thought that word was dumb. "Holy shit!" I curse again in Human at the little silver bead — it's a Niahhorru token and allows me to communicate with any other Niahhorru token. Ships are made out of the same material, allowing me to control this one without use of the pad built into the armrest. Or at least, it did, but I...I was sure I disabled it.

"You're not real!" I shout at the bead only to be rewarded when *laughter* echoes all around me. *It's coming from the ship! It's alive!*

I glance around at the emptiness beyond the walls. Planets, stars, asteroids, all listlessly floating by, minding their own business. And me, an intruder among them, listening to laughter that can't be real. *Maybe, I am crazy.*

"You didn't think you'd get rid of me that easily, did you Deena?"

"Shrov! How did you… I disabled it."

He breathes out very slowly and makes a clicking sound. "Deena, that isn't possible."

"You…you told me it was possible." I'm suddenly mortified. All those times I thought I had privacy and he was listening? He told me the command to disable it.

"I lied."

"You are a shroving sicko!"

"I liked listening to you when you thought I wasn't listening."

My impulse is to toss out my communicator, but I shove it into the pocket of my pants. Unlike the shirt, they're mens' jeans that belonged to my dad and they barely stay up on my hips — wouldn't, if I hadn't fixed them with a power cable. "Get out of my escape pod!"

"Your escape pod?" Comes the omnipresent reply. The thing I hate most about it? I don't know where to look.

So I just shout up at the ceiling. "Yeah! *My* escape pod. I'm escaping in it, aren't I?"

I believe that pod and its contents belong to me."

I hate the shimmery, slippery way he speaks. Hate it only because it affects me. I've heard that voice in the dark, late in the lunar, when I'm all alone. I've let its shivers wrack and wreck me. Let it get under my skin, into my bones. "You can have it back when you catch me."

"Make no mistake in thinking I won't."

"Big talk from a guy who has no idea where I am."

"Tell me and I'll know."

"Cute. Anyone ever called you cute before?"

"Centare, they have not."

"Well, I think you're positively adorable. Big bad pirate wandering space totally lost trying to find little ole' me. Just darling, really."

Silence. I think I hear him grumbling words to someone else, but they're all indistinct until he says, "Tell me where you are and I will punish you less."

I laugh at that. It isn't genuine so much as it is insane. I flip my hair up and down, my long locks spanking me in between the shoulder blades as I do. "You know, you're not very good at this. Don't you know bribery comes before threats?"

"Is this what Mathilda taught you?"

"Centare," I shudder. "Mathilda went straight for punishment. But that's not a step available to you right now, because you aren't here." Take that!"

He doesn't answer again, not right away. It makes me hungry to hear his voice and I hate how I pace around the pod, waiting...just waiting... The pod lurches again and I fall to my knees, banging them hard on the floor.

"Sit down in the xoking pod before you kill yourself on accident," Rhork hisses through the pod's completely invisible speakers. *Where is his voice coming from?!*

"You ain't the boss of me," I shout even as I waddle awkwardly over to the chair with the control pad. I sit and pull up a rendering of the nearby vicinity and my lungs both jerk. *I'm almost there. At the heart of this asteroid field, I'll be there. The first to reach the other humans in a hundred rotations. Maybe more.*

"Fine," he sputters, sounding momentarily *deeply* exhausted. I should know, I've had almost an entire rotation to study his voice's many shades and tones. It almost makes me feel sorry for him. Then I remember Svera, how she looked when I saw her on a slab waiting for Rhork to come and...*force* her. *I didn't think he was capable of that.* Even though I know that really all beings in this universe are truly terrible, I somehow thought he was above that.

I won't waste any regrets on him though. *No, he's just as wretched as everybody else.*

"Fine what?"

"Fine. I will bribe you."

"Sweet. Whatcha got, Rhorky bear?"

He growls, hating the condescending nicknames I've given him over the solars. This one he hates more than most. "If you tell me your coordinates, stay there and wait for me to come pick you up, I will not make you perform shekurr for my brothers."

"Oh wow. This is quite a bribe. Just picturing it now…sigh…*not* having to shove thirty monster cocks in me all at once."

"Don't make me do this the hard way, Deena," he says and his voice does get deeper, and does make my toes curl against the cold floor. I'm not wearing shoes. *Why would grandmother dearest give me shoes? That would make it easier to run.*

"Back to threats are we? So fast? Let me see… the things I'd rather do than do shekurr with you and your brothers?" I lift one hand and start to make a list. "I'd rather impale myself on an asteroid, throw myself out of an airlock, drink a hundred more of those nasty black tube drinks. You know what? Instead of thirty cocks all at once, I'd rather grow a cock out of each of my eyes."

Silence. "That is a wholly disturbing image."

I smile and kick my feet in the chair, having a jolly good time. "Yeah, well so is the image of me with you and all your brothers."

"How about just me?"

My smile falls. My feet still, toes barely touching the floor and only if I edge as far forward in my seat as I can without falling off. "Wh…what?"

"Does this image also disturb you?" He breathes and his voice is doing that dark, twisted thing it does for me. It dances in the dark, like some kind of sultry strip tease. I'm not…used to boys talking to me like that.

"Of course," I finally choke, but my voice cracks and I know that he hears it when he chuffs out light laughter. "It doesn't matter anyway." My fingers tense around the arms of my chair. I feel my face getting all hot and am glad he can't see me. *Not just because of my blush, but because I'm me.* "You're not going to catch me and even if you do, I'm not going down without a fight." Or flight. Right now, flight seems like the better option of the two.

"Hmm…" I hate it when he does that. It's like he's figuring something out. "You mentioned asteroids and I know that you aren't going to your human colony. We moved in the path you'd have needed to take to arrive here to intercept you, but imagine my surprise when you weren't here.

"I'm beginning to think, little Deena, that Svera gave you something very precious before she and her mate took off."

Shock, it hits me in the face. I blink. It comes again, this time, in the stomach. Because when I blink, I don't believe it. My little escape pod has just rounded the curved edge of one moon-sized asteroid and sitting directly in front of me is a satellite.

Shadowed by the asteroids behind it, it's illuminated only by very distant starlight — and the light of my bright little pod. The asteroids seem to be locked in its orbit, rotating very slowly. I start to follow the path that they take in my little bright beacon drawing nearer and nearer and…

"Deena. Did Svera give you the coordinates?"

"What coordinates?" I mumble, unstrapping myself from my seat and rising with complete and total awe. I approach the viewpane and press both palms against it.

Balesilha.

That's the word printed in huge block letters across the bit of it nearest to me. The satellite is a magnificent thing. *Huge*, I see why even the largest of these asteroids is caught in its rotation. There are three main components of the thing, two huge sections on either end that look like slowly rotating wheels and one huge sphere linked by enormous tubes — tunnels, bridges, whatever — between them.

The wheels are both silver and gleaming, shining like they were just built yesterday. The ball however, is inert and patchy with black and a sort of rust color that looks eerily like dried blood. Some bits of it, I see as I draw closer, appear mossy green. *Like vegetables after they've been left out too long.* I remember because one of my many protests was to deny all the food Mathilda gave me. I let the food spoil and eventually the meat and the vegetables grew these funny, fuzzy white and green spots. The sphere is the size of the larger asteroids I passed and the entire thing is that patchy white-green color. *Rot.* The word comes to me. *The color of rot.* And that's where my escape pod is headed.

"Deena, come back to me," his hard voice snaps and I jerk to attention, preparing for my little pod to dock. Preparing to meet the new humans! Oh my gosh, what will they be like? What will they think of me? I glance down at my clothes, my bare feet, the stains and smudges on my tee shirt. I sniff my arm pits and make a face. Well, I guess that can't be helped.

I tighten a few of my locks with my fingers as I jump eagerly from foot-to-foot. I refuse to answer Rhork as he speaks, whispering more orders to somebody. I'm getting close...super close! The giant sphere looks positively jumbo sized now as I approach it and we lock on to some port with a hiss.

"Deena, shrov!" Rhork curses. He almost never does. "Deena, you can't do this. This is my escape pod. You are *mine*." I don't know how he figures that, but it sounds pretty stupid from where I'm standing staring up at the ceiling, watching the black matter that makes up some of the ship part to reveal a rot-colored portal that's sealed shut.

The black matter slides down all syrupy and slow to form a single post with hand and foot rungs sticking out of either side of it. Cool. A ladder. I grab on and start climbing up. "Preciate your company these past solars, Rhork, but I'm off now. Don't expect to hear from me anytime soon."

"Deena," he says and I *hate* the way he says my name only because I hate him and I actually like the way he says my name, making me wish I didn't. "I'll take you to the ocean."

My foot slips from the rung its on and my arms shake with the effort it takes to hold the rest of my body up. *Crap. I'm real out of shape...* I wonder if that's what Rhork meant when he called me defective, not my leg. I glance down at the scar that circles it like a spiral and frown. It's kind of hard to walk up the ladder with my foot bent out like this, but it doesn't stop me. It hardly even slows me down.

"Nah," I say even though my heart does this annoying funny thing. It clenches. The ocean. *How many times has his melodic voice described it to me? How many times?* "I'll take my chances with the humans. Bye Rhork."

"Deena!" He shouts, and he shouts my name a dozen more times.

It takes me a long while to figure out the mechanism to open the latch on the other ship. It's so...ancient. No scanners or vein readers or weird syrupy black stuff. Just an old fashioned hand grip that I have to twist, twist, twist, then push in.

I'm sweating a little with the effort it takes to lift the mechanism up, but eventually, it's gritty surface gives and it locks. Hissssss. The doors peel apart in the center. How old-fashioned. I giggle.

"Rhork, it's dark in this ship."

"Shrov! Deena, do not go in. You don't know what you're getting yourself into…"

"Uhh, yeah, as if shekurr is a better option? I don't think so. Remember. Cocks in my eye sockets."

"Deena…" His tone makes me shiver. I doubt many have ever disobeyed it but, seeing as he's not here, I count myself among the few. Maybe the only. I smile a little bit.

"Is there a flashlight somewhere?"

"Deena…"

"Either, I go up in the dark, or you tell me where a flashlight is."

He hesitates, considers. I should probably have considered that he does in fact tell me where to locate a flashlight, rather than let me crawl up into the ship in complete and utter darkness, but I don't. Instead, as I strap the bright white direction lantern to my wrist and crawl into the ship, all I feel is giddy with excitement.

"Bye again, Rhork!" I shout down into the space and I quickly pull the latch on the inside of this ship to seal the door shut so I can't hear his answer.

I stand up and stretch my legs, sweeping my torch around. With a grin, I say, "Humans? It's safe! I'm me! I'm one of you! You can come out now. Want to hear my song about plants? It's in Meero, but it kind of translates."

And when I get no answer, I continue forward, sweeping my lantern light over the white walls. I hum quietly to myself and as I walk hall after hall, I start to wonder if maybe, I shouldn't have taken Rhork up on his offer to see the ocean.

And then I turn and see a person and excitedly hurry forward to greet him — her — *it*. I can't tell from here, but I shout eagerly, "Hello!"

————————

Xiveri Mates
Taken to Voraxia (Miari and Raku)
Taken to Nobu (Kiki and Va'Raku)
Taken to Sasor (Mian and Neheyuu) *standalone
Taken to Heimo (Svera and Krisxox)
Taken to Kor (Deena and Rhork)
Taken to Lemoran (Essmira and Raingar) *standalone
Taken to Eshmir (Ashmara and Jerrock)
Taken to Sucere (Halima and Jakka) *standalone

Xiveri Mates: SciFi Alien and Shifter Romance

Taken to Voraxia, Book 1 (Miari and Raku)

Taken to Nobu, Book 2 (Kiki and Va'Raku)

Taken to Sasor, Book 3 (Mian and Neheyuu) *standalone

Taken to Heimo, Book 4 (Svera and Krisxox)

Taken to Kor, Book 5 (Deena and Rhork)

Taken to Lemoran, Book 6 (Essmira and Raingar) *standalone

Taken to Eshmir, Book 7 (Ashmara and Jerrock)

Taken to Sucere, Book 8 (Halima and Jakka) *standalone

Population: Post-Apocalyptic SciFi Romance

Population, Book 1 (Abel and Kane)

Saltlands, Book 2 (Abel and Kane)

Generation 1, Book 3 (Diego and Pia)

Brianna, Book 4 (Lahve and Candy) – *coming 2021!*
more to come!

Brothers: Interracial Dark Mafia Romantic Suspense

The Hunting Town, Book 1 (Knox and Mer, Dixon and Sara)

The Hunted Rise, Book 2 (Aiden and Alina, Gavriil and Ify)

The Hunt, Book 3 (Anatoly and Candy, Charlie and Molly)
– *in production*

Printed in the USA
CPSIA information can be obtained
at www.ICGtesting.com
LVHW091055210124
769093LV00009B/583